Praise for *Married a...*

We hope you enjoy this book. Please return or renew it by the due date.

You can renew it at www.norfolk.gov.uk/libraries or by using our free library app.

Sophie Cousens, autho...

'Funny, feel-good and full of warmth, love and friendship'
Laura Kemp, author of *Under a Starry Sky*

'A witty, tender story that packs a real emotional punch.
I loved it!'
Nicola Gill, author of *The Neighbours*

'A heart-warming and joyous page-turner. Impossible
to put down!'
Holly Martin, author of *Sunrise Over Sapphire Bay*

'Enthralling and entertaining!'
Heidi Swain, *Sunday Times* bestselling author

'I couldn't put it down. What a wonderful, warm, wise
and witty book!'
Alex Brown, *Sunday Times* bestselling author

'Fresh, funny, and the perfect tonic for these gloomy times.
Totally relatable but at the same time, total escapism, and
it was so easy to race through the pages'
Lia Louis, author of *Dear Emmie Blue*

Claire Frost grew up in Manchester, the middle of three sisters. She always wanted to do a job that involved writing, so after studying Classics at Bristol University she started working in magazines. For the last twelve years she's been at the *Sun on Sunday*'s *Fabulous* magazine, where she is Assistant Editor and also responsible for the title's book reviews. She can mostly be found at her desk buried under a teetering TBR pile. You can follow her on Twitter: @FabFrosty, and Instagram: @therealfabfrosty.

Also by Claire Frost:

Living My Best Life

CLAIRE FROST

married at first swipe ~~sight~~

SIMON &
SCHUSTER

London · New York · Sydney · Toronto · New Delhi

First published in Great Britain by Simon & Schuster UK Ltd, 2021

Copyright © Claire Frost, 2021

The right of Claire Frost to be identified as author
of this work has been asserted in accordance with the
Copyright, Designs and Patents Act, 1988.

1 3 5 7 9 10 8 6 4 2

Simon & Schuster UK Ltd
1st Floor
222 Gray's Inn Road
London WC1X 8HB

Simon & Schuster Australia, Sydney
Simon & Schuster India, New Delhi

www.simonandschuster.co.uk
www.simonandschuster.com.au
www.simonandschuster.co.in

A CIP catalogue record for this book
is available from the British Library

Paperback ISBN: 978-1-4711-9385-9
eBook ISBN: 978-1-4711-9386-6

This book is a work of fiction. Names, characters, places and
incidents are either a product of the author's imagination or are
used fictitiously. Any resemblance to actual people living or
dead, events or locales is entirely coincidental.

Typeset in Bembo by M Rules
Printed and bound by CPI Group (UK) Ltd, Croydon, CR0 4YY

MIX
Paper from
responsible sources
FSC® C020471

*To Steve, for being with me
every step of the way.*

married
at first
swipe
~~sight~~

Prologue

Hannah gripped her dad's arm just below the crook of his elbow, her fingers turning white with the effort. She stood as straight and tall as she could in her too-new shoes, with her shoulders back and her other hand clutching a small but pretty bouquet of hydrangeas and asters. She swayed slightly, though she knew it wasn't because of the heels she was unaccustomed to wearing.

'You don't *have* to go through with this, you know, Hannah darling. We can call the whole thing off now, I promise. I can even tell him for you.'

'Don't be silly, Dad, this is everything I said I wanted,' she insisted. Though even to her the words sounded hollow and echoey. 'It *is* everything I want,' she tried again. 'Truly, I can't wait to walk down the aisle and begin the rest of my life with this man.'

Her dad gently loosened her grip on his arm and patted her hand. 'You always were a determined young thing, even when you were little,' he chuckled softly. 'But remember that you aren't alone on this journey. Whenever things get hard – and believe me, things *will* get hard – your family will be here to love and support you. It might be you walking down that aisle, but you're not doing it alone. You've got your great big, hulking dad by your side for one thing!'

'And me! You've got me too, don't forget,' her small half-sister piped up from a few feet in front of them, where she'd been devising some kind of complicated dance set to a tune in her head only she knew. 'And Mummy said I look like a princess today, so I will wave my magic wand and cast a spell to make everything all right,' she added triumphantly, brandishing her flowergirl wand that was actually a plastic stick with a star attached to the end, drooping under the weight of the glitter that had been liberally applied during a crafting afternoon a few days before.

Hannah and her dad both laughed, and the intensity in the tiny room dropped a few notches.

Noticing Jess waving, Hannah's dad turned to his daughters. 'I think that's our cue.'

He paused to look at Hannah. 'Ready?'

She removed a stray piece of glitter from her dad's cheek. 'Ready.'

As the rows of people in the large room swivelled to look and smile at their little procession, Hannah only had eyes for one person: the man waiting for her at the altar. He slowly turned around and their eyes met.

Finally she got her first ever glimpse of the man she was about to marry.

JANUARY

Eight months earlier

Chapter 1

Jess

One of the few qualities Hannah had inherited from her dad was his ability to mix the strongest, most moreish gin and tonics known to humankind. Which was why she and Jess were already halfway through the bottle of 'small-batch, artisan gin, distilled just three times a year when Mercury is in retrograde' at 7 p.m.

'Andy and Pippa must have been very grateful to send you a bottle of such wanky, overpriced gin,' Hannah said as she glugged the rest of the clear liquid in her glass. 'Though I'm definitely not complaining. It tastes delicious.'

'I'm so happy they're engaged.' Jess smiled. 'They really do seem made for each other. And the fact they met through Save The Date means I'm even happier. So if they want to send me a bottle of Mystic Meg's tears, I'll drink it. And on that subject, you need to do your bartender bit again – we need filling up. Plus, I've just remembered, I've got a packet of crisps in my bag that I didn't eat at lunchtime – cheese and onion McCoys will go perfectly with a big G and small T.'

Once they were both happily sipping and crunching away, Jess nudged her best friend and said, 'So, how did your second date go the other night? I haven't had a chance to ask you properly.'

'Well, let's just say I must have been very drunk to agree to a second date as there's definitely not going to be a third.'

'Why? He seemed all right when I checked out his profile on the app. His pictures looked fairly normal and he didn't say he was ideally looking to marry a woman aged sixteen to twenty-one.'

'But neither did he admit to still living at home aged thirty-nine or his bedroom being a shrine to *The Avengers*. He saved that information for last night. Oh, and Captain America is his favourite character – despite everyone else knowing he is the shittest of all the Avengers.'

'You can't write someone off because they have bad taste in comic-book characters, Han!'

'I'm sorry, did you miss the bit where I mentioned he lives at home with his mum and his room boasts an Incredible Hulk duvet set complete with matching curtains? And to top it all off, when he said on his profile he was a "video games developer", what he *actually* meant was he plays *Call Of Duty* on his PlayStation all day, but is hopeful that very soon Sony will notice his brilliance and offer him the CEO job. And his name is Barry.'

'Urgh, okay, fair enough,' Jess said, making a face and

giggling. 'Onwards and upwards, hey?' she added, clinking her glass against Hannah's.

'Well, I'm not sure how much further there is to go *downwards*. Anyway, I thought the whole point of me working for your dating app is that I get to find love and live happily ever after running an Insta-perfect beach bar in Colombia with my gorgeous husband.'

'You're not the greatest advert for Save The Date, that's for sure,' Jess replied, earning a mock outraged face from her friend. 'Though you finding the man of your dreams isn't the only reason you work here, surely? What could be better than actually getting paid to spend eight hours a day with your best mate?'

'Getting paid to spend eight hours a day with your best mate drinking gin?' Hannah suggested. 'Shall we have one more for the road?'

'No, I'd better not have any more or I'll make the twins drunk when I kiss them goodnight. Although it is Friday, I suppose, and I might need to drink through the rest of the weekend in preparation for my meeting at the bank on Monday.'

'What meeting? Is everything okay?' Hannah asked, her eyes wide.

'The bank called me when you were out at lunch and asked me to come in to discuss the business. But I'm sure it's all fine,' Jess added quickly in her most smart, capable businesswoman voice. Hannah continued to eye her keenly. 'I wasn't going to say anything until after the meeting because

I didn't want you to stress, Han. There's probably nothing to worry about anyway.' Hannah took a gulp of gin and smiled, and Jess's shoulders relaxed a little.

'I'm sure whatever it is, it's just a blip.' Hannah nodded. 'You've done so well launching Save The Date in the first place, and there's no other app out there for people who want to settle down and get married, rather than just hook up or go on a few dates. Our USP is still our strongest asset.'

'Listen to you and all your technical talk – we'll make a businesswoman out of you yet. No more working in crappy bars on the other side of the world for you!'

'I'll have you know that all the bars I've worked in are very high class, actually!' Hannah laughed. 'And six months ago I was only in Italy, hardly the other side of the world.'

'True, but six months before that you were in Peru or somewhere equally far away, and before that you were in Oz, if I'm not very much mistaken! Right, three gin and tonics is probably three too many, so I'd better go and rescue Tom from the clutches of two eight-year-olds and make sure they get to bed.'

'Can't Tom put himself to bed?' Hannah joked. 'Okay, boss, you go and marshal the twins into their rooms and I'll tidy up in here before I go,' she said, glancing around the small summerhouse at the bottom of Jess and Tom's garden that formed Save The Date HQ.

'What would I do without you?' Jess smiled, giving her friend a hug. 'Have a fab weekend and see you on Monday, unless you fancy coming round for a roast on Sunday?'

'I'd love to, but Scott and Jules have invited me for lunch and you know I can't pass up the opportunity for some Auntie Hannah cuddles with Leo.'

'Indeed! Well, give Sir Chubby Chops a kiss from me, won't you?'

'Jess, it's rude to call Scott chubby even if he is my brother!'

'*Ha ha*, you're so funny. Remind me not to let you loose on the gin again. But give them all my love.'

'I will. See you next week.'

Jess glanced up at the dark Mancunian clouds sweeping across the already grey sky as she made her way past the huge trampoline in the garden and up the path to the back door of the large home she shared with Tom and their twins, Sam and Lily.

Before she reached the back door, she turned to wave at her oldest friend. Jess had created the 'office' a year before, when she realised she needed more space than just the kitchen table from which to run her business. It was only six months ago that she had asked Hannah to be her right-hand woman, working out of the summerhouse and earning a fair amount more than she had from the bar work she was used to in Australia, Argentina or wherever else in the world she'd found herself. Jess had been pleased but surprised when Hannah had accepted the job as it meant she would be spending the foreseeable future in Manchester for the first time in years, but when she'd said as much, Hannah had revealed the real reason she was keen to stick around.

'I know I've been a bit – okay, a *lot* – here, there and

everywhere the past few years, but coming back here for Scott's wedding and helping you out with ideas for the app made me realise the joy of working during the day and having evenings to myself. I think I'm done with lock-ins until two a.m. and the inevitable hangover that *forces* me to have a large Maccy Ds as soon as I wake up, a cycle I then repeat for as long as I can stick with the job. And now Scott and Julia have had Leo, I've decided it's time for me to put down some roots nearby, too. Plus, what's not to love about getting paid to dick around with you every day?'

Jess had rolled her eyes, but she couldn't have been happier to have her best friend so close after years and years of rushed, broken phone calls with her from the other side of the world.

The pair of them had always been chalk and cheese – even back in those early years of secondary school they'd joked that Hannah was chalk (easily changeable and a bit flaky), while Jess was cheese (solid, immovable and, Hannah liked to add, a bit smelly). When they played netball during PE, it was Hannah who was chosen as the flighty, quick-on-her-feet wing attack, while Jess was always the dogged, dependable goal defence. But somehow their friendship just worked. And from the age of fifteen, Tom had been a part of that friendship too. Jess started going out with him at the end of Year 11, just as she and Hannah were celebrating the last of their GCSEs and their imminent sixteenth birthdays. Tom had seemed impossibly grown-up to the two of them as he was about to start his last year of school, was having driving lessons and went to the pub with his mates every

Saturday night after finishing his job on the deli counter at Sainsbury's. Jess and Hannah, meanwhile, were still at the having-sleepovers-and-sneaking-a-sip-from-their-parents'-vodka-bottles stage, and both sat wide-eyed as Tom regaled them with stories of his friends being sick into pint glasses and uni open days. When she snogged Tom for the first time, Jess could never have imagined that she would still be kissing him almost twenty years later. Although, she had to admit to herself, there was quite a lot less lip action – or in fact, action of any kind – between them nowadays.

The three of them had spent a lot of time hanging out together, whether they were lounging in Jess's room helping Tom – who Hannah quickly nicknamed Tank after her favourite TV show as a kid – revise for his mocks or driving round town in his old banger screeching along to guitar bands at the tops of their lungs. Jess had always been careful to make sure her friend didn't feel like a spare part, and once Tom's A levels were out of the way, they spent the summer in beer gardens with a whole crowd of his mates, trying to look old enough to drink. Hannah even had a few snogs and, after too many cider and blacks, the odd grope with a few of the lads, but nothing that even came close to what Jess and Tom had. And when things got serious and Tom announced he was going to take another twelve months out on top of his gap year so he and Jess could go to uni together – much to his parents' annoyance – Hannah couldn't have been happier for her best friend, saying drunkenly but solemnly one night, 'Jess, you're like the sister I never had, and Tank, you're like the brother I wish I did have instead of the arrogant, entitled stoner my parents refuse to ever criticise!'

Now, eighteen years later, Jess opened the back door and was met by a cacophony of wailing (Lily), laughing (Sam) and shouting (Tom). She briefly thought about closing the door and retreating back to the summerhouse, but instead she took a deep breath, a step inside and smiled brightly before beginning what was very much her second job.

Chapter 2

Hannah

That evening, Hannah tipped the last of her glass of wine down her throat and wondered when her life had changed so much. Even just a year ago, a Friday night would have involved working behind a bar on the beach in Bali or Bondi and then drinking rum with the locals, but now the most excitement she got was a FaceTime call with her friend Dee in Oz, who seemed to be having the time of her life on the Gold Coast and had even met a bronzed god called Ade. It was 6 a.m. their time and they hadn't been to bed after staying up to watch the sunrise over the sea. But after twenty minutes of Dee waxing lyrical about how she was living her best life, bronzed god Ade had started giving her a foot massage that definitely hadn't ended at her ankle and she'd started to rather lose focus on their conversation. Not wanting a front-row seat at her friend's sex show, Hannah had promptly said her goodbyes – she liked Dee a lot, but not *that* much.

13

Now, she absent-mindedly reached for her phone and pulled up the Save The Date app, which notified her she had some new suggested matches. Unfortunately, as nice as Steven, John and Philip said they were, their pictures suggested they were either mummy's boys à la Barry or corporate types who left their socks on during sex. Groaning, she closed the window and instead clicked on what she could admit to herself – but definitely not Jess – was her favourite of all the dating apps. She logged into her profile and pulled up her saved matches and scrolled till she landed on:

Matt, 34

A doctor who doesn't need a stethoscope to make your heart beat faster.

They'd messaged a couple of times the previous week but hadn't arranged to meet. Noticing the app showed him as 'active', she sent a message asking if he was free for a drink the following day, before she could overthink it.

His answer came back within a minute.

> Hannah! So my medical jokes won you over
> eventually – go me! Sure, a drink sounds
> great. I'm in the middle of my last night shift
> of the week at the mo (and yes, I'm on my

break rather than messaging from a patient's
bedside, before you ask!), but I only need
a few hours' kip as I need to get back into
day shift mode for Monday, so let's say a late
lunch at the George and Dragon on the high
street – does that work for you?

Hannah agreed, although she was surprised at both his
choice of pub and timing. She wasn't sure she'd actually
been inside the George and Dragon, but it definitely
fell into the category of 'old man pub' rather than 'cool,
hipster, impress-your-date bar'. Oh well, she didn't have
anything to lose, and she still had the whole of Saturday
morning free for herself. Maybe she'd finally get round
to joining the gym. She picked up her phone again and
opened WhatsApp.

Hey, Tom, feels like we haven't caught up
in ages. I'm finally going to get off my arse
and join a gym – I need to find one near here
that's cheap but not filled with posers. Any
thoughts? x

Her phone lit up with a notification that meant Tom was
still awake.

A gym without posers is like a school without
naughty children! I go to the leisure centre

one sometimes (it's PAYG) as it's pretty
decent. Catch up soon. x

That was tomorrow morning sorted, then.

After wheezing her way through twenty minutes on the
cross-trainer and (almost) ten on the rower, Hannah stood
smugly under the less-than-powerful shower in the leisure
centre changing rooms, thankful she'd remembered to bring
her own shampoo and conditioner and didn't have to rely
on the white slime dripping from the soap box on the wall.
She rinsed her hair, wrapped her towel tightly round her and
gave her full attention to her imminent date. Matt looked
handsome enough in his profile picture and his messages had
painted an image of a wise-cracking but caring guy looking
for someone fun and interesting to have a relationship with.
Whether he'd live up to this in the flesh remained to be seen;
she could but hope. She spent longer than normal drying
her long, dark locks *and* straightening them (she hoped Matt
felt honoured), then, glancing at the clock on the far side of
the changing room, she realised she only had ten minutes
to make the fifteen-minute walk to the pub where they'd
agreed to meet. She hastily smoothed on some pressed
powder, swiped mascara somewhere close to her lashes and
added a cloud of blusher to her cheeks, before stuffing her
gym kit into her bag and shoving her feet into her Converse.

By the time she arrived at the George and Dragon, she
was already regretting the blusher; she'd forgotten how

tomato-red her face went after even the shortest gym session. She sniffed her armpits delicately, trying to remember if she'd applied deodorant after her shower, but then realised there was nothing much she could do about it now. Anyway, Matt was a doctor and had surely smelled worse than slightly fragrant pits.

Hannah pushed the door open and was hit by the peculiar odour only found in old pubs – a not unpleasant mixture of ale, cleaning fluids and damp bar stools forever infused with cigarette smoke. She stood in the doorway checking out the groups of ageing men surrounded by empty glasses, the cute old couples slowly forking fish and chips into their mouths, and, right in the corner, an unruly-haired man around her age sipping a pint of Guinness and staring intently at a yellowing menu.

Hannah strode over to him. 'You're Matt, I'm guessing. I'm Hannah. Obviously.' She grinned, before plonking herself down next to him on the fake-leather banquette.

'Excellent guess, ten points to you! Now your reward can be the choice between scampi and chips, chicken and chips or maybe pie and chips – what do you fancy?'

'I think I'll go for chips and chips,' she laughed. 'I'll go and order if you want?'

'No, I insist. Do you definitely not want anything with your chips? Fine, but I'm telling you now there'll be no stealing my scampi. Right, chips and chips and a glass of wine for the lady?'

'No, a pint of lager for me please.'

They performed a complicated dance as Matt tried to pass her and Hannah ended up crouching on top of the seat.

'Liking your moves,' he said, raising his eyebrows and sauntering to the bar.

Three pints later, Hannah felt like she hadn't stopped laughing for hours. Matt had been regaling her with hilarious stories about patients with various kitchen implements stuck in various parts of their bodies, as well as some warts and all tales about what happens when overworked medics let loose and go clubbing.

'God, my face hurts!' she cried, taking a large gulp of what seemed to be a magically refilling pint glass. 'I absolutely do not want to know what happened to that thermometer in the end.'

'It's even worse than you're imagining, I'm afraid. What about you – you must have some wild stories about bungee-jumping in Mexico or full-moon parties in Koh Samui?'

'Full-moon parties? I'm not some gap-year student bragging to their mates about how many neon cocktails they drank from a fish bowl on the beach before they vommed all over the cute guy from Wolverhampton they met out there! I'll have you know that when I do wild, I do wild.'

'I stand corrected and I apologise profusely for tarring you with a gap-year student brush.' Matt held up his hands as he laughed. 'So when you say wild, exactly how wild do you mean?'

'I've done white-water rafting in Costa Rica, climbed into a volcano crater in Iceland and had a rifle pointed at me in South Africa. And obviously, I've got roaring drunk on a beach in practically every country I've ever been to, and probably vommed all over countless gorgeous guys, although I can't remember any of them being from Wolverhampton.'

'Quite wild then,' Matt agreed and nodded his approval. 'So, what's been the best thing you've ever done?'

'The best thing ... Okay, do you want the version I tell everyone who asks me this question, or the actual truth?'

'What about both?'

'The best thing I've ever done is swim along the Barrier Reef. It's the most awe-inspiring thing in the entire world.'

'Good choice, can't really argue with that. And what about if you are being properly honest?'

Hannah tipped the rest of her drink into her mouth and swallowed hard. 'The best thing I've ever done is walk along the beach on the edge of the Gower Peninsula in the middle of a massive storm complete with thunder and lightning with the man I thought I was going to marry.'

There was silence as Hannah looked into the bottom of her empty glass, then Matt cleared his throat. 'So you're saying the best thing you've ever done is in Wales? As in *Wales* Wales?'

The weird tension that had enveloped them was immediately broken and Hannah burst out laughing again. And then suddenly neither of them could stop. They were just beginning to pull themselves together when Hannah started hiccupping madly, which only set them off again.

'We're getting some strange looks from the locals,' Hannah managed to say between laughing fits.

'Then maybe it's time to get out of here,' Matt said, chucking her jacket at her. 'Oi, don't forget this,' he added, picking up her gym bag and accidentally scattering sweaty trainers and her bright pink sports bra across the floor. By the time they'd gathered everything up and made it outside, they were both close to hysterics.

'Oh my god, did you see that poor old man's face?' Hannah wheezed. 'I thought he was going to have a heart attack right there and then. You'd have had to resuscitate him on the sticky pub carpet.'

'I'm not sure we'll be welcome in there again,' Matt replied. 'Almost killing half the punters with shock does not go down well with the landlord! Christ, I haven't laughed that hard in forever. Are you all right, I've got an inhaler if you want one?'

'Don't set me off again! But hark at you and your hero doctor act. Where are we going now anyway?'

'Back to mine? I've got a few beers crying out to be drunk.' She grinned. 'Beer, you say? I'm in!'

Two hours later, Hannah found herself walking past the pub in the opposite direction, back towards her own flat. Though it was only eight o'clock in the evening, her hangover was starting to kick in, as were the feelings of self-loathing and regret. Why had she allowed herself to sleep with him, she wondered miserably. She could blame it on the beer – she'd certainly had enough and it had been a long time since the bowl of chips in the pub. But she knew being pissed wasn't the only reason. It had been the adrenaline rush; the thought that she really shouldn't be in a stranger's bedroom removing her underwear; the desire to shake up her life and relive that fun and carefree feeling she had when travelling; the need to bury that memory of walking along the beach and towards a shared future in Wales.

And that was all fine. She was young, free and very single. The only problem was that Matt apparently wasn't.

She'd left him snoozing in bed while she went to the bathroom and for a mooch around his terraced house, which while small boasted what was obviously a high-end kitchen-diner and was kitted out with a wealth of Bluetooth speakers, sound systems and definitely-not-Ikea furnishings. Clearly medicine paid far more than being an office manager for a small dating app. There wasn't a huge amount of personality in Matt's home, she'd mused as she'd wandered through to the living room. But there she'd found a wall adorned with more frames than an art gallery. There were photos of Matt and his mates, one of him in graduation robes with his parents and lots of pictures of him with a gorgeous blonde lady. At first Hannah had allowed herself to be convinced this could be Matt's sister – he clearly carried the handsome genes himself, after all. But her eyes had landed on a small photo with a large white mount and modern frame that showed the pair of them locking lips in a very un-sibling-like way. That, coupled with the array of candles and plants trailing their way over the bookcase that contained authors such as Marian Keyes, Liane Moriarty and Sophie Kinsella, had made her think Matt's grasp on the truth was not as healthy as some of his patients in the hospital.

'Is your girlfriend away at the moment?' she'd asked casually as she'd returned to the bedroom and seen Matt's eyes were half open.

'What? What do you mean?' he'd said. He was going for puzzled, but Hannah could see the fear in his now fully awake eyes.

'Well, she's obviously not here so I just wondered where she was,' Hannah had replied.

'I ... We ... I'm about to break up with her,' he'd blustered. 'But she's away with her job so much and I'm working loads of shifts, and ...' he'd tailed off.

Now Hannah let herself into her flat, poured herself a pint glass of water and ran a deep bath, adding obscene amounts of expensive bath oil for good measure. She tried not to think about how she'd bolted from Matt's bedroom with as much dignity as she could muster while hopping into her clothes, and had legged it out onto the pavement before he'd a chance to realise what was happening.

'What is wrong with people?' she asked out loud into the empty bathroom. When the universe didn't deign to reply, Hannah sighed. Deep down she knew she was not only annoyed at Matt, but also herself. Of course, she couldn't be expected to know that, despite being on a dating app, he had a girlfriend he wasn't sure if he wanted to break up with. But she was supposed to be looking for someone to spend the rest of her life with, not a one-night stand on an evening he wasn't seeing his girlfriend.

She heaved herself out of the water, her limbs aching – although whether that was from the gym or the energetic sex she'd just had she wasn't sure – and chose her softest cotton pyjamas from her drawer. She snuggled into bed, gently placing over her legs the brightly coloured blanket G-ma had knitted for her to take to uni. More than fifteen years on, it was a little dulled and grubby and had more than one fraying piece of wool where the stitches had come undone, but it was still one of Hannah's most prized possessions, and tonight she needed all the comfort blankets she could get.

Hannah's grandparents had been a huge part of her life when she was younger. Every Sunday afternoon, she'd adored hearing them reminisce about their marriage and how they moved from Cornwall up north when Gramps got a job at an aircraft manufacturing firm, and then brought up her mum Joan. But the story she'd loved to hear more than any other was of how a young Vera had met a dashing Robbie at a village fete in Cornwall when he was home on leave from the army one Saturday night.

Hannah had been devastated when Gramps had passed away during her last year of uni, but it was seeing how upset G-ma had been that had truly broken her. She became terrified that G-ma would die of a broken heart – which she'd discovered on the internet was an actual thing. Her mum had told her not to believe everything she read, but Hannah had never really listened to her mum's advice back then, and even now she didn't talk to her about relationships, especially as Joan had spent the last nine years alone and bitter, watching Hannah's dad settle down with Charmaine and their 'surprise' daughter, seven-year-old Seraphina.

When she was growing up, Hannah had been able to talk to G-ma about anything, but there were definitely things she would never tell her grandmother now – like sleeping with not-so-single Matt. Not because she thought G-ma would be shocked or that it would get back to her mum, but because she didn't want her to worry. Since Gramps had died, her grandma had spent all her time telling Hannah how much she wanted to see her settle down and be happy. It was one of the reasons why G-ma loved Jess so much – she thought she was a good influence on Hannah, being married to her childhood sweetheart in their own home with two gorgeous children. And despite her naturally adventurous, impetuous nature, Hannah wanted to make her grandmother proud and find that forever relationship that she and Gramps had had.

Her phone lit up beside her with a message from Matt. She ignored it and instead spent the next half an hour scrolling through one social media platform after another. Every post she looked at seemed to involve loved-up couples who had got engaged on Christmas Day a few weeks earlier and were still dining out on their happy news. Hannah could only think of one other day more awful to propose, and that, *obviously*, was Valentine's Day, which would no doubt fling up another hundred vomit-inducing 'romantic' pictures into her timeline. *Have some imagination please, people!*

She'd promised Dee she'd try to make it over to Oz soon, but the prospect of getting the money together for the flights and accommodation when she was barely able to save a tenner a month after paying the rent on her tiny, slightly dingy flat and keeping herself in red wine, was depressing and not a subject she wanted to dwell on. It wasn't as if Jess paid her badly, but everything seemed to cost so much in the UK compared to the laid-back life she had bumming around South America and Australia. Plus, she knew that if she did go out to Brisbane, she'd never want to come home again, which not only wasn't fair on Jess at the moment, but meant she'd miss out on all things Leo. And if there was one shining beacon in her life it was her seven-month-old nephew.

Hannah had been shocked to say the least when her brother Scott had sent her a message just over a year ago to say his girlfriend of four months was pregnant and, oh, did she want to come to their wedding in nine weeks' time? She'd presumed her ex-stoner, still-a-child older brother would never settle down and was happy living in his bachelor bedsit that was really their mum's garage, which Joan had converted especially for him when their dad had left. But, if even Scott had managed to find long-term love, why couldn't she?

Chapter 3

Jess

Jess had hatched big plans for her weekend. However, instead of having a long bath, reading her book and not allowing herself to consider the worst possible scenarios for Monday's meeting at the bank, she'd spent much of the time making the breakfast/lunch/dinner, tidying up the breakfast/lunch/dinner things, skimming off the top layer of the never-ending laundry pile and cleaning the bathroom. All the while biting her tongue at Tom, who was happy enough telling her to go and relax, but never actually offered to do the chores that kept her from doing so. Who did he think was going to clean and tidy? The chores fairy? He forced her to sit down mid-way through Sunday morning to eat the bacon sandwich he'd made, but the crumbs he'd left on the kitchen side only wound her up further. When he tried to help her wash up their dishes, she finally snapped.

'Just leave it, will you! I might as well do it myself, like everything else in this house. Don't you have to get back to watching TV?'

'Jess, sweetheart, I know you're stressed about Save The Date—'

'Don't call me "sweetheart", you know how much I hate it. And, yes, I'm stressed that the business I've worked so hard on for the past few years is at the mercy of the bank and could be about to collapse, leaving both this family and my best friend with the possibility of having nowhere to live.'

'It's not going to collapse, I'm sure, the bank will just—'

'Oh, you're sure are you? You do know we're mortgaged up to our eyeballs, and it's not as if you're bringing in the megabucks? Or maybe you've won a huge commission to paint a portrait of the Queen and I just don't know about it?' She stared at him. 'Or maybe you've been sitting back and waiting for those commissions to come to you and have then been surprised when they haven't.'

'I have been pitching for work, but there's not a lot out there at the moment. Though I'm hoping to sell a couple of the red and yellow abstract canvases through Pete's gallery – he's pretty confident they'll work well in Liverpool. Look, Jess, I'm just worried about you.'

'Maybe you should be more worried about how we're going to pay the mortgage and all the bills.'

'I am, and I'm working as hard as I can. I'm owed a bit of money from that wedding I did the photography for, so once that comes in along with the pieces Pete is taking, things will feel a lot better.'

'Well, you'd better go and chase that money then, hadn't you?'

Tom gently folded the tea towel over the cooker handle and gathered his phone and coffee cup from the table. 'Jess, sw— *darling*, we are both on the same side on this. I want Save The Date to succeed as much as you do, but most of all I want you to be happy.'

Jess knew that was her moment to apologise, but her instinct was to keep her mouth shut in case she said something even worse. She turned back to the sink.

Tom sighed softly. 'I'll go and pick the kids up from their play date and give you some time to yourself. Please stop washing up and go and relax.'

Jess made a noise approximating the word 'thanks' and carried on scrubbing the chopping board that was already clean. She knew Tom was just doing his best, but sometimes it felt like his best wasn't enough. She dried her hands and swept her arm across her eyes to stop the tears that seemed to have gathered there from falling. She was tempted to make the most of the free living room and watch something she actually wanted to on TV, but she knew she'd only feel like she should be working. Instead, she pulled Sam's A4 notebook from the bottom of the towering pile of paper on the chest of drawers and opened it at a clean page. She wrote the words 'Save The Date' in the middle, drew a circle around it then searched the almost-blank page in front of her for inspiration.

She was staring into space when she suddenly heard the

sound of the front door closing and two hungry children in need of snacks.

'Muuuum, can I have a biscuit, what's for lunch?' Lily sang loudly as they barrelled into the kitchen, stopping briefly by her chair for an arm hug and kiss before making straight for the cupboard.

'There are grapes in the fruit bowl and you can have one of those flapjacks. Grapes first, Sam, please. It's quite late, did Dad take you to the park after you left Ollie and Grace's house?'

'Yes, but we were hungry and he didn't bring any snacks so we had to come home,' Sam replied through a mouthful of flapjack.

Jess gritted her teeth. 'Okay, well, why don't you two get your homework done now and then after lunch we can do your reading and then watch a movie together.'

'We watched *Moana* yesterday so it's not movie night again till next Saturday,' Lily piped up, before Sam gave her a scowl and a shove. 'Ow, that hurt, Muuuuum!'

'You're right, but I thought we could all have a treat. You might even be able to have some popcorn, but only if you're both very good,' she replied firmly. They nodded and grinned at each other, their disagreement already forgotten at the thought of Saturday-night treats the evening before school.

Despite all four of them enjoying their evening snuggled on the sofa in front of *How To Train Your Dragon* (for the hundredth time), and a taciturn peace being restored between Jess and Tom, the next morning they were all suffering. Tom hadn't argued when Jess had told him her plans for the evening, but that hadn't stopped his eyebrows rising at her relaxation of Sunday to Thursday rules, and she knew if he so much as thought the words 'I told you so' when she was trying to wrestle two overtired and fractious eight-year-olds into their school uniform at 7.45 a.m., she would likely explode.

'But I don't want to go to breakfast club, Mummy,' whined Lily, her eyes filling with easy tears. 'I want to have toast and chocolate spread with you.'

'Well, I'm afraid you can't this morning and you need to get in the car now as it's time to go. And you, Sam, come on, where are your shoes?'

'Dunno,' he shrugged, patently paying more attention to the football cards he was holding than to his irate mother.

She bit her lip until it hurt and managed not to shout too loudly, which thankfully averted a full-blown meltdown from either children or adult. Eventually, they were both strapped into their seats and Jess breathed a sigh of relief, before realising she'd left her glasses in the house. She considered driving without them, but realising how tired her eyes were already, she swore under her breath and opened the car door. 'I won't be a second. Please don't kill each other in that second, okay?' she said, giving the twins a hard stare. They barely looked up from their comics and cards so she ran back into the house.

'Everything all right?' Tom asked as he poured water into his coffee cup.

'Yes, everything is absolutely fucking perfect, obviously,' she spat, locating her glasses and trying not to notice the hurt look on Tom's face. She hated herself for being so horrible to him, but she couldn't seem to stop herself. She dropped the twins off and was back home in double-quick time. She couldn't bear to see Tom give her his disappointed look again, so she sidled upstairs and ran herself that overdue bath. Not that she'd have more than fifteen minutes to soak in it before she needed to be in the summerhouse and getting on with work, but that was better than nothing, she decided.

She was just dozing off in the warm cocoon of bubbles, when she heard a knock and saw Tom's head peeping round the bathroom door.

'I've brought you tea and flapjacks,' he said, placing them on the side of the bath. Jess watched him hesitate before he knelt down beside the tub and gently washed her back with the expensive shower gel he'd bought her for Christmas then massaged her shoulders. She leaned back into his touch and closed her eyes.

'Do you remember when I used to do this, back in the days before the twins,' he whispered. 'Back in the days when all we had to worry about was each other.'

'Mmm, those were the days,' Jess replied sleepily. 'Not that I'd ever change us having the twins, obviously.'

'Of course,' Tom agreed. 'But being parents is definitely

not easy.' He paused. 'Maybe we need to be a bit kinder to ourselves and admit when things are hard and allow ourselves to be imperfect. Like at the moment, for instance.' He squeezed Jess's shoulder.

She sighed. 'I know. You're right. There's just so much going on. I'll try, I promise.' She turned her face up towards him and kissed him. For that second it was good to feel the familiar softness of his lips and she missed him as soon as she pulled away and looked at his wrist. 'God, is that the time, I need to get dressed.'

Despite it already being almost nine thirty, the time she and Hannah usually started work, Jess made sure she spent more than her usual two minutes applying her make-up and brushing her hair. She smoothed on a comfy but grown-up-looking maxi dress and even added some silver hoop earrings for good measure.

'Looking hot, wifey!' Tom smiled from the bedroom doorway.

'Thanks,' she said, brushing her lips to his cheek. 'I'm sure it will make all the difference with the bank manager. You won't forget you're picking up the twins from school today, will you?'

'Of course not.' He smiled again, pulling her into a hug. Jess wriggled away and hurried down the stairs, but her steps were lighter than they had been for days.

'Just the small issue of saving my business from the clutches of the bank to sort now,' she muttered to herself as she made her way to the summerhouse at the bottom of the garden. Hannah was already at her desk and tapping away on her keyboard.

'You're eager this morning!' Jess said in greeting.

'Lots to do and I know you have your meeting this afternoon.' Hannah smiled encouragingly.

Jess nodded grimly. 'Yep, indeed. Thanks, Han, I appreciate it.'

They worked in companionable silence although Jess couldn't stop herself from glancing at the time on the top right of her laptop every few minutes. Finally, she gave in, made some coffee and pulled out the emergency packet of biscuits from her drawer. 'I've got an hour before I need to leave for my meeting, Han, so tell me something fun that's going to cheer me up! How was your weekend?'

'Well, I'm not sure my weekend was as fun as it could have been, unless you count going on a date with a man you later find out has a girlfriend he "hasn't quite got round to breaking up with yet".'

'Oh, Han,' Jess replied sympathetically. 'Well, at least you didn't sleep with him, I suppose.' She saw her friend's expression. 'Oh, *Han!*'

'Yep. But how was I to know a good-looking man on a dating app with his own place and a good job wasn't already coupled up? Although you'd have thought I would have guessed. All the good ones are clearly taken.'

'All the good ones are definitely not taken,' Jess replied swiftly. 'Oh my god, you didn't meet him on Save The Date, did you?' she asked, horrified.

'No, don't worry.'

'Well, why weren't you on Save The Date instead?'

'I can't win, can I?' Hannah grinned. 'None of my new matches looked like my type so I tried a different app for once. God, how hard can it be to find a hot, fun yet unattached man to settle down and live happily ever after with? I think I need to find a mad scientist who can clone Tom for me – he seems to be the only decent man around. You two are so happy together after almost twenty years, so he must be doing a whole lot of things right.'

'Hmm,' Jess replied non-committally. She hadn't talked to her best friend about how frustrated her husband was making her feel. It wasn't that she didn't think she'd be on her side exactly, more that she wanted to protect her. Hannah had always held up Jess and Tom's relationship as being the pinnacle of married bliss. It didn't help that Hannah's parents' marriage had been less than happy, and when they were teenagers her friend had confided in her about the arguments and raised voices that provided the soundtrack to her life. Jess knew that now was not the time to start confessing how unsupported and – if she was honest with herself at least – *trapped* she was feeling at home. 'I don't think any man, or in fact woman, is perfect, Han,' she said instead. 'Every relationship has its ups and downs and I'm not sure "happily ever after" actually exists. Maybe happily most-of-the-time ever after is a better goal.'

'G-ma and Gramps were always happy,' Hannah shot back. 'And they'd been together fifty years!'

'I'm sure your grandparents also had their bad days when everything the other did annoyed them,' grimaced Jess. Seeing her friend still look unconvinced, she hurried the conversation on. 'Anyway, there must be at least one man on Save The Date that you'd go on a date with? The whole point is that they all want the same as you – to meet The One and settle down. If my app can't find my amazing best mate a husband then what is even the point of it?'

Hannah laughed, then abruptly stopped, before grinning broadly.

'Hannah? I know that look. What are you planning?'

'I just had a brilliant idea . . .'

'When you say brilliant, why do I instantly feel nervous?'

'Because you know I have all the best ideas and you'll just be annoyed you didn't have it first! Anyway, drum roll please . . .'

Jess waited anxiously.

'You should use Save The Date to find me a husband!' Hannah sat back and grinned while Jess looked confused.

'But, Han, isn't that what we've already been doing? You're signed up to the app and you haven't met anyone you like. What's the difference with your idea?'

'The difference is I wouldn't be doing the choosing. My happily married-with-children successful best friend would decide for me. Quite frankly, I trust you more than I trust myself at this point.'

'Ha! And what if I chose wrong? That would be absolutely hilarious. Imagine, I could match you with any of the hundreds of men you've already swiped past and there'd be nothing you could do about it. I could set you up with Geeky McGeekface who not only loves Captain America, but also dresses up as him on special occasions – including on his wedding day. Imagine your face when you walked down the aisle and realised you were going to have to marry a man dressed as the worst Avenger. I'm almost tempted to say yes just to make that happen. *Almost.*'

'Oh my god, can you imagine?' Hannah winced. 'No, I'd have to set some ground rules to stop that from ever happening.'

'Deal!' Jess agreed, laughing. 'I knew you would cheer me up! Although it really is time for me to go and see the bank. I'm not sure I'll be back before you leave – in fact, you should go home early today, don't wait around for me to get home. I'll tell you what the bank said in the morning, don't worry.'

'Right you are, chief!' Hannah saluted, before getting up to give her a hug. 'Just tell them you have an amazing office manager who has the very best ideas and Save The Date will be fine, I'm sure. But in all seriousness, J, try not to worry and listen to what they say and then let's take things from there, okay?'

Jess smiled and hugged her friend back, although no amount of positive thinking could get rid of the heavy feeling in the pit of her stomach. She'd been over and over Save The Date's financials, and there was no getting away from the fact that the business was still in debt and would likely be in debt for a while to come, bar a minor miracle. She just had to hope that it wasn't a minor miracle the bank was going to tell her she had to produce if they weren't going to withdraw their loan. She didn't say any of this to Hannah, however, and instead picked up her carefully curated folder of all the business's good points and dragged her feet out of the office and towards her car, her nerves jangling as much as the car keys in her hand.

Chapter 4

Hannah

'So, how did it go?' Hannah asked the next morning before Jess even had a chance to shut the door and remove the winter coat the freezing weather outside demanded. She shivered as an ice-cold breeze blew around the summerhouse and, not for the first time, she wondered what on earth had possessed her to return to Manchester when she could be feeling the blissful heat of the summer sun in any number of countries far away from the north-west of England. 'What did the bank say?' she asked again impatiently when Jess didn't immediately answer.

'Shall we have some coffee?' her friend replied with a small smile. 'And I brought us a couple of croissants that the kids turned their privileged little noses up at because they're not the chocolate ones they're used to.'

'The twins' loss is very much our gain,' Hannah said, eyeing up the pastries hungrily. 'I know it's not even ten o'clock, but I'm starving. Seriously, going to the gym should come with a health warning. I always eat double what I normally would after a workout, even one that only lasts twenty-five minutes. Here you go, coffee strong enough to stand your spoon up in, just as you like it. Now, are you going to tell me what happened yesterday afternoon while I scoff a croissant?'

Jess's smile didn't reach her eyes and she sipped her coffee slowly before taking the seat opposite Hannah at their little office's 'meeting table' and fiddling with a biro. 'Okay, so, I don't want you to worry, but I need to be honest with you about the financials.'

Hannah tried to rearrange her anxious expression into something more business-like and supportive, but in the end settled for taking a huge bite of her croissant and nodding.

Jess produced the folder of paperwork – or 'plastic wallet of doom', as Hannah often thought of it – she'd taken along to the bank the previous day and piled the sheets onto the table between them. Hannah felt her eyes start to glaze over at the sight of so many spreadsheets.

'I'm not going to bore you with lots of facts and figures,' Jess began, making Hannah immediately feel better. 'But this is the document I wanted to show you.' She pulled out a slightly dog-eared sheet from the bottom of the pile and laid it in front of Hannah. 'This is how many paying users we have, and this is how much money they bring in a year.'

'But that isn't much more than my salary!' Hannah said, looking directly at her. 'What about *your* salary?'

Jess shifted uncomfortably in her supposedly comfy chair. 'Well, I haven't really been paying myself one for the last twelve months or so.'

Hannah was appalled. 'So how have you and Tom been paying the mortgage and buying the kids' school stuff, and all the other bills that seem to go with being an adult? I don't understand.'

'Well, I obviously had my redundancy money from my marketing job—'

'But that was, what, nearly two years ago now? And didn't you use some of that to set up Save The Date in the first place?'

'Ye-es, along with a loan from the bank. But Tom's art business brings in a bit of money too, don't forget. And we took some equity out of the house, plus we had a few investments.'

'Right. I don't know much about these things having never owned a house myself, but I know you said when you bought this place that the mortgage was scarily huge, so it must be even bigger now?' Hannah looked at her questioningly. 'And did those investments work out?'

Jess couldn't meet her eye.

'Shit, Jess, just how much of your finances are tied up in Save The Date?'

'A lot,' she replied quietly, fidgeting with the side of the chair.

'And if the app doesn't get more paying users, what happens?'

'The bank will pull out their loan, the business will fail, I won't be able to pay you ... and we might have to sell the house.'

Hannah looked at her wide-eyed. 'Fuck.'

'Yep, that about sums it up.'

'Does Tom know?'

It was Jess's turn to look shocked. 'Of course he knows, it's not something I'd keep from him!'

'You kept it from me,' Hannah shot back. 'Sorry, I shouldn't have said that. Your finances are none of my business.'

'Except in this instance they are,' Jess said sadly. 'Anyway, Tom's working as hard as he can, I'm sure. It's not like he can just churn out paintings every day – and he'd still have to sell them even if he did. Anyway, let's concentrate on Save The Date. The finance gurus reckon if we can double our paying users within the next six months and then continue to grow them at a steady rate for a *further* six months, we could start to get ourselves out of this mess.'

'Well, that doesn't sound too horrific,' Hannah said, pulling up her sleeves.

'Except when you think that it's taken eighteen months to get to where we are now,' Jess replied with a sigh.

'But you didn't have me on board for that first year, so it doesn't really count.' Hannah grinned. 'Okay, so we need something big that's going to make a splash and entice a huge amount of people to part with their money very quickly, as well as gain the attention of new users in the long term.

Something none of our bigger competitors are doing or would maybe even want to do, as that's what sets us apart. Something that will mean everyone hears about Save The Date and makes them want to get involved.' She wrote down bullet points in her notebook as she spoke and then looked at the page in front of her. 'What else?'

'You're right, it needs to be something to do with our USP. What can we do with Save The Date that Tinder or Bumble or any of the others can't?'

Silence stretched between them as they racked their brains for something, anything, creative that would pull in the punters. Jess tapped her fingers on the table as tumbleweed swirled through her mind, only interrupted by thoughts of whether she'd remembered to defrost the sausages for the twins' tea and if she'd bought a birthday card for Tom's brother.

'You know ... there's always my ide—' Hannah started before Jess cut her off.

'No, Han. I'm not pimping you out just to save my dating app! I don't even understand how you think you marrying a stranger would drive people to sign up in the first place.'

'Well, I've been thinking about that,' Hannah said, her heart quickening with excitement. 'You know earlier this week—'

Suddenly the door opened and Tom came striding in. 'Knock knock, I come bearing gifts of real filter coffee and muffins!'

Hannah and Jess turned to stare at him.

'What? Oh sorry, have I interrupted? I'll come back in a bit,' he added.

'No, no, I'll have a muffin, Tank – that croissant barely touched the sides.' Hannah smiled, and he was quickly relieved of the food and drink before Jess pulled her desk chair over to the table for him.

'I was just telling Hannah what the bank said yesterday.' Jess grimaced. 'We're trying to come up with some way of doubling our subscribers in the next few months and we have precisely nothing.'

'Well, not *nothing*,' Hannah said. 'Look, both of you just hear me out and then let's see what we think, okay? So you know last week when Andy and Pippa sent that bottle of gin to announce their engagement and say thank you?' Hannah began. Her friend nodded, though Tom looked blank. Clearly Jess had decided that what was drunk in the Save The Date office, stayed in the Save The Date office. 'Well, anyway, it made me realise that what we need to do is celebrate our successes and make sure our customers know that real people are using the app and finding their soulmates. That's the whole reason people sign up to us: to find The One so they can live happily ever after. But we know from the bank's doom and gloom that not enough people are buying into that dream of wedded bliss, so *that's* what we need to sell harder.'

Tom chewed his lip. 'Right, that makes sense. But how are we going to do that?'

Hannah could see Jess frowning at her, so she focused all her attention on Tom. 'We show them what the app could do for them. Publicly. We prove that it really does work – just look at Andy and Pippa. We show them that anyone – even a loser like me – can find love and get married!'

'But you haven't found love, have you?' Tom asked, confused. 'And you're not getting married – that I know of anyway,' he added laughing.

'Not yet, but what if Save The Date set me up on the ultimate blind date?'

'Hannah . . .' Jess began.

'I still don't quite understand,' Tom interrupted.

'Okay, in simple terms it would work something like this: Jess finds me the perfect match via Save The Date and then we sell the idea that the app can find anyone The One, even poor lonely thirty-something me, and I trust the company so much that I agree to marry my match on our very first date. We'll place a few stories in the press to create a bit of a stir, then we'll get them to follow up with me and my perfect husband a few months down the line and everyone will see how happy we are and want a bit of that happiness themselves. The app goes crazy, more and more people who want to get married and settle down subscribe, meaning the pool of people to choose from is even bigger, so more and more users find their perfect match and set a date for their wedding – and, bingo, we've created a self-perpetuating circle that ensures Save The Date becomes a success.'

'But do you even want to get married, Hannah?' Tom asked.

'Yes,' she said simply. 'If you mean do I want to find

someone I love enough – and who loves me enough – to spend the rest of our lives having adventures together, then yes.'

'Well . . . wow!' Tom said. 'I mean, it's clearly crazy, but it will definitely get people talking. Although I'm still not quite sure how it will mean we get a load of subscribers in the short term and get the bank off our back.'

Hannah's excitement began to diminish as she realised she definitely wasn't sure how that would happen either.

'What if we put out a call for guys to take part?' Jess suddenly said. 'We know we have more women than men signed up to the app at the moment, which isn't ideal when we're trying to cater to everyone. So doing a subscription shout-out for eligible men who are up for the date of a lifetime should not only beef up our male members, it should also . . . What? Why are you both pissing yourselves?'

'*Beef up our male members*?' Hannah smirked, before nudging Tom and dissolving into giggles again.

'God, you two are so childish,' Jess scolded, but Hannah could see she too was trying not to laugh. 'Now I can't remember what I was saying! Right . . . it should not only boost our male member*ship*, it should also create some early publicity and buzz around the app's USP.'

Hannah made an effort to straighten her face and say something helpful. 'That's a great idea, J. And to give us a bigger reach and boost memberships we should come up with a special offer for both men and women, whether they want to put themselves forward to be my blind-date husband or not.' Warming to her theme, she added, 'And we should do some focused Facebook ads directed at single people in their late twenties and thirties, as they don't cost that much and should reach our target audience. And we also need to leverage people like Andy and Pippa who have already found love through Save The Date. Have you asked them for testimonials or anything yet, Jess?'

Jess shook her head, clearly annoyed at herself for not thinking of that sooner.

'Then let's not only get them to write something for the website, but also ask them if we could share their engagement picture and use it on our social channels, and maybe even write a press release to get out to the media. I mean, we all need a good-news story when the world around us is falling apart like it seems to have been lately!'

'You're right, Hannah,' Tom nodded. 'As far as I'm aware, Save The Date hasn't done much press at all since launch, has it, Jess? And that's not a criticism,' he added. Hannah glanced at Jess's frown and Tom's fearful look and decided to step in quickly.

'No, we haven't, but we should definitely start now, right, Jess? I guess if this is going to be a truly blind-date wedding, not only will I not be able to meet my groom, but he also won't be able to see me, so we can't use a photo of me in our call-out for a would-be Mr Edwards. So let's use Andy and Pippa to launch the search for my husband. What do you think?' Hannah turned her gaze full on Jess, who had been uncharacteristically quiet.

'I'm just not sure,' her friend said, shaking her head.

'Jess, let me at least give it a go. If it works then I end up with a gorgeous husband I love for the rest of my life and you end up with a successful business that will mean you don't need to worry about stupid bank managers. And if it doesn't work, well at least I'll have had fun trying! If I'm truly honest, life has been feeling a bit stale the past few months, despite the joy of spending more time with you guys and the twins, and my family. I've been missing that adventure and thrill-seeking you know I crave so much. And this feels like the perfect opportunity to jump into something exciting and potentially life-changing in all the right ways.'

'You really are serious about this, aren't you?'

'Yes, I am. You're thinking of this as if you're the one who's going on the marriage blind date, so you're never going to be on board because it's the last thing on this earth you'd do. But for me, it makes perfect sense – okay, not *perfect* sense, but you know what I mean.' She smiled at the look on her friend's face. 'You started Save The Date because you saw a gap in the market for people who want long-term, grown-up love. I'll never forget you writing that email telling me about the conversation you'd just had with a couple of the mums at school who struggled using dating apps. The guys they matched with always seemed to be up for one thing only, and weren't interested in a long-term relationship. I could feel your excitement even though I was thousands of miles away, and when you asked me if I thought you were mad to take a punt and start Save The Date – you'd even come up with the name, for god's sake! – I immediately replied telling you to go for it, as I'm sure you knew I would! I know you think I should be finally growing up and settling down, so this is my slightly mad way of doing it. I know I'm taking a chance, but isn't that what you did setting up the business in the first place?'

Jess still didn't look completely convinced. 'But what if you get hurt in the process? I'm not sure I can deal with the responsibility of promising you sunshine and roses for the rest of your life only for you to end up heartbroken and divorced.'

'That's the real world, though,' Hannah said thoughtfully. 'Whoever I end up marrying might turn out to be a dick, whether I've met them thanks to my best friend's amazing matchmaking skills or drunk in a dodgy club in Cuba. Isn't that the chance we all take when we agree to marry some-one? Except you two, obviously – you were always meant to be together for ever. And you'd have me to deal with if either of you tried to leave! Which is why both of you should be involved in choosing my husband-to-be.' She caught Jess's raised eyebrow and quickly added, 'Though of course you'd be the one in charge, Jess.' She saw her friend's face relax just a little so she delivered the knockout blow. 'If I don't do this, I might just pack in the whole finding a man thing for good.'

'Han, your love life hasn't been *that* bad up till now,' Jess reasoned.

'Define bad . . . I'm sick of going on first dates with boring Barrys and moron Matts for god's sake!'

'Who are Barry and Matt?' Tom asked.

'You don't need to know,' Hannah and Jess said at the same time. Hannah smiled and reached for her friend's hand. 'Jess, I need to do this. I know we all want what we don't have, but from where I'm sitting and looking at you two and your gorgeous twins, married life looks pretty bloody perfect. Is it so wrong to want a bit of that?' Hannah watched as Jess's eyes moved to look at her husband and her face broke into a smile.

'Believe me, it's *definitely* not bloody perfect. But you're right, I don't know what I'd do without Tom and the kids now.'

Hannah noticed tears were pricking at her friend's eyes and she herself had to blink hard a few times, but then she stood up and declared, 'Okay, so that's settled then!'

'I'm not sure I actually agreed to anything,' Jess protested.

'I'm sure I heard you say yes, right after you'd said what an amazing man you'd married yourself!' Tom laughed, and suddenly the three of them were hugging and laughing and cheering like they'd won the lottery.

'What just happened?' Jess said when they'd all calmed down a bit. 'I feel drunk. Though is it too early for one of your special gin and tonics, Han?'

'It's only midday,' Tom laughed. 'And sadly I've got a call with a prospective client in a few minutes so I'll have to leave you to it. But don't go agreeing to any more harebrained schemes when I'm not looking, Jess, I know what you're like now!'

'I'm still not sure I agreed to this one,' Jess answered,

shaking her head again. 'Although before you go, Tom, in all seriousness, if we are going to do this I think we all need to agree that if any of us feel this ultimate blind date thing is getting out of hand – especially you, Hannah – we will pull the whole idea. Without meaning to sound trite, no amount of money can buy happiness, and if there's a choice between my best friend being happy and saving this business, my best friend wins out every single time without fail. We can deal with whatever financial mess we're faced with, but I can't deal with knowing I've made you miserable, Han. So we need to promise we're going to be honest with each other at all times throughout this process.'

'Of course,' Hannah nodded. 'I really want to do this, but I also really want us all to be friends at the end of it, so I'll definitely let you know if you start pissing me off!'

They all laughed slightly hysterically and Tom gave them both a hug before racing back to the house to make his call. They watched him go and when it was just the two of them, Jess walked over to the desk, dumped the papers on top of it and declared, 'Right, I'm not sure how I follow any of that, but I'm about to add "Find Hannah the man of her dreams" to the top of my to-do list, so I'm going to be pretty busy for the next few weeks, which means unfortunately you're going to have to do the dreaded certificate updates this month, Han. Bad luck!'

Hannah groaned but smiled. 'I'll let you off, seeing as how you've got the best excuse ever!'

*

That evening, as she waited for the ping of the microwave to tell her that her baked potato was ready, Hannah steadfastly ignored the notifications lighting up her phone to tell her she had received four WhatsApp messages from Matt. What was the point in reading his pathetic excuses? And anyway, Jess was about to find her a husband so Matt was very much out of the picture now.

Later, in a post jacket-with-cheese-*and*-beans coma, she idly scrolled through the messages before remembering she wasn't supposed to actually read them. She decided she might as well reply seeing as how Matt could now see the blue ticks showing she'd opened them.

> Hi Matt, thanks for your messages, though
> I definitely didn't need that much detail
> about the state of your current relationship.
> It's always complicated, isn't it? Anyway,
> I think it's only fair to tell you that I've just
> agreed to get married to someone myself,
> so I won't be responding to any future texts
> from you. Good luck and hope you manage
> to finally find the courage to break up
> with the girlfriend you've told me so much
> about. Hannah x

Hannah put down her phone with a big smile on her face and absent-mindedly began humming a tune she only later realised was 'Here Comes the Bride'.

Chapter 5

Jess

Finding Hannah the man of her dreams was a pretty daunting mission, Jess concluded the following week. She'd contacted Pippa and Andy, who had been delighted to help launch Save The Date's search for the perfect groom, and the press release was drafted and almost ready to go, along with social media ads and emails to everyone already on their mailing list. One minute she worried that no one would put themselves forward to be part of such a mad scheme, while the next she fretted thousands of people would apply and she'd never be able to decide between them all. And even if she did think one of them would be a good match, would Hannah agree? Jess had spent a whole evening flicking through her friend's old Facebook images to get a snapshot of the kind of guy she usually went for, but one tanned, long-haired beach-bum bartender tended to look fairly similar to another after a while, and now she was more confused than ever. It was all so much responsibility. She was actually holding her best friend's future in her hands.

Jess had been Hannah's friend for over twenty years and truly believed she knew her inside and out. But she also knew that there were times in their lives when they hadn't seen each other as much as they would have liked, especially when Hannah was on a different continent for months on end; plus, although Hannah spent a lot of time with Jess's family, Jess only saw Hannah occasionally with *her* family. And even then it was with just her mum, or maybe with her dad and his family. She needed to build up a bigger picture of Hannah and the different – and difficult – relationships in her life in order to make sure she matched her with the right man.

'Why not take a couple of afternoons off work and hang out with her mum, her brother and her dad and his family each day?' Tom suggested, when she voiced her worries to him on the sofa that night. 'You don't have to tell them the plan is for her to marry the man you match her with, just that you want to find her the right man, and as you run a dating app, you want to make sure the algorithms or whatever are working properly.'

'Mr T, you are sometimes a bit of a genius!' she smiled.

'Sometimes? I think you'll find it's all the time,' he replied, yawning. 'Although sadly my genius doesn't stretch to where Sam has stashed his PE kit – do you know where it is? Their teacher told me at pick-up that Sam says he's lost it so won't be able to do PE tomorrow at all.'

'Is it not in the cupboard under the stairs with Lily's?' Jess frowned.

'I don't know, I didn't know that's where it lived, and I forgot to ask Sam about it earlier because he was chatting away about some Pokémon thing that I didn't understand on the way home. I thought he would have talked to you about his kit.'

'Well, it's lived in the cupboard for the last three years – after they've dumped it on the floor and I've sorted through it, washed it, ironed it and put it back in the bag, obviously.' Jess replied, irritated her husband had so little clue about the mundane minutiae of their lives. 'And before you say it, no, I'm not better at remembering these things than you, I just listen better and have no choice but to sort things out. That reminds me, did you see that email from the school about inset days next term?'

'I saw something in my inbox, but I didn't read it,' Tom answered, yawning again. 'Right, I'm off to bed, are you coming up?'

Jess rolled her eyes. 'I'll just locate the PE kits, update the calendar with the inset days and be up soon.'

Her exasperation seemed to be lost on Tom as he merely replied, 'Okay, see you shortly. Oh, did I mention I can't do school pick-up tomorrow as I've got a call and I've also got a meeting in town on Wednesday? You'll be able to swap with me though, won't you?'

'Do I have a choice? Though we do have a thing called a calendar, you know, where we're both supposed to note things like that down?'

'I know, but if I just tell you that's much easier; I know you'll always remember these things,' Tom said, giving her a kiss on the cheek as he went upstairs.

Half an hour later, PE kits checked and placed in the hall ready for the following morning, calendar updated, plus a prompt added to her phone for closer to the time to remind Tom about the inset day, Jess had texted Joan, Scott and Hannah's dad John and arranged to see each of them over the next week, having very briefly explained that she wanted to talk to them about the sort of man Hannah should date. It had been too late to call Hannah's grandma, but she'd emailed her as she knew how much Vera enjoyed using her iPad. All she had to do now was tell Hannah, and she wasn't quite sure what she was going to think about her plan.

'So you're going to see my parents, grandma and brother to talk about me, but I'm not allowed to come too?' Hannah asked the following morning after Jess had broken the news to her.

'Yep, that's about the size of it!' she laughed. 'While I'm at it, I Facebooked Dee and Johanna, and although Dee is obviously in Oz and Johanna is somewhere I can't even pronounce, I'm going to email them some questions and they're going to send me their answers.'

'Myanmar. Or at least that's where she was last I heard. She's working for a humanitarian charity over there; she's amazing. Though I'm surprised she's got time to indulge you in your ridiculous questions!'

'They're not ridiculous, Han, they're going to help me find you a husband – there's nothing ridiculous about that. Would you rather I just did eeny meeny miny moe? Because I can, you know?'

'Of course not, it's just a bit weird you speaking to my family and friends without me being there, that's all.'

'But if you were there, do you think they'd actually say what they really think?' Jess reasoned.

'Have you met my mother? Though maybe the others wouldn't, I'm not sure. Fine, go and see them, but don't blame me when you realise how weird they all really are!'

'Well, they are related to you, after all!' Jess grinned.

She'd arranged to start with Joan, Hannah's mum, as she lived the closest. In fact, she was still in the pretty semi-detached house Hannah had grown up in. The only difference now was that Hannah's dad lived a ten-minute drive away with his second wife and their daughter. Not that Jess really wanted to mention that to Joan, as she knew she was still rather prickly about the situation.

'Jess! So lovely of you to pop over,' Joan cried as soon as she opened the door and ushered Jess inside. 'I thought we could have a glass of Pinot Grigio while we chat,' she giggled girlishly once they were ensconced on her three-piece suite.

'Joan, you're so naughty, it's only two o'clock!' Jess laughed. 'But go on, I'll have a very small glass – I'm driving, sadly.'

Joan fussed around with side tables and coasters, but finally she relaxed and sipped her wine. 'So, this sounds exciting: you're trying to get Hannah to finally settle down, I hear?'

'Well, it actually all came from Hannah,' Jess replied earnestly. 'She's asked me to help her find a man she can be with long term, seeing as how we both work on Save The Date. It sounds like she'd definitely like to settle down. So I wanted to ask you what you thought of any of her previous boyfriends.'

'She rarely deigns to bring them round to meet me,' Joan said rather bitterly.

'I don't think she's had many, erm, steady boyfriends recently, so maybe that's why,' Jess said gently. 'But what about before then?'

'Well, she was abroad so much before then, so I suppose I've only really met the boys she used to go out with when she was a teenager, and they all seemed far too unambitious for her. But I suppose when you're that age, all you're interested in is beer and girls,' she tittered. 'Except for your Tom, Jess, he's always been a nice boy. At least your mum has never had to worry. But with Hannah, she's never been interested in settling down with anyone.'

'There were a few guys she met when she was abroad, weren't there?' Jess pressed. 'Did she tell you anything about them?'

'There was a man she met in Fiji, who she liked, I think. He was from Australia or New Zealand, or somewhere like that, and she took him to Wales, I think, although goodness knows why; it was soon after that it fell apart, from what I can work out. She never brought him home to meet us, that's for sure, and she just stopped mentioning him so I didn't like to ask what happened. As I said, I don't really know anything about my daughter's love life, and I'm sure that's the way she likes it!' She smiled a little sadly, before topping up her glass and offering the bottle to Jess, who had hardly touched her own wine and politely waved it away.

'Okay, what kind of man do you think Hannah *should* date then, especially if she is looking for a long-term relationship?'

'She needs someone who's going to balance her out,' Joan replied immediately.

'What do you mean?'

'Well, you know what she's like, always rushing headlong into things; she needs a man who's going to make her stop and think before she runs off to the nearest hot country to "find herself" again.'

'So someone who's going to complement her adventurous nature, but help keep her feet on dry land?' Jess smiled.

'Exactly!' Joan agreed. 'I keep telling her she needs to realise she's not in her twenties any longer. But you're right, he has to also have that exciting, exploring streak about him. I can't imagine Hannah with anyone too boring, like an accountant or tax adviser. He has to have something about him to keep her interested. And he needs to be intelligent. Hannah is so clever; if only she put her mind to things, she could be a real high-flyer in a big company. No offence to your company, Jess, of course, but you know what I mean. She could have walked into any job after university, like my friend Mary's son, who's a top lawyer down in London now, but instead she found herself behind a bar in yet another beach resort. But you've got to let them do what they want, I suppose,' she sighed.

'I'm already finding that with my two, and they're only eight.' Jess nodded. 'They'll be teenagers before I know it! So what do you think is the most important thing to Hannah in a relationship?'

'Gosh, I've never really thought about it, you'd probably have to ask her.'

'But what do you *think* might be important to her?' Jess pushed.

'I don't know. Hopefully that he's kind. Oh, and funny. Hannah has always loved to joke around, as you know, and doesn't take anything too seriously, more's the pity! And that he seems like he might be good with children I suppose.'

'Has Hannah ever talked to you about having kids?' Jess asked tentatively in case she was crossing a line.

'Not directly and definitely not recently,' Joan said. 'But she's always liked children, hasn't she. When she was little, she used to tell me she wished she had a little sister to play with. She had Scott, obviously, but I think she fancied bossing around a younger sibling and she was desperate to dress up all her dolls in pink baby clothes.'

'I didn't know that,' Jess said, intrigued.

'She grew out of it, I suppose, and then she became as thick as thieves with you at secondary school so didn't need a sister anymore. And I can remember having to tell her off for bossing *you* around so much in those first few years. Thankfully, that was another thing she grew out of.'

'Ahh, she still does her fair share of that now!' Jess laughed. 'I've taken up too much of your time already, but I wanted to ask you one final question. Is there anyone – apart from an accountant or a tax adviser – you think Hannah definitely shouldn't date?'

'A cheat,' Joan answered crisply. 'Hannah would hate to be humiliated and I would hate to see her hurt. Once a man has cheated, he's a cheat for life, believe me. No matter what the circumstances, there's never an excuse, never.'

'Yes, right. Okay, that's everything, I think.' Jess smiled awkwardly. 'Thank you, Joan, you've been so helpful, and hopefully I'll be able to find Hannah the perfect match.'

'If anyone can, you can, Jess,' Joan said warmly. 'I know Hannah really looks up to you and your marriage to Tom, and she loves those dear children of yours, too. You must bring them with you next time you come and we'll bake some biscuits. Hannah and Scott used to love mixing the dough together when they were little, although they'd always squabble over who got to lick the bowl, the little terrors!'

Jess smiled. 'The twins would love that, I'm sure. Thanks again, Joan.'

She was a bit late making her way over to Hannah's dad John's house the following afternoon, after the bank called her to confirm everything she'd already discussed with the adviser in person the week before. Sadly, Save The Date's financial position was no less precarious than it had been then, and hearing it all again had upset and destabilised her, which meant she'd then missed the correct turning off the main road and had to double back on herself, adding to the delay.

'I'm so sorry I'm late, I can't believe I went the wrong way, even with the sat nav telling me what to do,' she gabbled as John showed her into the kitchen, with its large table and fridge covered with paintings and crayon-filled pictures.

'It's not a problem at all, Jess,' he said as he made them both tea. 'Charmaine will be back from the school run with Seraphina soon and they'll both be so pleased you're still here. We were saying last night how long it is since we've seen you. Although we haven't actually seen Hannah for a while either, I must invite her over for Sunday lunch. Anyway, you said you had some questions?'

'Yes, that's right. I've promised Hannah I'll help find her The One, but I can't do it on my own, which is why I wanted to talk to you about the kind of man you think she should go for.'

'In my dad role, I obviously don't think any man out there is good enough for my little Hannah,' he laughed. 'But I do think she'd love to have someone to settle down with now she's finally putting down some roots back home and not always on a flight to wherever the next big thing is. So I'd say someone who can let her be herself without clipping her wings, but also makes her want to stay in one place for an extended amount of time, with that place hopefully being local. It's been so nice having her back home for the past six months, and I know her mum appreciates it too.'

'I saw Joan yesterday,' Jess nodded. 'She was telling me that back in the day Han always wanted a little sister, which I didn't know.'

'For a while, she'd ask us every day if she was getting a new baby sister like so many of the other kids in her class and she'd point at her mum's tummy and ask if she could listen for the baby's heartbeat. I think she even told her teacher she was going to have a sister at one point and poor Joan had to explain to them that no, she wasn't pregnant. I think Hannah thought that if she wished for it enough, a baby would just appear! Sadly, it wasn't to be, but thankfully she met you a few years later, and I know she sees you as the sister she never had, Jess.'

'Me too.' Jess smiled, her throat tight with emotion. 'Any other qualities you think her perfect match needs?'

'To tell her how much he loves her every day. I know Hannah adores her grandmother, and her poor grandfather before he passed away – sadly my own parents never got to meet her as they both died when Scott was tiny – and she often talks about their amazing relationship. I know me and her mum didn't always have the best marriage, but I always loved Joan. I just wish I'd told her more often. I'm trying not to make the same mistake this time though,' he said, before clearing his throat. 'Listen to me going all soft! I just want Hannah to be happy and with a man who adores her. Everything else is a bonus. Ah, I hear the sound of a hungry little girl. We're in here, darling,' he called.

'Daddy, we made insect houses at school today and then Mrs Wilson read us all a story about a boy who had a funny eye and got laughed at except by one nice little girl in his class and then they became best friends and went on a magic carpet together. It was awesome.'

'Everything is awesome at the moment, isn't it, darling. Say hello to Jess and then you can have a snack. I think Mummy has put one in the fridge for you.'

With that, Charmaine walked into the kitchen. 'Jess, it's so lovely to see you, it's been far too long. You should come over with the twins for a play date with Seraphina – shall I send you some dates?'

'That would be lovely,' nodded Jess, aware that she'd also promised to take them over to Joan's at some point. At this rate, she'd be seeing more of Hannah's family than she did her own parents.

'We were just talking about Hannah and her new man. Well, the new man Jess here is going to find her.'

'I hope he's handsome!' Charmaine said. 'Hannah is so pretty that she needs a good match in the looks department.'

'Noted!' Jess said, while trying not to laugh at John's face. 'Anything else?'

'Hannah would like to marry a painter,' Seraphina announced through a mouthful of carrot and houmous.

'Really, why do you think that, darling?' her dad asked.

'She told me,' she replied importantly. 'She was plaiting my hair and we were talking about why she didn't have a boyfriend and she said she hadn't found anyone who made her tummy whoosh enough. I asked her who would do that and she said someone creative and I asked her what creative means and she said like a painter and I said that we had a painter coming to paint our hall tomorrow and I could ask him if he had a girlfriend if she wanted, and then she laughed but I don't know why.'

'Wow, you do have a good memory, Seraphina!' Jess laughed. 'I think someone creative sounds perfect for Hannah.'

'She's a lovely kid,' Jess said to John and Charmaine as Seraphina went upstairs to change out of her school things.

'She is,' John agreed proudly. 'And it's nice to see her and Hannah getting along so well. Scott is a bit more distant with his half-sister so she doesn't have the same kind of bond with him, but she adores Hannah.'

'And Hannah adores her too.'

Jess was slightly dreading her meeting with Scott. She'd arranged to meet him in a hipster café in the Northern Quarter in town at his suggestion, and she was quite glad time would be fairly tight. She wouldn't have more than three-quarters of an hour before she had to get back to pick the twins up – Tom apparently had another meeting he couldn't move.

So, it meant a massive schlep into town for a very short amount of time. Jess being Jess, she'd managed to arrive half an hour early, despite her attempts not to be, so she was already on her second latte by the time Scott arrived. He was as good-looking as he'd always been, with his strong jaw and cheekbones. His eyes were the same chocolate brown as Hannah's, though where her hair was dark and glossy to match, his was a dirty blond that was gelled neatly at the front, except for one lock that fell across his forehead in what he probably thought was an attractive way, but which annoyed Jess immediately. She was secretly happy to see the telltale grey bags beneath his eyes that showed he wasn't immune to getting up in the night with the baby, plus she was glad to feel none of the frission of attraction she'd experienced throughout her teen years whenever she'd seen him – despite being with Tom for much of them. She'd once let slip to Hannah that she thought her brother was pretty hot, and her friend had ripped the mick out of her mercilessly for a whole year afterwards.

'Scott, hi!' she called as she saw him glancing round the café and missing her entirely.

'Jess, I'd have known you anywhere! Looking gorgeous!' He grinned. 'I'll just grab a coffee.'

'So how are you?' she asked a couple of minutes later as they sipped their drinks.

'I'm really good. I've got loads of work on at the moment. I manage construction sites so I've got literally hundreds of people that I've got to make sure are pulling their weight and not taking liberties. It's hard work, but they all respect me, you know, so it's all good.' Jess tried hard not to pull a face, but she softened as he started talking about Julia and Leo. 'And of course there's the small matter of me being a dad now! Which is crazy and brilliant, though nobody tells you you're going to feel ... well, feel so much, really. And Julia is just amazing. Seriously, I thought I knew what love was but it wasn't until I saw Julia feeding Leo that I *knew*, if you know what I mean. Has Hannah shown you pictures? Here, look at this one I took yesterday when I came home from work – they were both spark out on the sofa, bless them.'

Jess grinned in recognition of the exhaustion of motherhood, though was also sure she'd never looked as beautiful as Julia did asleep *before* she'd had the twins, never mind afterwards. 'He's gorgeous, and Hannah clearly loves spending time with you all,' she said.

'Yeah, she's very sweet with him, although she has also taught him to blow raspberries, which Julia's not quite so happy about! It is actually really nice to have her back here in Manc, though I can't understand why she didn't stay in Oz or wherever she was, I know I'd be out there like a shot if I could. Anyway, what's all this about finding her a man? She didn't mention anything to me when she was over the other weekend.'

'Well, I think she's up for settling down and wanted it to be back home. I'm trying to find her the perfect match through my dating app and I wondered if you had any thoughts about why her previous relationships haven't lasted and what the right kind of guy for her is like?'

Scott looked surprised at the question and rubbed his eyes. 'I guess all the guys she previously went out with were just not right for her – or she wasn't right for them, anyway.'

Jess suppressed a sigh. 'But why do you think that is?' she probed.

'Well, she's very headstrong, isn't she? If she doesn't want to do something then she's not going to do it, which might put some men off. And she's quite independent. Even as a kid she was always climbing trees or off reading in a corner on her own. Most of my mates had their sisters trailing round after them wanting to be part of our crew, you know, but Hannah was never like that. She's always been independent and guys just sometimes want to look after their birds and be that hunter gatherer, whereas Hannah never seemed to need that.'

'Okay, what about Hannah's *good* points,' Jess asked, raising her eyebrows. 'What do you think she brings to a relationship that other women don't?'

'God, do you know how weird it is thinking about my sister getting it on with someone!' Scott made a vomit noise and Jess wondered whether she should just give the whole thing up and go home and scroll through the Save The Date database for men who were nothing like Scott, as clearly that was now her first prerequisite. As Hannah's best mate, she surely had to actually *like* her husband-to-be.

'Maybe just think about their first date, rather than them "getting it on" then,' she said.

'Right, got ya. Okay, so I'll say one thing for Hannah and that's that she always has good chat. Some women look ten out of ten but as soon as they open their mouth they drop to a five out of ten, you know what I mean? Hannah always has something to say or a great story about when she went travelling or whatever. And obviously she's a good-looking girl – she is related to me after all!' Scott found his own joke hilarious and chuckled to himself for a good sixty seconds before carrying on.

'So, yeah, she's funny, got something to say and is pretty. Any bloke would be lucky to have her, I'd say. Though you might want to let them meet me first and I can check them out for you and see if they're sound.'

'I'll keep that in mind.' Jess smiled politely. 'Right, thanks so much, Scott, it's been lovely catching up and thanks for all your help, it's been invaluable.' Invaluable in helping her realise that Scott seemed to be just as much of an idiot as he had been when they were teenagers and he had been Hannah's hot but stupid older brother. She could only hope for Leo's sake that Julia was less of an idiot, otherwise she pitied the poor child's chances at school.

'Ahh, mate, it's been so cool. Say hi to Han from me and tell her Julia will text her tomorrow, yeah?'

Jess wasn't sure why he couldn't send his own sister a text saying hi, but she nodded and hurried to catch the bus back to the safety of school pick-up and snacks on tap. She and Tom might have their problems, but at least he wasn't a misogynistic little idiot like Scott.

The following day, she was glad she'd left her visit to Hannah's grandma till last as she knew it would be a welcome relief after her coffee with Scott. She drove over to

Vera's sheltered-accommodation flat after doing the school run and was touched to see she'd gone to the trouble of getting her best china out for her arrival.

'When you're my age, you take every opportunity possible to use the posh tea things,' Vera said, waving away Jess's protests. 'And anyway, it was Carla who set it all out nicely like this – she's the lady who comes in to help me twice a day, and she's a total sweetheart, except when she's trying to get me to do something I don't want to do, and then she's a nightmare!'

'I can't imagine you doing anything you didn't want to do, Vera!' Jess smiled as she poured the tea and helped herself to a biscuit from the plate the older lady had pushed towards her.

'No, well, you'd be right there,' Vera chuckled. 'Now, what can I do for you, young Jessica? This is about our Hannah, I presume?'

'That's right. She might have told you that I've promised to find her a man through Save The Date, my dating app? Yes, so I wanted to chat to you and the rest of her family to see what kind of man you think would be most suited to her.'

'Now this is the kind of conversation I like!' Vera rubbed her hands together. 'Although I do have to say that I wouldn't count myself as an expert in these kind of matters. As you know, I have only ever loved one man in that kind of way – and I've never met a better man than my dear Robbie.'

Jess saw her eyes start to mist over and cursed herself for not being more thoughtful. 'But you are an expert when it comes to Hannah,' she said quickly.

'Well, in my opinion what that darling girl needs is someone who will not only treat her right, but who will also make her think differently about things from time to time. I often think Hannah has quite set views and she isn't one to change her mind once she's decided something. That can obviously be a very positive thing, but I get the sense my granddaughter isn't very good at compromise. You remember that boy she brought back from god knows where and she was all set on marrying after some walk on a beach in Wales? Well, she told me she split up with him because he thought playing the guitar was a profession not a hobby and she disagreed. Now, she may well have been right as I never had the pleasure of hearing this boy play, but it was definitely her way or the highway, so he chose the highway. I remember talking to her at the time about letting people have the space to be whoever they truly are, but if I'm honest, I'm not sure she took much notice of what her aged G-ma was telling her!'

'I can't remember what she told *me* was the reason for them breaking up,' Jess confessed. 'Especially as about a week later she flew off to Argentina or somewhere and it was a struggle to even get her to text me regularly!'

'That sounds like my granddaughter!' Vera smiled. 'Anyway, you've also been talking to Joan and John, I hear – you must tell me what they said when you asked them these kind of questions!'

Jess laughed but did as she was told and Vera did a lot of nodding and eyebrow-raising to show she did or didn't agree with what other people had said, as well as doing some uncanny impressions of her own daughter.

All too soon it was time for Jess to jump in the car and make her way back to the office for a phonecall with the web developer. Before she left, she washed up the tea things and put them away, and made sure that Vera was going to eat the sandwich the Meals on Wheels team had left with her that morning.

'You are a good girl, Jessica.' Vera smiled at her. 'But you make sure you find darling Hannah the right man, won't you. Or you'll have me to deal with!'

Jess laughed as she let herself out of the flat, though she knew that G-ma had only been half-joking.

Chapter 6

Hannah

'So, how have your interrogations of my family been going?' Hannah asked Jess on Monday morning, trying her best to sound nonchalant. 'Scott mentioned you'd gone for a coffee?'

'Why, are you worried they've divulged your darkest secrets to me?' Jess teased. 'It was interesting actually, though some were more helpful than others.'

'God, tell me. Did Scott spend most of the time talking about himself? Did Mum tell you what a disappointment I am to her? Was G-ma incredibly nosy? And did Dad get all soppy?'

'Maybe, a bit! Although your mum never said you were a disappointment – if anything it was the *opposite* – so shush.'

'What did they all say? Come on, tell me,' Hannah ordered.

'I'm not going to sit here and replay every conversation for you, I've got better things to do. As have you, Han, or have you finished updating all the certificates and permissions you were working on yesterday?'

'All right, boss, I'm on it!' she replied. 'But I'm finding it really hard to concentrate on anything except what my nearest and dearest spilled about me. I don't even know what you asked them.'

'Just questions like what they thought of your previous boyfriends and what qualities they thought you should be looking for in a long-term match.' Jess shrugged, continuing to tap away at her keyboard.

'And? Did they say they hated everyone I've ever gone out with and thought I should set my sights on a sugar daddy so I never have to work again?'

'Hannah! How many coffees have you had this morning?' Jess sighed. 'Look, they were all really supportive, although your mum and dad admitted they didn't know much about the guys you went out with when you were travelling, but luckily Johanna and Dee helped fill in the gaps over email. The consensus was you probably tend to go for men who aren't that well matched to you in terms of life goals and plans. It's almost like you're protecting yourself from having a long-term relationship by choosing guys who won't make it beyond six months. It feels like you're waiting for men to do the dirty on you, so you tend to get in first and end the relationship early.'

Hannah's eyes widened. 'Ooh, listen to you, Dr Freud!'

'But you're not denying it's true? Interesting . . .' Jess said, pushing her laptop away.

73

'Don't be ridiculous. I just haven't found someone I want to be in a long-term relationship with – which is why I've asked *you* to find me The One as you're so successful at everything and clearly I am not!' She stuck out her tongue and Jess laughed. 'Don't you think you should be asking me the same questions you asked everyone else? Surely my views on what's gone wrong – and what's gone right – with my exes are even more important?'

'But, on past evidence, you don't seem to be the best judge of who's right for you – hence why I'm in charge of finding you a husband,' Jess reminded her.

Hannah nodded in defeat. 'I know and you're right. I definitely don't trust myself to find the right man and I definitely *do* trust you, and possibly Tom. I meant it about you being successful in everything you do – that's just who you are and always have been. So, yes, I'm glad you're in charge of finding me a husband, it's just a bit weird not to feel part of the process. I am the one marrying this man, after all.'

'Right, okay, if it makes you happy.' Jess consulted the notebook she'd been jotting down thoughts in all week. 'What do you think was missing from all of your previous relationships that meant they didn't last?'

'God, have you ever heard of leading someone in gently? Okay, well I think none of my relationships have lasted long term because of the situation. Either I've been moving to another country or he's starting a new job that means working nights, or something like that.'

'Right. And not because you've got bored or he is happy

working in the same bar in the same town and you want to spread your wings somewhere else?'

'I mean, maybe,' Hannah shrugged. 'Sometimes I do get bored in the sense I suddenly realise I don't really fancy them after all. But you know how much I'm up for settling down now.'

'Are you, though?' Jess asked, eyeballing her closely.

'What, me saying I want to get married to a stranger isn't enough evidence for you?' Hannah replied incredulously.

'I'm just checking you haven't changed your mind, that's all. What qualities do you think are important in your future husband? Obviously I called him "long-term boyfriend" not "husband" when I was talking to your family, but I did also mention I was searching for The One for you. Anyway, qualities?'

'Tall, dark and handsome is far too obvious – and I'm definitely not bothered about the tall bit, being five-foot two myself – but I do definitely need to be attracted to him. I want the infamous spark – and when I say spark, I mean complete fireworks, obviously. And he needs to make me laugh until my stomach hurts. I'll never forget seeing you and Tom belly-laugh on your wedding day. I can't remember what it was about, but seeing the two of you sharing some secret joke together was just as heart-warming as watching you say your vows, to be honest. What else? Oh yes, he needs to be happy sharing a bottle of wine of an evening – is it too shallow to say someone who doesn't drink is immediately out of the running? Oh well, I've said it! But beyond all of that, I want someone who I can love as much as he loves me, so we're on an equal footing. If he's too good-looking or successful, I'll feel like I'm punching above my weight, but if he's lacking in the attractive stakes and has a job he doesn't care about, I worry I'll think I can do better.'

'That's quite a list! Though it's interesting you haven't mentioned about him needing to be kind,' Jess commented. 'Yet it's a word that came up time and time again when I spoke to other people.'

'Christ, what are you, my therapist?' Hannah said, wriggling around in her seat. 'Of course I'd like him to be kind. No one in their right mind would say they want an unkind partner, would they?'

Jess raised her eyebrows but didn't respond. 'One last question then: what is the ultimate deal-breaker? What's the one thing that would immediately make you run back down the aisle screaming "I don't"?'

'That's a great question.' Hannah grinned, but slowly her face become more serious as she really thought about her answer. 'God, it's actually really hard. I mean if they opened their mouth and spoke like Jacob Rees-Mogg then that would probably send me sprinting out the church. Or if they were a massive cokehead or already had four children by four different mothers, that might make me reconsider.'

'What if they already had one child or had been married before?' Jess probed.

'I guess as long as they were divorced it wouldn't matter. And I suppose them having a child would complicate things, but I haven't really thought about it. I think if they didn't like dogs, that would be a deal-breaker; you know how much I want a border collie at some point in my life.'

'Really, you've never mentioned it!' laughed Jess, turning round Hannah's computer to see her screensaver of five border collie puppies playing in some long grass. 'What about if they didn't like travelling, would that be a deal-breaker?'

'Do you think there are people out there who don't like to go places?' Hannah frowned. 'I mean, I'm not saying he has to agree to a year backpacking in the Himalayas, but I might struggle to have anything in common with someone who has never left Manchester, as much as I'm a Manc through and through.'

'All right, *our kid*!' Jess giggled, doing a rubbish impression of the Gallagher brothers.

'Why have I got a stronger Manc accent than you and I've spent the last ten years travelling around the world?' Hannah shook her head.

'I'm just well-posh, me. Anyway I'd better take another look at this press release, then I'll get you and Tom to look at it tomorrow, before we send it out on Wednesday.'

'This is quite a weird thing to do, isn't it?' Hannah suddenly said twenty minutes later, breaking their companionable silence.

'You mean someone else finding you a husband? I guess it is for us, but in India and Pakistan, women's families often introduce them to a man they think it would be good for them to marry.'

'True,' Hannah said. 'And I'm always reading articles about British Muslims who've had arranged marriages and are really happy twenty, thirty years down the line, so it happens in this country too. It just feels strange leaving the decision of who I should marry to someone else.'

'You can always say you don't want to marry whoever I choose for you – you know that, don't you, Hannah? Whether we're two months before the big day or two minutes before you walk down the aisle. No one is going to think badly of you, I promise. And even if you do get married, you still have the options of an annulment or divorce. Again, no one is going to judge you.'

'I know.' She nodded. There was silence for a few moments, before Hannah spoke again. 'Kindness is really important in a husband, you're right,' she said. 'I hadn't really thought about it before, but I'll never forget that old-fashioned gentleness and chivalry Gramps always had. I don't mean holding doors open and stuff, but small things like bringing each other cups of tea in bed and writing little love notes to each other and showing you're thinking about the other, that's what's important to me; a man who is kind.'

Jess smiled at her. 'Then that's who I'll find.'

Chapter 7

Jess

It had been quite a fortnight. After the press release had gone out, Jess had somewhat naively expected her inbox to go crazy with groom applications within the first fifteen minutes, or at least for the media to come calling. Neither of these things happened. But while they may have got off to a slow start, by the time the deadline for applications was up, Save The Date had created a mini storm – online at least.

The company's Instagram post featuring a cute picture of Andy proposing to Pippa had racked up more than five thousand Likes, and their Facebook post had been shared thousands of times. While it might not have made front-page news, a couple of online sites based in the north-west had picked up the story, and Pippa and Andy's local paper, the *Bristol Post*, had run a feature about them, which had boosted subscriptions, too, so much so that membership numbers were up by thirty per cent. And although they obviously hadn't hit the magic figure the bank had set them, not to mention the fact that most of the new members had made use of the discounted subscription fee, they were pretty pleased with themselves.

'Now we just have to keep hold of these members and build on the figures. Easy, right?' Jess said as she, Hannah and Tom sat in the summerhouse chomping on biscuits and toasting their success with large mugs of coffee.

'Oh, and there's the small matter of sifting through over a hundred applications from men eager to be Hannah's husband!' Tom grinned.

'Just a small matter,' Hannah agreed. 'I think it's only fair that I have a quick scroll through the applications inbox and weed out any no-hopers.'

'Absolutely not!' Jess shook her head. 'This is a blind date, remember, and you've put your trust into my hands. And Tom's, I guess. I'm going to whittle the list down to ten, at which point I'll ask them some more specific questions to help us eliminate seven more. Then, I'll meet each of the three remaining potential grooms for a coffee. Basically, Han, I'm doing all that pre-date getting-to-know-you chat and the actual first date for you. It's going to be so much fun!'

'Is it, J?' Hannah grinned. 'Can I remind *you* how long you and Tank here have been together? It'll be nineteen years in May, won't it? That is a long time. A long time in which you've clearly forgotten how tedious it is weeding out the time-wasters, mummy's boys and perverts. Wait! You've *never* actually had to do that, have you? Oh my god, welcome to my world! Tom, she is going to need all your support, believe me!'

'Don't worry, me and the kids are going to be her wing-family, and whisk her away from any weirdos she meets in coffee shops. Although it's going to be a bit strange seeing my wife go on dates with men right under my nose!'

'Actually, that is weird,' Hannah agreed.

'The things I do for my best mate, eh,' Jess said. 'Imagine if I ended up falling for one of the handsome grooms-to-be!' As soon as the words were out of her mouth, she wished she'd kept that thought to herself. While her comment had clearly tickled Hannah, Tom's face betrayed the fact he wasn't quite so at ease with the situation. Things had been okay-ish between them for the past few weeks, in that they hadn't had any big arguments – although Jess had bitten her tongue a fair few times at Tom's inability to help run an organised household – and she was eager to keep it that way. 'Not that that would ever happen, obviously,' she added quickly.

Tom cleared his throat. 'Right, well, I look forward to seeing the fruits of all our labours. Let's hope they're not all right plums. I'd better get some work done so I'll see you later.'

Hannah guffawed loudly as Tom made his way back to the house. 'Tank is such a good sport,' she said. 'I hope my new husband is going to play along with my mad schemes like he does with you.'

'Mmm,' Jess replied non-committally. 'Talking of your new husband, I'm going to spend a few hours this afternoon going through the applications before school pick-up. Would it be safer for me to work from the kitchen table rather than sit two metres away from you? I know you and I know not being able to see my screen will be torture!'

'You could stay in here and I could have a teensy look every half an hour maybe?' Hannah replied hopefully.

'Han! Looks like I will be retiring to the kitchen this afternoon. But maybe when I go and pick the kids up you should knock off early and go to the gym or whatever to take your mind off it all.'

'Yes, boss!'

By the time three o'clock rolled around, Jess didn't know whether to laugh or cry. They'd indeed had over a hundred applications, but she'd immediately moved more than half of them to her 'NO' folder within seconds of starting to read their no-more-than-two-hundred-word paragraph about why they wanted to apply. Reasons ranged from 'Getting married will finally make sure my crazy ex gets the message I don't want to be with her' to 'My sister has just had a baby and now I want a family as quickly as possible, too'. Then there were the ones she was tempted to put in the 'MAYBE' folder because they were in need of someone to make them feel better, like the man who wrote 'I rarely leave the house so find it difficult to meet any women, let alone one who would marry me'. But she also knew there was no point adding him just because she felt sorry for him; he clearly wasn't going to be a good match for her outgoing, wanderlust-obsessed best friend.

It had taken her longer than she'd anticipated, and she was left with forty emails to read through properly, so once she'd coaxed the kids into bed, put the dishwasher on and cleaned down the kitchen worktops, she joined Tom on the sofa where he'd turned on some gruesome-looking Netflix drama. She opened her laptop and pulled up the MAYBE list. This time, before she even started to read their reasons for applying, she opened the image attached to each email. While she didn't want to resort to a Tinder-esque judgement based on looks alone – especially as that would go against one of Save The Date's core values – she also knew that the man she eventually chose as Hannah's groom needed to be someone her friend would fancy at first sight – or at least within a few weeks of getting to know him.

She glanced at her own husband lolling next to her. He definitely wasn't looking his best in tatty tracksuit bottoms and a grey paint-splattered T-shirt, but even after almost nineteen years together she still appreciated his blue eyes, kind face and slightly crooked teeth.

He turned and saw her smiling at him. 'You all right, love? Oh, damn, that's what I meant to remind you about – Lily said the school is having some kind of bake sale tomorrow and the twins need to bring a cake in.'

'I haven't seen a letter or anything,' Jess said, puzzled. 'Are you sure she didn't mean next week?'

'Well, she told me about it when I picked the kids up last Friday and I totally forgot to tell you, sorry. Have we got anything in the cupboard they can take? Or if not can you drop into Sainsbury's before drop-off tomorrow? I've got a meeting about that possible commission first thing, otherwise I'd do it.'

Jess stared at her husband, but his attention was already being drawn back to the screen by the sound of someone being stabbed multiple times. 'I'll just go and sort that out then,' she said through gritted teeth.

'Thanks, love.' He smiled at her before turning to watch the victim die dramatically in a pool of his own blood.

She closed her laptop and put it on the side in the kitchen before opening the treat cupboard and staring hopefully inside. She pulled out the emergency Swiss roll she'd hidden at the back and had been intending to eat in three large slices with a giant cup of coffee when only 'plastic cake', as she liked to call it, would do. If she sprinkled it with icing sugar and put it in a tin, maybe none of the other mums would be any the wiser, until someone actually ate it, at least. Normally, she spent the evening before one of the school's sales baking a Victoria sponge that, try as she might to make it look professional, was always obviously home-made, from the cream spilling out of the centre to the slightly burnt bits round the side. The irony that she was now desperately trying to make a professional cake look more home-made wasn't lost on her, and it only served to increase the anger currently bubbling up inside her. Once the Swiss roll was dusted and placed on some greaseproof paper inside a tin, she strode into the living room ready to unleash her fury at Tom's inability to pass on the simplest message – only to find him snoring on the sofa with the TV still showing various people beating the crap out of each other.

'Typical,' she fumed to herself. 'Bloody typical.'

She was still furious the next morning, so when Lily piped up with, '*Muuuuuum*, have you made a creamy cake for the bake sale today?' she replied tightly, 'No, your father failed to tell me about it, but we have got this lovely-looking Swiss roll instead so don't worry.'

'Isn't that the one that was at the back of the treat cupboard?' Sam asked, peering into the tin. 'I wasn't looking in the cupboard, obviously, because I know that's naughty. Lily must have told me about it.'

'I did not!' Lily yelled. 'You are such a liar, Sam!'

By the time Jess had prevented world war three, they were running late and she had to rush the twins into school with Lily carefully carrying the tin.

'Good morning, Lily, good morning, Sam,' smiled their teacher.

'Good morning, Mrs Simmons!' Lily chorused brightly while Sam muttered his reply and headed over to join his friends. 'Mrs Simmons, we brought a Swiss roll from the treat cupboard for the bake sale because Dad failed to tell Mum about it, but Mum made it look like she baked it, which is good, isn't it?' And with that, she skipped into the classroom.

Jess's cheeks flamed and she looked anywhere but at Mrs Simmons. 'I'm sorry, we've both just been so busy and—'

'Oh don't worry at all, Mrs Taylor, at least you remembered, unlike some other parents, and you made the effort to put it in a tin and everything!' She grinned and her eyes twinkled, but Jess barely returned her smile before walking quickly back to the car.

'God, I felt like I'd been reported to the headmistress, thanks to Tom's stupidity,' she moaned to Hannah when she finally got to the office. 'I was so embarrassed. What, what's so funny now?'

'Oh, it just made me think of us at school when I'd make you skive PE or ask to copy your homework and you'd get really funny about breaking the rules even a tiny bit. You are such a goody-two-shoes!'

'Why get into trouble when you can just do things properly in the first place?' Jess huffed. 'That's what made me so annoyed about the cake sale. If Tom had only told me, then I wouldn't have had to get so annoyed last night.'

'No, you'd have spent the whole evening trying to make the perfect cake instead. Jess, I'm saying this as your best friend, but sometimes you need to chill the fuck out!'

Jess stared at her, unsure what to say, until she saw Hannah's lips twitch and they both started giggling. 'I know, but I can't help who I am. As you say, I've always been like this, so there's no helping me now.'

'One of these days I'm going to bake you some brownies that will *definitely* make you chill out!' Hannah laughed. 'Although knowing you, you'd take them to a bake sale and it'd be the kids who ended up horizontal, not you!'

'Mmm, brownies . . .' Jess groaned. 'With all this talk of cake, I could eat a whole tray of them right now! And on that note, I'm going to spend another afternoon in the kitchen reading through applications, so you'll need to run things in here later – is that okay?'

'No problem, captain! In the meantime, in the absence of any cake, shall I at least make us a large cup of coffee and we can see if there are any of those old digestive biscuits in the bottom of your drawer?'

By the end of the following week, Jess had managed to whittle the list of applicants down to ten hopefuls and get them to email over answers to a few additional questions, so she and Tom had as much info to go on as they could at this stage. All ten sounded normal and didn't look like Jack Nicholson in *The Shining* (she still couldn't fathom why 'Dean from Bristol' had decided to send a photo of himself posing as his favourite horror-movie character. Needless to say, he wasn't among the ten she'd chosen).

After dinner on Friday night, with Lily at a sleepover and Sam in bed reading thanks to the promise of pancakes for breakfast if he was good, Jess topped up both her and Tom's wine glasses and thrust the laptop onto the table in front of him. 'Right, let's go through the candidates and their answers to the questions I sent over, and we'll each give them a score out of ten and see which three come out on top,' she instructed, reaching for her notebook.

'Yes, Lord Sugar,' Tom deadpanned.

'Tom, I hope you're taking this seriously – this is Hannah's future we're talking about here, not some poxy gameshow.'

'I am taking it seriously! But you have to admit it is a strange way to set someone up on a date.'

'On a blind-date wedding,' Jess corrected. 'And, no, now I've been working on it for a while, it doesn't sound as strange as I thought it would. It actually makes a lot of sense for someone's friends and family to be involved in finding them the perfect match. After all, we just want Han to be happy. I'm thinking about adding an element of "what my loved ones say about me" into Save The Date actually – you, know, a bit like that old dating site where your friend had to write your profile for you?'

'Do you remember going to that dinner party at Pat and Susie's house years and years ago when we'd just left uni and everyone was trying to be all grown-up, and we all got hor-ribly drunk and ended up persuading Lisa we should rewrite her profile for her? She got loads of messages from weird men with strange fetishes for months afterwards, even though she deleted everything we'd written the next day!'

'God, I'd totally forgotten about that! Poor Lisa, especially as she ended up marrying Awful Justin. Urgh, I think I'd rather have a man with a strange fetish than that greasy-haired, obnoxious oik. Anyway, enough chat and more looking at grooms-to-be.' She nudged her husband. 'What do you think about Brian from Slough?'

'He's called *Brian*.' Tom pulled a face.

'He can't help his name — that's his parents' fault, not his.'

'And he lives in *Slough*.'

'Right. But what about him as a person? He sounds nice, no?'

'I guess. But he's a bit run-of-the-mill, isn't he? Surely Hannah deserves someone a little, well, cooler?'

'Okay. What about this one?'

'Yes! It should definitely be him.'

'Are you basing that solely on the fact he's called Tom?'

'Maybe . . .'

'I knew we should have done this before opening the wine. If you're not going to take this seriously—'

'I am, I promise, sorry,' Tom apologised, pulling his most puppy-dog-eyed contrite look. 'Tom does sound okay, though, and he lives in north Wales, which isn't very far away. Have you thought how it's going to work out if Hannah's groom lives in Devon and she's here in Manchester?'

'I know, location is definitely something to bear in mind,' Jess admitted. 'Although I think Brian in Slough is the furthest away of any on the shortlist, and I've made sure most of the others live within a sixty-minute drive. So we're saying Tom is a possible, yes?'

'Yes. And I like this other guy's application, too,' he nodded, pointing at the screen.

My sister has slightly strong-armed me into this, but I know deep down she's right. Two years ago I thought I had it all – I was engaged to the perfect woman and we were happily planning the rest of our lives together, but then everything changed. To be honest, it's taken me a long time to get to a point where I feel like I want to settle down with someone again. And maybe that someone could be Hannah. The old me loved travelling, eating weird and wonderful foods and playing guitar in a rubbish band. And the new me likes these things too, as well as pints in proper pubs, live comedy shows and listening to other people play guitar in non-rubbish bands. Now I'm up for a challenge and an adventure – and what's more adventurous than a blind-date wedding!

'That's Toby. I liked him too,' Jess agreed, 'but I was a bit worried he had too much baggage.'

'Maybe, but at least he's been honest. And he's, what, thirty-eight? Who doesn't have baggage at our age?'

'True. Okay, he's in. Do we need one more to add to our shortlist?'

Another glass of wine later and Tom had dismissed each of the seven other applicants as being 'too strait-laced', 'too sexist' or 'too vegan'.

'Maybe you only need to meet the two we've shortlisted to start with at least,' he suggested, draining his glass.

'No, I think we should go through the others again tomorrow, when we *haven't* drunk a bottle of wine between us. We don't want to miss anyone out.'

However, the following day Brian and co. seemed no

more appealing to either of them. 'I'd better call Toby and Tom and set up meeting them for coffee,' Jess said, shutting her laptop. 'It's so weird to think that one of them could end up being married to Hannah!'

Chapter 8

Hannah

'I bring *pains au chocolat*!' Jess announced triumphantly as she walked through the door one Wednesday morning a few weeks later. She threw down her car keys and a slightly sweaty paper bag and marched over to the coffee machine. 'Large mug of caffeinated drink to go with it?'

'Yummy! Actually, I'll have a nice cup of tea for once, please,' Hannah replied, looking up from her laptop and smiling at her friend's cheeriness. 'What's brought the pastries on? Not that I'm not grateful,' she added quickly as she ripped open the bag, filling the office with the smell of butter and chocolate.

'Oh, nothing much, just that I've found my best friend a husband.'

There was a beat of silence while Hannah processed what she'd just heard. She knew Jess had been out meeting prospective husbands at the weekend and after school, dragging the kids and Tom along as her 'wing-family' to watch from a distance as promised. But she had no idea they'd actually gone ahead and chosen someone – and that he had said yes.

'You mean, you've actually found someone who's as mad as me? Who is actually up for going through with this?' She paused, weighing up the likelihood of that outcome. 'Does he look like a gargoyle?'

'What happened to just wanting someone kind?' Jess laughed. 'Now the truth comes out – it's about what they look like after all! Well, you'll be pleased to know that Toby is very handsome indeed, I think.'

'Toby?'

'Yes. Your husband-to-be is called Toby.'

'Toby.' Hannah rolled the syllables round her tongue to see how they felt. 'Okay. What else are you going to tell me about him?'

'Nothing,' Jess said smugly. She reached for a pastry and stuffed half a *pain au chocolat* into her mouth.

'What? You have to tell me more than that!' Hannah cried. 'I know the idea is to marry a stranger, but I need *something* to go on.'

Jess continued chewing and looking smug. Hannah continued eyeballing her.

'Oh, all right. His name is Toby and he lives within half an hour's drive of here.'

Hannah immediately opened Facebook and typed 'Toby' into her search bar. After scrolling and tapping for a few minutes, she ruled out all but one of the possible candidates – all the others were either married, old enough to be her grandad, young enough to be her child, or were actually the Toby Carvery pub down the road. It left only the account of Toby Richards, who appeared to be a friend of a friend of Scott.

Hannah looked up from her screen aghast and turned it round to face her friend. 'Jess, I trust you with my life, but if you have matched me with a Toby whose profile picture is of his right bum cheek, I will never speak to you again. I cannot marry a man who moons.'

Jess giggled naughtily. 'Deal-breaker noted. But you'll be pleased to know your Toby's name is not Toby Richards, and to the best of my knowledge he does not moon.'

'But you don't know for sure?' Hannah's eyebrows shot up.

'No! Funnily enough it wasn't on the list of questions I asked potential suitors. And I don't remember you explicitly mentioning it as something to be avoided. But the questions I *did* ask your Toby have led me to believe he is not a mooner.'

'You'd better be right. Also, you've used the phrase "your Toby" twice now. It sounds weird.'

'But he is about to be your Toby! Would you prefer "your husband-to-be"? Because that isn't weird at all, obviously.'

'Point taken. What about "Toby-to-be" as a compromise?'

Jess laughed at her friend. 'Fine, if that makes you feel better. And just so you know, you definitely won't find him on Facebook because I made him deactivate his social media accounts, or at least make them private. Now you need to do the same, I'm afraid. I know how lax you are with your Facebook settings, so you'll need to change those, and make your Insta and Twitter private too.'

'What? We never discussed this. I'm barely even on Twitter anymore, and I only use Facebook to check up on mad exes and potential dates.'

'Well, thankfully, the only potential date you need to worry about now is your Toby-to-be.'

'I thought we were dropping the "your"?'

'Sorry, I got confused with all your demands. Right, come on, change those settings and I might even let you in on an exciting part of the plan.'

'The plan?' Hannah asked, her voice an octave higher than she'd intended. 'What plan?'

'Questions, questions!' Jess replied oh-so smugly. 'Sort those privacy settings and I'll explain all.'

'You are loving this far too much,' Hannah grumbled, but nevertheless she did as she was told. The problem was her best friend knew her too well and there was no way she was going to jeopardise finding out some vital information by trying to break Jess's rules at this early stage – she'd save that for later when she really needed it.

'Well, I've got to get my kicks somewhere, haven't I? You do realise I'm going to be living my life vicariously through you for the next six months? It's the most fun I've had since Tom and I decided to start "practising" trying for a baby!'

'Ha! I remember those few weeks when all you did was grin dreamily at me when I asked how Tom was. That was when I saw you at all – most of the time you were at home, naked, with a self-satisfied smile on your face.'

'Until I got pregnant with twins and quickly found myself unable to waddle up the stairs never mind shag on them!'

'Jessica Taylor, did you just say the word shag?' Hannah laughed. 'All this talk of getting your kicks has clearly got you overexcited. I'm not sure I've ever heard you say that word in my life!'

'Maybe I'm not as prim and proper as you think!' Jess said in what Hannah could only presume was her seductive voice and therefore made her burst out laughing. 'What? I love that the idea of me being anything other than a boring old mum has you wetting yourself.'

'No, it's not that, it was that voice! It was like a cross between Marge Simpson and Elvis!'

'And there was I thinking it was like Marilyn Monroe . . .'

Hannah snorted and they both convulsed with giggles, leaving them unable to speak for the next few minutes, until Hannah started hiccupping and had to grab an emergency glass of water.

'J, I love you,' she declared between gulps. 'This is why you're the person to find me The One.'

'What, because the closest I've got to using my "Marilyn" voice recently is to gently try to wake my husband up when he's fallen asleep in front of the TV at nine p.m., only for him to wake up in an absolute panic as he was having a nightmare that someone was whispering threats to kill him into his ear?'

'Yep, that's exactly why,' Hannah replied. 'The very fact

you're trying to be seductive towards the man you've been with for two decades means you must know something millions of others don't. And now you can pass the secret to a happy marriage on to me. And my Toby-to-be.'

'So he is "yours" after all, is he?' Jess grinned, before more seriously adding, 'If you're looking for the secret to a happy marriage, I definitely don't have all the answers, believe me.'

Hannah looked up from her computer and stared hard at her friend. 'But you and Tank are happy,' she said, raising her voice a little at the end of the sentence but refusing to make it a proper question. 'You still make each other laugh, you have two beautiful kids who make me unbelievably proud to be their godmother, and you both run successful businesses.'

'Well, one of our businesses is a little more successful than the other,' Jess replied with a wry smile. Hannah didn't smile back. 'Han, look, of course me and Tom are fine, stop worrying. Haven't you got enough to think about with the small matter of your engagement, anyway? Although at least you've stopped that stupid Facebook search. And as a reward I'll explain the next part of the plan.'

Hannah was immediately like a dog that had been promised a walk and was waiting for its owner to pick up the lead. 'Yes, tell me the plan, finally!' she panted.

'All right, well, although you can't contact each other on social media – and I will be checking, believe me, so no underhand messaging, okay? – you *are* allowed to learn a little more before you walk down the aisle. I'm going to get both of you to write letters to each other every few weeks, which I'll publish on the Save The Date blog for the world to read.'

'Right, but when *is* the big day?'

'Oh yes, that's the other thing I was going to tell you,' Jess laughed.

'Hold on,' Hannah said, rising from her chair. 'You cannot just casually slip into conversation when my wedding day is! It needs a build-up, a fanfare, or at least a drum roll, you heathen!'

'Sorry, it's not as if I've ever arranged a blind-date marriage for my best friend before. I didn't realise there were rules,' she shrugged. 'But if it makes you happy . . .' She drummed her palms rhythmically on the desk. 'I am pleased to announce the wedding of Hannah Laura Edwards to Toby *Something Something* – no, I'm not going to tell you his full name, no matter how hard you stare at me – on Saturday the fourth of September at Castlefield House in Manchester at three p.m. Ta-dah! Do you think you might be able to make it?'

'If I can't, then Houston, we have a problem!' Hannah laughed. 'Although do you mean September the fourth *this* year, as in just' – she counted off the weeks on her iPhone calendar – '*four* months away?' She looked up at Jess with a frown.

'I do indeed, Han! Lots to do and so little time to do it. I remember when Tom and I got married, his mum spent months and months telling me I should only have traditional roses and freesias in my bouquet. I got so annoyed I ordered some out-there tropical things, which inevitably they couldn't source, so I ended up with boring roses and freesias like everyone else.'

'I honestly can't remember the roses or freesias at your wedding – although I'm sure they were lovely,' Hannah added quickly. 'I think I was more interested in the fit barman. Oh, and the fact the bar was free until we sat down to dinner!'

Hannah thought back to that weekend and it seemed like a different lifetime, even though it was less than ten years ago. Jess had appeared so grown-up to her, sweeping down the aisle of the small but pretty church she'd been christened in as a baby, in her huge, heavy dress that pulled her in in all the right places and then sprayed out in a full, hooped skirt she had to be careful not to fall over. Hannah had been her bridesmaid, tripping up the aisle in heels she wasn't used to wearing, clutching the stalks of the bouquet that had been shoved into her hands as she'd got into the car with her mum and Jess's mother. Although she couldn't remember the flowers thanks to the vast number of pints of lager she'd sunk in an attempt to impress the hot barman, she would never forget the calmness that had washed over Jess that day and her absolute certainty she was doing the right thing in marrying her child-hood sweetheart. Hannah knew that even now in her thirties she'd never felt that sense of serenity and contentment, and it certainly didn't look like her wedding day in four months' time – *four months' time!* – was going to be filled with any sense of calm. She glanced over at Jess, who had a faraway look on her face.

'Earth to Jess!' Hannah laughed, waving her hand in front of her friend's face. 'I'm sorry that I have to pull you out of your reverie, but what happened in your honeymoon suite stays in the honeymoon suite, okay?'

Jess snapped back into the present. 'Ha! I hate to be the one to smash all your clichés, but by the time I'd managed to get myself out of my straitjacket – I mean dress – Tom had fallen asleep, slumped on the chair in the corner of the room, midway through getting undressed. I had to practically drag him into bed, take off his socks and shoes for him and prise the bow tie he was somehow clutching from his hand – he'd been wearing a neck tie so I still have no idea where that came from – and then he started snoring. By that point I was so exhausted, I couldn't even be bothered to take my make-up off and brush my teeth, so when we woke up the next morning, I had dragon breath, panda eyes and a fake eyelash sticking to my cheek. Welcome to married life!'

'Classy, J, classy. Although at least you made it to breakfast. I remember I took one look at the scrambled egg the hotel had laid out and had to run back to my room! Much to the disgust of my mother, obviously, who lectured me for weeks afterwards about the etiquette of sipping "champers" at weddings rather than gulping down pints of Fosters, and how I would never be asked to be a bridesmaid again if I carried on being such a "ladette". It was during her *Daily Mail* phase and she blamed a lot of the world's problems on pint-drinking girl-power women, to be fair. I've a good mind to ban champers-sipping from my wedding entirely and only serve Stella.'

'Are you turning into Bridezilla already?' Jess laughed. 'Although it's almost worth it to see Joan's face when she's handed a pint of lager!'

'That's if she comes to the wedding – you can guess how she's going to feel about the idea of a blind-date marriage.'

'She'll calm down and she's got four months to get used to the idea, what could go wrong? Plus, you're her only daughter, so she's not going to miss out on her mother of the bride moment, is she.'

'She can be pretty stubborn, can old Joan.'

Jess grinned. 'Like mother, like daughter, then.'

'Me? I'm not stubborn!' Hannah cried.

'Okay, not stubborn, but you're definitely strong-willed,' she replied calmly. 'There aren't many people who would force their best friend to find them the man they're going to marry in the ultimate blind date.'

'I'm not quite sure I forced you.' Hannah smiled. 'Anyway, enough talking about my mule-like behaviour. What's all this about a blog?'

'Well, as you can't actually meet or see what the other looks like before the big day, I thought you and Toby could write to each other and talk about how you're feeling. But instead of it just being between the two of you, I'll post the letters on the website so everyone can read them. That way we can build on the publicity and buzz we've already started to create and hopefully get the public excited about the wedding of the year. As we discussed, at this point you'll both be completely anonymous, other than your first names and any information you choose to share with each other, and whoever reads the posts, obviously. It won't be until after the wedding that we reveal your photos to your adoring public.'

Hannah noticed Jess shifting uneasily in her chair, a sure sign she was worried what her friend would think about putting her feelings and emotions out there, not just for Toby to see, but for anyone who clicked on Save The Date's website.

'Writing publicly to each other makes sense, I guess,' Hannah said thoughtfully. 'After all, this isn't just about me finding a husband, it's about me finding a husband thanks to Save The Date and telling all the single people out there that they can do it too, right?'

'Yes, but I want to make sure you're happy first and foremost,' Jess replied quietly. 'You might want to think about exactly how much you give away, and I've said the same to Toby.'

'It's not as if we're going to be identifiable to anyone who doesn't already know us and know the situation though, right? The whole idea is that we only give away to each other bits about our personalities and how we're feeling, not our names, addresses and jobs. I'm interested to know what Toby thinks about the whole plan though,' she added, raising her eyebrows at her friend and smiling sweetly in an attempt to get her to spill some more information about the stranger she was due to marry in just a few months' time.

'Understandably, he has been pretty nervous about the whole thing,' Jess admitted. 'As you know, I read through every single applicant's reasons for wanting to be part of this, and once Tom and I had narrowed it down, I emailed Toby some extra questions to find out a bit more about him, then we went for coffee and finally I called him at the end of last week to tell him I thought he was the right man for the job – your Mr Right, in fact. Every time I've spoken to him and seen him he's become more and more invested in the whole process and he was so excited when I called him the other day. Shocked, yes, but then immediately ridiculously excited. He's so lovely, Han, he really is.'

'Well, I should bloody hope so if I'm going to spend the rest of my life with him!' Hannah grinned. 'But if you told him at the end of last week, how come you're only telling me now?' She glanced at her friend suspiciously.

'I wanted to give him a cooling-off period. It's a big thing he's agreeing to and I wanted him to be sure it was what he wanted. Plus, I wanted to give him a chance to tell his family and friends what he's signed up for. But don't worry, I spoke to him again last night and he said he was surprised at how behind the idea everyone has been, even if they do think he's slightly unhinged – his words, not mine. He was a lot calmer about it, although he asked lots of questions about the blog. I think he found focusing on the details he *can* control rather than all the things he can't was the best way forward – which is what I know I would do, too.'

'Oh my god! Jess, have you matched me with basically the

boy version of you? Other than me marrying Jason Momoa, that would be my absolute dream!'

'Don't get too excited – I'm not sure I'd go quite as far as to say he's the male version of me. For starters, there is no way on this earth I would agree to marry someone I had never met!'

SAVE THE DATE

Meet our blind-daters with a difference ...

Save The Date is *the* dating app for people seeking The One. If you're looking for someone you'll be celebrating your golden wedding anniversary with fifty years later (#oldromantics) then we're the app for you – and we can prove it ...

To show you that it really *is* possible to find true love online, we're putting the app to the ultimate test: one girl, one boy and one happily ever after. But, there's a twist. The only things our couple know about each other are their first names, and that the first time they'll meet will be at the altar on their wedding day!

You can follow our blind-daters on their journey to wedded bliss right here on our Save The Date blog. And if you're still looking for that special someone to share your life with, download our app and become a member – and make sure you take advantage of our discounted subscription fee.

So, without further ado, let's meet the bride and groom to be ...

Dear Hannah,
   My name is Toby and I'm ... well, I'm very soon going to be your husband (that is definitely one

of the strangest sentences I've ever written! And somehow typing them into a blog on the internet that will instantly leave a digital footprint makes this whole thing excitingly/scarily real). I can't believe how nervous I am, writing this all down, knowing you will read it, but for what it's worth, here are my answers to Save The Date's first three blog questions:

Describe yourself in three words:
Kind, tech-loving, work-in-progress

What fictional character are you most like?
I'd love to say Mr Darcy after he stops with all the Pride, but I'm probably more Donkey from Shrek.

What's your favourite hobby?
As I work in IT, I spend a lot of time staring at a computer screen, so when I'm not in the office I love getting outdoors, playing five-a-side after work, maybe taking one of my sister's dogs for a walk, going to gigs (both comedy and music) and winning the pub quiz with my mates (or, if I'm being honest, losing the pub quiz with my mates).

I'm looking forward to reading your answers . . .
   Until next time,
   Toby x

Dear Toby,

Right, well, I hardly know where to start with this. I think it might be the weirdest letter I've ever tried to write, but I suppose the first thing to say is: hello! I'm Hannah, Han, or even Spannah, depending on whether you're talking to my mum, my friends or my brother. And, I'm going to be your lawful wedded wife in a few weeks! Which is both crazy and amazing! I'm not really one for exclamation marks, but if any situation calls for copious amounts of them, it's this one!

Describe yourself in three words:
Fun, adventurous and up for breaking the rules!

What fictional character are you most like?
Nancy Drew. I'm pretty nosy, love a challenge and often find myself a bit out of my depth, but obviously I triumph in the end.

What's your favourite hobby?
I love to travel. I'm aware this sounds both privileged and #basic – who doesn't like to go on holiday a couple of times a year? – but I really love visiting different countries and finding out about different cultures, even if that's just what locals like to drink and where they like to drink it. I've been to the worst of places – I will never forget the flea-infested

hostel in Colombia I went to on my three-month backpacking trip after I graduated and had used my last remaining credit card to buy the flights and only had twenty quid of my overdraft left to play with. And the best of places – the tiny shack I shared with three other girls overlooking the beach in Chubut, Argentina, beats any five-star hotel, not that I've stayed in any.

Well, that was short and sweet wasn't it? Anyway, I do hope our wedding day will be filled with drinks, dancing and debauchery – and did I mention drinks?! I can't wait to see you there.
    Hannah x

Chapter 9

Jess

Jess chuckled to herself as she finished reading and formatting Hannah's blog on Sunday night. It was obvious she and Toby were both nervous about writing to each other in such a public way, and Jess wondered what the outside world would make of them. Would they think the pair were crazy to have signed up for such a thing? Would they think Save The Date – and Jess by association – was completely irresponsible for encouraging them to do so? Or would they buy into the excitement of it all and realise that some people need to be brave and put themselves out there – occasionally in a slightly crazy way?

'Well, there's only one way to find out,' Jess muttered to herself as her mouse pointer hovered over the Post Now button. She squeezed her eyes shut and clicked, then took a shaky breath in. However, she knew that the hard work had only just begun; unless she started shouting about the blog post, it would only ever get a few hundred views from people who were already subscribed to the app. Once she'd composed messages across all Save The Date's social channels and set them to go live first thing the next morning, she began writing emails to local and national media again in the hope one of them might bite and run the story.

By eleven o'clock that evening, Jess was exhausted and fell into bed next to Tom, who was already snoring lightly. But just minutes later she heard a loud thump coming from the next room, followed by a moment's silence, then the inevitable '*Muuuuuuuuum!*'

Sighing heavily, Jess shuffled her way across the landing to her daughter's room, her work for the day seemingly still not done.

Jess was woken the next morning, not by the kids or Tom, but by her phone vibrating and lighting up across her bedside table. She grabbed it quickly, along with her favourite hoody that was lying in a heap near the bedroom door, and padded her way downstairs. She filled the kettle and unlocked her phone, which immediately lit up with social media notifications. She glanced at the clock on the kitchen wall, surprised it was already 7.30 a.m. and the rest of the house was still fast asleep. She turned her phone face down, thinking she'd deal with all of that later and braced herself to wake up cranky children and an equally cranky husband, none of whom could ever be called early risers.

An hour later, everyone was washed, dressed and fed, and

she'd headed off at least two arguments between the twins before they'd become all-out war, so she was congratulating herself by making that cup of coffee she hadn't quite managed to have earlier. Luckily, it was Tom's day to do the school run, so she happily waved goodbye to her brood, although not before retrieving a discarded lunchbox from the side and shoving it into Sam's bag as he tripped out the door with his head in a superhero comic.

Finally, she was able to pick up her emails and check her social media. She was shocked by what she saw.

She grabbed her cup of coffee and an extra piece of toast and decamped to the summerhouse, where she logged into the Save The Date website and saw the blog had already had five hundred views, and her Facebook post had been shared almost a thousand times. When she opened her email she even found a message from the *Manchester Evening News* asking to interview Hannah and Toby. Jess knew how amazing that kind of exposure would be, but it simply wouldn't be possible without revealing their identities. She quickly tapped out a reply, saying Hannah and Toby weren't able to do any press as yet, but she would love to set up an interview with Andy and Pippa, who could also talk about the #marriedatfirstswipe project.

A quick scroll through the replies to Save The Date's posts revealed some very definitely negative responses to the idea of a blind-date wedding, with people saying it was just a PR stunt or all set up, but there were also messages of support and encouragement, urging Hannah and Toby to go for it and saying how brave they were.

Jess looked up from her computer and spotted Hannah walking along the garden path towards the office, looking flustered. Her excitement quickly turned to worry about whether her friend had seen any of the negative responses to the blog.

'Sorry I'm late, Jess, I had to hang around for ages at the doctor's this morning. Sometimes I wonder why I bother waiting nearly a month to get the coveted first appointment of the day, because they're always running late even at that point. And to make matters worse, I forgot to charge my phone overnight, so the minute I tried to get online it bloody died. I couldn't even stalk people on Insta while I was waiting! Anyway, sorry for going on, how are you?' She'd finally looked up from plugging her phone into her laptop to make eye contact with Jess.

'I'm really well, thanks, Han! The blog posts have gone up and are getting a great reaction. I'm just about to check subscription numbers now, in fact.'

'Oh my god, I can't believe I forgot they were going live this morning. I'm dying to see what Toby's written!'

Jess laughed. 'Okay, well, you look at the blog while I make us a drink.'

'I can't believe you didn't send it to me before it went live, J!' Hannah said, furiously clicking through to the website on her laptop. 'I know Toby won't have seen mine till this morning, but there have got to be some perks to me being your best mate and all that. Right, here we go. God, he sounds even more nervous than me, doesn't he? Oh, I like the work-in-progress as a description. Mr Darcy, fine, but Donkey from Shrek? Okaaaay. But he likes the outdoors and beer and is a bit rubbish at pub quizzes, which I'm on board with. And it sounds like he has friends, which is also good.' Hannah took a breath. 'Well, that's not a lot to go on, but he sounds nice? I hope he doesn't think I've waffled on too much, especially that bit at the end about drink and debauchery at the wedding – Jess, you totally should have cut that out!'

'I'm not here to edit you, Han,' her friend said gently. 'You want Toby to get to know the real you, don't you?'

'Maybe! Although I still can't believe I used the word "debauchery" in my first communication with the man I'm going to marry. Have you heard anything from him this morning?'

'No, not yet, but I'll send him a message in a minute to make sure he knows the blog is live. I have just checked the system, though, and we've had fifty people sign up to the app today already and it's only half past ten!'

'That's amazing, Jess,' Hannah said, looking up from her screen.

'I know, it's brilliant. The click-throughs from the Facebook post are especially high.'

'Oh shit.'

'What? What's wrong, Han?'

'Facebook. My mum's on Facebook.'

'I know, I'm friends with her on there. So?'

'But my mum can't find out I'm getting married through Facebook.'

'What do you mean? You must have chatted to your parents about it last week? I've been meaning to ask you what they said, but things have been so busy . . . Han, you *have* told your parents you're marrying Toby, haven't you?'

'No.' There was a pause. 'I've told G-ma, obviously, and I was going to get her to talk to Mum but she said I needed to do it, and there just hasn't been a good time.'

'Hannah!'

'But you know what my mum's like. Dad will likely be fine about the whole thing if he thinks it will make me happy, but I just wanted to put off the conversation with Mum for as long as I could. And to be fair, I didn't know you were going to shout about the whole thing from the rooftops quite so much!'

'But, you did! I talked to you about the blogs and how we'd share them publicly to help increase our subscriptions and build interest for the big reveal when you're back from honeymoon,' Jess said, completely bewildered. She was annoyed at herself for not checking that Hannah had told her family before Save The Date shared the news, but she couldn't understand how Hannah hadn't predicted this whole situation. Seeing the fear and worry on her best friend's face, she softened and added gently. 'Look, Han, why don't you text your mum now and say you're coming over for an early lunch and tell her then? Joan probably hasn't looked at Facebook this morning and your dad isn't even on social media, is he? So he won't know anything about it, and you can tell him after you've been to your mum's.'

'Don't you need me here if it's all kicking off?'

'Don't worry, I'll manage. Go and see your parents. Maybe take your mum some flowers or something to butter her up a bit?'

'Okay, but I don't think this is going to go well,' Hannah sighed, gathering her coat and bag. 'After I've texted them, I'll turn off my phone. I still hardly have any battery. I'll let you know how it goes later.'

'It will be fine, I'm sure,' Jess said with a conviction she didn't feel as she hugged her friend. 'I know they might be unconvinced to start with, but they'll come round eventually, I promise.'

'We'll see,' Hannah replied, unplugging her phone. 'Speak to you later.'

Jess guilt-ate three biscuits in quick succession once Hannah had gone. She wished she'd offered to go round to Joan's with her. As much as Hannah was 'fun, adventurous and up for breaking the rules', she was less good at the emotional side of things, especially when it came to her mum. Their relationship had always been a bit complicated, and Jess just had to hope that Joan would be able to put her own views aside and simply be there for her daughter.

Jess was super busy all afternoon, but she kept half an eye on her phone, waiting for Hannah to call. Then Toby sent her a WhatsApp message and her stomach lurched a little.

Hi Jess, hope you're not too busy today – I
saw there was a pretty big response to our
letters. I know it's really unlikely anyone will
know it's me, but I'm a bit worried about
someone at work finding out. While I've of
course told my friends and family what's
going on, I haven't spoken to anyone in the
office about it and I don't want to alert them
to it until further down the line. Anyway, if
you have a spare minute today, let me know
if there's anything else you think I should be
doing to protect my identity. Cheers

She could hear the worry in his message so she gave him a
call, which he answered within one ring. Thankfully, she
managed to reassure him that he wouldn't be identified by
anybody until they were ready, and she placed her phone
back down on her desk with a sigh, before it immediately lit
up and vibrated again, displaying 'Hannah' on the screen.

'Han! How are you? How did it go?'

There was silence for a few seconds before she heard a
strangled sob and Hannah gasped out, 'I can't believe you've
made this happen – you're supposed to be my best friend.
There's no way I can get married to a stranger!'

Chapter 10

Hannah

Hannah lay on her bed, wiped her hand across her stinging eyes and took a gulp of wine from the large glass of Pinot next to her. She'd deliberately left her phone face down on her desk by the window so she wasn't tempted to text either her family or Jess, as she knew they – and she – had said quite enough already. She hated arguing with anyone, let alone people she cared about, and she would generally try to walk away from conflict. But sometimes she had to speak up – and this was definitely one of those times. It was one thing to argue with her mother – god knows how many times they'd disagreed when she was growing up, as well as when she was an actual grown-up – but it was another thing entirely for her to fall out with Jess.

Hannah struggled to think of any other time they'd argued over the years. Sure, they'd had some honest conversations with each other – often when Jess tried to lure Hannah home from whatever mad adventure she was on, when all she really wanted to hear was that it was fine for her to bum around in the sunshine a bit longer – but they'd always stopped short of saying anything either of them would regret.

She suddenly remembered a moment when they were in Year 8 at school. They had been best friends for over a year, and had seen all the girls in their form fall out over something as trivial as homework or fancying the same boy. Not to feel left out, she and Jess decided they would have an argument too, so that they could say they'd fallen out, before quickly becoming best friends again. But neither of them could bring themselves to say anything even remotely mean to the other. Even Jess, who would work herself into a proper bad mood if a teacher so much as told her off, couldn't make herself angry enough to shout at Hannah. Instead, the pair started giggling uncontrollably in their history lesson and found themselves being sent outside to calm down by Mrs McGee.

But twenty-two years later, it seemed they'd managed their goal. And it was mostly Hannah's mum's fault, she mused. She had known her parents wouldn't be ecstatic at the news she was marrying a stranger, but she'd hoped they'd support her. Apparently that was too much to ask of her mother.

Joan had greeted her and the supermarket flowers she'd proffered with a suspicious frown.

'Hannah, you shouldn't have. Really, I mean it. You'd better come in now that you're here – though aren't you supposed to be at work? You haven't done something to make dear Jess fire you, I hope?'

'No, Mum, I just ... I just have the afternoon off so thought I'd pop round to see the 'rents – well, one of them – like a good daughter!'

'Hannah, please don't use that term, it makes my role sound so transitory, like you can change me if you get bored.'

Hannah had smiled as her mum filled her in on her friends' lives, her friends' grown-up children's lives, and even the lives of their grandchildren who Hannah had never met, nor was ever likely to. She had been shaken out of a gentle daydream by her mum's abrupt, 'So, as nice as this is, I'm presuming this visit has a purpose? Please don't tell me you want to flit back to Argentina or Aleppo or wherever.'

'No, Mother dearest, I'm staying in Manchester, for the time being anyway. You haven't spoken to G-ma, have you? No? Then I have some news.' She'd taken a deep breath and had spilled out the whole plan in a slightly wavering voice, which, now that she thought about it, she was sure her mum had pounced on. Joan had immediately made her phone her dad, put him on speaker and tell him the news so he could talk some sense into her.

'You seem to listen to him more than you do to me, though god knows why!' she'd said.

In some ways, her dad's soft response to the news had done more to shake Hannah's belief she was doing the right thing than her mum's eruption into tears that the family was going to be brought into disrepute. 'Is this what you really want, Hannah?' he'd merely asked

Hannah had tried to remain calm in front of her mum,

but if she was honest, seeing her mum so upset had pushed a button somewhere inside her, sending her right back into teenage mode, and she'd shouted at her, 'You're never proud of anything I do. Is it because I'm not darling Scotty boy, who spent so many years smoking weed and cheating on women until he finally managed to grow up? I've always been second best and nothing I do is good enough for you, apparently. I'll never match up to golden boy, but you can never just be happy and support me, can you!'

Thinking back to the argument, Hannah wasn't proud of what she'd said, especially as she was well aware of how much both her parents had helped her out when she'd run out of money while backpacking in Bali, and how her mum had helped her find a flat when Jess had offered her the job at Save The Date.

But then again, Joan had hardly been the better person, and had instead shouted, 'No, we can't be happy for you marrying a complete stranger. Can't you see what a ridiculous, embarrassing proposal that is? And now you're telling me it's going to be all over the internet? We'll be a laughing stock!'

'Why are you so obsessed with what people think?' Hannah had screamed. 'Anyway, we're not being identified at the moment so no one will connect poor, sad little Hannah who can't get a husband with Perfect Joan and her perfect life! I'm getting married whether you like it or not, and you can't stop me!' she'd screeched, ever more teenage-like.

'Well, don't think I'm coming then!' her mum had thundered.

'Fine!' Hannah had grabbed her coat and made for the door, before realising her dad was still on the other end of the phone in her hand and had heard every horrible thing she'd just said. She'd quickly turned the speaker off and brought the phone to her ear. 'Dad? I'm guessing you heard that.'

'Don't worry, your mum will calm down, darling, she always does.'

But as she ended the call with a promise to speak to him properly the following day, his words had done little to reassure her. She'd slammed the door behind her and given in to the angry tears pooling in the corners of her eyes. Her anger had seemed to increase with every step she took towards the bus stop and then she had looked at her phone and had seen Jess had sent her three messages asking how it had gone.

That conversation had not gone well either.

Hannah knew she'd been pretty horrible to her friend. Deep down, she also knew that none of this was Jess's fault, and it wasn't like Hannah had been forced into the idea of a publicly arranged marriage. But she was hurt by the thought that maybe Jess *was* putting her business before their friendship. Anyway, the damage was done now, however much she wished she could undo it.

She took another gulp of her wine and ran her hand along G-ma's knitted blanket beneath her.

The following morning she messaged Jess to ask if it was okay for her to work from home as she couldn't really answer any calls unless she pretended her name wasn't Hannah, which she was bound to forget to do. Jess agreed immediately, and followed her message up with a second, asking how she was and whether she was okay and whether they could have a glass of wine in the pub that night. Miserably, Hannah pushed her away and told her she just needed to be on her own for a bit.

> I'm a bit tired to be honest. Another time
> though. It looks like subscriptions to the app
> are still going strong.

Jess had replied promptly:

> Yes, the figures are looking great. Could you
> deal with the membership inbox today, do
> you think, as there are loads of questions
> from new users and people thinking about
> signing up?

Finding it easier to talk about work than how she was really feeling, Hannah had responded:

> Yes, of course. I'll get onto that now. Let me
> know if there are other things you need me to
> do as well.

Their messages continued in the same stilted, semi-friendly but professional manner for the next few days, and Hannah couldn't help but feel sad every time she received one, as it served to remind her how very weird things were between them.

She'd not heard anything from her mum since their argument, though her dad had called her a few times and she had been round to Scott and Julia's. Between attempts to teach Leo to stick his tongue out at his parents, she had told them the news about her planned blind-date wedding but also mentioned that now she wasn't sure she was going to go through with it. They'd both been really lovely and supportive, and Scott said that she shouldn't let Joan put her off the idea if it was what she truly wanted, adding that he'd pop round to their mum's the following day and take Leo as a distraction to try to get her onside if she wanted. Hannah was surprised at her brother's thoughtfulness – he definitely wasn't known for his empathetic nature – and she'd thought to herself for the hundredth time that Julia was a very good influence on him. Boosted by their enthusiasm, she'd agreed to Scott's plan. A few days later he reported back that Joan hadn't ranted about the situation as much as he thought she would once he'd explained he and Julia thought it was a good idea. Hope swelled in Hannah's heart, but she knew she should take Scott's optimism with a pinch of salt as he always presumed their mum hung off his every word. Though, to be fair, it seemed she often did.

Feeling more buoyed, Hannah tentatively asked her dad if he thought there was any way her mum would accept an invitation to go wedding–dress shopping with her at the weekend. His answer was typically John-like: succinct but sincere. 'It's always worth a try, Hannah my dear, but I have to be honest, it doesn't sound like she's at the point where she'll accept yet. Do you want me to ask Scott to try to bring her round a bit?'

Hannah grimaced and said no, she'd sort it herself. She realised she probably couldn't win either way – if she didn't invite her mum, she'd never hear the end of it; but if she did invite her, it was likely to be a no. She glanced up at the birthday card Jess had given her a few months ago and she'd kept on her desk, and nodded in agreement at the words: *Don't grow up, it's a trap!*

She spent the next ten minutes typing and deleting various versions of a text to her mum, before eventually settling on:

> Hi Mum, I know you're still getting your head round my wedding plans, but I'm going dress shopping on Saturday and I'd really like you to be there. Are you free around lunchtime maybe? x

The reply didn't come back until the following morning, and it was as Hannah expected.

> I'm afraid I've already agreed to lunch at Mary's on Saturday. I hope you enjoy your shopping trip. Make sure you take Jess with you. Mum x

She texted her dad with an update and he replied:

> Sorry it's not better news, Hannah darling.
> She will come round in time. She's a good
> woman, your mum. Can't wait to see you
> looking a million dollars. Dad x

Hannah was struck yet again by how different the language John used about his ex-wife was compared to the constant digs and put-downs Joan had adopted. Although it was always going to be easier for her dad; he'd moved on so quickly with Charmaine and his new life, whereas sometimes it felt like her mum had never truly moved on at all – it certainly seemed she hadn't dealt with any of the hurt and anger she felt when John revealed he had a new 'lady friend' just weeks after moving out.

She sighed and wondered whether she was really doing the right thing. If her parents couldn't make their marriage work after knowing each other for more than twenty years, then could she really expect her marriage to a stranger to be successful? Or maybe that was precisely why she and Toby *could* be happy – because they didn't know each other?

She sighed again.

Later that day she checked her online banking app and saw that her dad had transferred £500 to her account with the reference 'wedding dress fund'. She welled up as she sent him a grateful text, and wondered whether it was only blind-date brides who spent most of their days crying, or if everyone about to get married was close to tears at all times.

She met Jess outside Selfridges in Manchester on Saturday, just as the sky was moving from its regular light grey hue to full-on blackened storm clouds.

'Quick, inside before we get drenched,' panted Jess as she trotted over to Hannah, planted a kiss on her cheek and pulled her through the doors. 'Right, I'm thinking we start with Whistles and Self-Portrait and then move up the price brackets if we need to – what do you think?'

'Yes, sounds fine,' Hannah replied, rather shell-shocked. She had been about to launch into a short speech she'd been rehearsing all the way into town, but now didn't seem the time.

'Excellent. Now I know you don't want a big flouncy meringue and are determined to go for something a bit different, but I've been looking online and I do think there are a couple of gorgeous white but cute dresses, and also some beautiful jewel-coloured ones that you'll love, so I hope they have them here.'

'All right, Gok Wan!' Hannah laughed, relaxing her shoulders as the escalator took them up past rows and rows of intricate, lacy bras that probably cost more than Hannah's monthly rent.

'If you're not careful, I'll do the full-on Trinny and Susannah when we get to the lingerie department. Now, let's do this. And then we can have a drink to toast our shopping success, and I'm warning you now, I'm already thirsty. No pressure, obviously.'

They spent the next hour picking out dresses that might work, laughing at many hideous dresses that definitely *wouldn't* and gazing at beautifully cut designer dresses that they couldn't bear to add to the maybe pile as they'd both have to rob a bank just to pay for one of them. Eventually, they whittled the dresses down to a possible six, and Jess ushered Hannah into the next available changing room.

'I'm going to stand just out here, but let me know when you need zipping up. Don't try to do it yourself – you'll either rip the dress or one of your muscles, okay?'

'Yes, sir, whatever you say, sir!' Hannah saluted her. 'When did you turn into such a bossy-boots?'

'When I started having to marshal two children into their school uniforms every day,' she replied with a grin. 'Come on, let's get the first one on. Start with the green full-length one. I know it's a bit out-there as a wedding dress, but it's really going to complement your eyes.'

Hannah was surprised how much she enjoyed trying on the array of dresses they'd chosen. Usually she wore skinny jeans or a denim skirt and black tights in the winter, and cut-off shorts or, if she was pushing the boat out, a flirty ditzy-print dress in the summer, and she certainly didn't own anything like the ladylike gowns in front of her.

'I like this one,' Jess nodded in approval at the deep-red satin Ghost dress she was currently modelling.

'I like it, but I don't really feel like me in it, if you know what I mean,' Hannah said, twisting and turning to get a better view of herself in the mirror.

'Han, I love you, but I'm not letting you get married in denim shorts and a vest top, which is what you'd buy if I weren't here, I know. Your mum would kill me, for one thing. Although, to be fair, there's a high chance she might already be plotting to poison me. Sorry, too soon for Joan jokes?'

Hannah couldn't help but laugh. 'Yes, definitely too soon. And, yes, she probably already wants to kill you. But I think maybe I'm first in her firing line, so don't worry, you're safe for a little while.'

Jess gave her a sympathetic smile, but knew when to change the subject. 'Okay, not this one then. Try the white Whistles one next. It's the most "weddingy" of all of them.'

Hannah pulled the curtain across and fanned her increasingly warm face. 'Why do they always make changing rooms the hottest place on Earth? I'm not even wearing any clothes and I'm boiling. And before you say anything, yes I am trying this dress on, I just needed a second without some expensive fabric next to my burning skin. Seriously, they need to get some fans in here or someth—'

'Han? Are you all right? Hannah?'

'Yes, I'm fine,' she whispered and pulled the curtain back.

'Oh. My. God. Han, you look amazing. Oh, it's perfect. Christ, what is wrong with me, I don't know why I'm crying. And now I've set you off too, no!'

Hannah swiped at her eyes. 'I feel like me, just a grown-up, more bridal version of me!'

'Quick, let me get a photo. Perfect. Well, I think we're done here. You'd better take it off before you get mascara down it. Once we've paid then we can go have that drink!'

Half an hour later, they were each holding a large glass of wine in the Royal Exchange Theatre bar and gazing at the large yellow Selfridges bag at Hannah's feet.

'Cheers to an excellent shopping trip!' Jess said, clinking her glass against Hannah's.

'Cheers indeed!' she cried, taking a ladylike sip to match her new-found ladylike feeling. 'Thank you for coming with me,' she added more quietly. 'And I'm sorry for the way I spoke to you on Monday. I was horrible. I was upset and angry and confused, but I should never have lashed out at you, Jess. This whole thing was my idea in the first place and I should have spoken to Mum and Dad about it immediately instead of putting it off till I absolutely had to.'

'I'm sorry too. I should have checked that you'd spoken to your parents – and asked how it had gone. I felt like the worst person in the world after your phone call on Monday, I really did. Of course, it's amazing Save The Date is getting loads of exposure, but not at the expense of your happiness. This is about you more than it is the business and always will be, Han.'

The two of them smiled shyly at each other for a second before Jess broke the moment with a laugh. 'It looks like we've had our first argument then. But at least we don't have to pretend to be annoyed with each other for no reason now – I can't believe we tried to do that when we were kids, it's ridiculous!'

Hannah grinned. 'Ahh, those were the days, when all we had to worry about was that everyone else was falling out with each other and we weren't. Now I'd happily swap that problem for all of mine! Anyway, you need to tell me some more titbits about Toby. I loved his blog, but he didn't give that much away and it's killing me trying to guess what he's like.'

'Han! I've told you, I can't tell you any more – it's not like he's going to find out anything more about you, so it's not fair. Although I need you both to write another blog this weekend, so you can read his next one when it goes live on Monday or Tuesday. That's not long to wait, is it?'

'Yes! It's far too long,' moaned Hannah. 'I was thinking the other day that I guess I'm *actually* engaged, although I never had a proposal, which is weird. We've kind of missed all of that bit out, haven't we? We've gone straight to jail without passing go, so to speak.'

'Jail? Marriage isn't like jail, Han! Well, not most of the time anyway. Although you just wait till you and your Toby-to-be have been together so long you can tell exactly what the other is thinking without them doing more than blink in a certain manner – and believe me, it's rarely something good. Then they ask you what's for tea, even though they know what's in the fridge just as much as you do, or they moan they haven't got any clean pants, even though they haven't put the washing machine on for weeks, or say—'

'Argh, stop!' Hannah said, looking mock-alarmed. 'Married life is going to be all sunshine and roses, no?'

'I hate to break it to you, Han, but it's really not. Although it doesn't usually feel like jail.'

'Well, if I can have anywhere near as sunny and rose-smelling a relationship as you and Tom do, then I'll be on to a winner, I think.'

Jess didn't reply and instead busied herself topping up their glasses, but Hannah prodded her. 'You and Tank are definitely all right, aren't you? All of this stuff with Save The Date and the wedding and everything isn't too much?'

'We're fine. We're both just busy, that's all. Oh, I better get this,' she added, pointing at her phone and in Hannah's opinion looking a bit too relieved at the interruption. She waved at her friend to pick up the call and concentrated on sipping her wine as Jess moved towards the door and away from the hubbub around them. When she came back a few minutes later, her face was flushed.

'Oh my god, you won't believe this! That was a producer from *North West Tonight* – they're interested in doing something on Save The Date and the wedding! Nearer the time, of course, but they just need to work out the details, and that's why they wanted to chat to me. This could be big! But only if you and Toby want it to be big, obviously,' she added quickly.

'Well, as long as we both actually make it down the aisle and don't kill each other on our honeymoon, then I guess it will be fine!' Hannah laughed.

'Yay! Cheers to that! Although we can't get too drunk as I need you to write that blog post this weekend!'

SAVE THE DATE

Find out more about our blind-daters with a difference ...

Wow! Our first blog has had a GREAT response across social media. You've all been so supportive towards Hannah and Toby, the strangers who are being brought together at the ultimate blind date location: The Altar!

So, if you're looking for love at first swipe, or if you're on a slightly more sedate search for Mr/Mrs Right, then subscribe to Save The Date and download our app now! Join hundreds of others who are looking for long-term love, just like you.

In the meantime, let's hear how our bride- and groom-to-be have been feeling over the past week ...

Dear Hannah

Holy guacamole! F@%$!

I'm not sure I was prepared for that level of interest/excitement/disbelief from random strangers about our impending nuptials, were you?! (You're definitely right about there being a time and place for exclamation marks!)

I really enjoyed reading your letter last week. You're already starting to take shape in my head – not physically exactly, as I don't know whether you have blonde hair, brown eyes or a massive

carbuncle on the end of your nose (although as
long as you wear your carbuncle with pride, who
cares!), but the kind of person you are. I love that
you're up for an adventure (I guess there's no bigger
adventure than marrying someone you've never
met – thanks Save The Date!), and have been to
some really interesting places.

I've spent my whole weekend thinking about
my answers to this week's STD questions (I've just
realised that STD doesn't just stand for Save The
Date . . . !) and trying to get the right blend of
funny/interesting, but my sister has just given me
a lecture about overthinking, so instead I'm simply
going to be honest.

What's your relationship history?
Does it sound a bit lame to say I've only been in
one long-term relationship? Well, even if it does,
that's the truth. It was two years ago, and it's taken
me a while to get back into the dating game. I
guess that's why I'm happy to let Save The Date take
away all the stress and awkwardness around finding
someone I'm suited to.

What scares you?
Lots of things. When I was younger I used to be
fearless, but I suppose the more things that happen
to you, the more wary you become. I was definitely

scared about what my family and friends would say about all this at first, but I can safely say I am glad I let my sister talk me into this blind-date wedding.

What's your favourite food?
Finally a question I don't need to overthink! It's chip shop chips, all crispy and chunky and coated liberally in salt and vinegar.

Until next time,
Toby x

Dear Toby

Thanks so much for your letter last week – it was ace to start getting to know you, albeit with the rest of the world looking over my shoulder! That is the first time I've ever written the word 'albeit', by the way; not sure what came over me . . . Maybe it's because I'm writing an actual letter rather than firing off a load of WhatsApp messages. The past week has been pretty crazy, but knowing I would soon be finding out a little more about you has really helped – although Save The Date have ramped up the intensity of the questions this week, haven't they!

What's your relationship history?
I've been engaged once before. It was under very different circumstances. Unsurprisingly, since first-date weddings aren't exactly an everyday

occurrence in my life! I was working in a bar in Fiji around ten years ago and had the very definition of a whirlwind romance with a guy from New Zealand. I invited him back to the UK, and we lived in this amazing bubble in a holiday cottage in Wales for a few weeks. But then reality caught up with us and I think we both realised we wanted different things and it was never going to work. He went back to Fiji and I said I'd follow him, but instead I ran off to Australia and sent him an email from Sydney airport breaking up with him. But it was definitely for the best. Now I'm in a very different place – I'm not going to run off to Australia in the next few months, I promise! I've dated a few other people but I have been very much single for the past six months. Well, until now, as it seems I'm engaged!

What scares you?
I try not to let too much scare me, although, looking back now, there are things I definitely shouldn't have done. Though you'll have to wait till we're actually married and are sipping cocktails on our honeymoon for me to tell you about them! But I suppose this whole blind-date wedding scares me a bit – I mean, it would be weird if it didn't, right? Oh, and I have coulrophobia. I know it sounds made-up, but it is a real, if slightly ridiculous, phobia – of clowns. When my brother and I were

kids, our parents took us to the circus. While we were waiting for it to start, he told me some super-scary story about killer clowns, then as soon as it began and a clown came on, I was convinced they were coming to kill me and began screaming like a banshee. Embarrassed, my mum hustled me towards the back of the tent, at which point I was promptly sick all over the feet of the poor people sitting on the second to last row of chairs. Mum made us all leave and go home without seeing any of the rest of the show.

What's your favourite food?
Whenever I'm travelling, the one thing I always crave from home is chip shop sausages. Not posh, farm-fresh, 100% pork organic sausages, oh no. Proper brown-skinned, processed meat that comes with a scoop of salt-and-vinegar-drenched chips and a wooden fork stuck in the middle.

Right, I know what I'm having for my tea tonight! I still can't wait to meet you at our wedding (apologies for all the drinks and debauchery stuff I mentioned last week, I was definitely a bit overexcited about everything!).
Hannah x

Chapter 11

Jess

Jess breathed a sigh of relief as she finished prepping Hannah and Toby's blogs ready to go live the following day. With every new letter from them both, she became more and more certain that they were a good match.

'I can't wait for them to meet,' she said to Tom, sighing happily as she closed down the Save The Date website and opened her email on her laptop, which was resting precariously on her knees on top of the duvet. 'And the app is doing all right, too, which is good. Although we'd be getting *so* much more coverage if only they were available for interviews.'

She sighed again, although this time not so happily.

'But if they do that – and meet each other or even see each other on TV – it won't be a blind-date marriage anymore, so you'll lose the very idea you're trying to promote,' Tom pointed out, with just a hint of exasperation.

'Well, *obviously* we can't reveal anything about them *before* they get married,' Jess replied shortly. 'But I'm hoping to persuade them to do some press afterwards. If I can keep the local media onside until after the honeymoon, then hopefully it will get picked up by bigger outlets once they broadcast it. And if that doesn't save the business, I don't know what will!'

'Haven't subscription numbers rocketed already, though?' Tom said, looking up from his book and catching her gaze. 'Do you really need to do all that promo afterwards?'

'We're well on our way to hitting our target membership numbers, but the business could still go under at any point. *You* know how close to folding we've been, even if I haven't quite told Hannah. So anything we can do to grow the business and shore up finances for the future has got to be worth it.'

'"Grow the business"? You're not on *Dragons' Den*, Jess, this is me you're talking to!'

'There's nothing wrong with talking the talk to help you walk the walk, Tom,' Jess replied. She felt rather than saw him explode into giggles in bed next to her, and immediately felt her hackles rise. 'I don't know what you think's so funny about me trying to save my business so I can pay the mortgage and buy school uniform for the kids.' Before she could stop herself, she added, 'Not that you'd understand. It's called having ambition and wanting a better life. You should try it some time, Tom.'

'Oh, right, so it's my fault that you have to sell your best friend to the press, is that it? Not that you've told her how much you plan to use her, I bet. I'm not ambitious enough with my own business, so it's down to you to support the family while I put my feet up in my office sketching a few drawings for clients – is that really how you see it?'

Deep down Jess knew she should lower her voice, pull back and not let herself be dragged into the argument any further, but she ignored the quiet voice in her head telling her to walk away and gave into the fireball of worry and anxiety in her stomach. 'Well, funny you should say that but, yes, we *can't* survive on the pocket money you bring in, so Save The Date *has* to work. And, yes, that does mean I have to rely on Hannah to help me, but what other choice do I have? Is it wrong to want to be financially secure so we can give the kids what they need?'

'Pocket money?' Tom spat. 'Have you listened to yourself recently, Jess? And as for giving the kids what they need, they need *us*, not material possessions. And even when you're here, you're not here. You're glued to your laptop or tapping away on your phone. You're even on your computer in our bed for god's sake. Where we should be doing anything other than typing emails. Can you even remember when we last had sex? I can. It was six months ago. Since then you've seemed far more interested in exploiting your best friend for the sake of your dating app than in your marriage and family.'

Jess recoiled from her husband and stared at him open-mouthed for a second, before her brain truly registered his words. Then she said slowly, 'Are you saying I'm a bad mother, Tom, because it sounds very much like that to me?'

'Of course not!' Tom lowered his voice a little. 'I know you love the twins and you're a great mum; I'm just saying that sometimes you could be more present, that's all.'

'Right. Because that's not what it sounded like to me. And as for me exploiting my best friend, I think you'll find it was Hannah herself who suggested she get married to a stranger, not me.'

'I know that, I just think we have a duty of care to her. It's Hannah for god's sake.'

'We? Sorry, I thought this was all me, all my fault, that I was the bad person here—'

'Look, Jess, I'm sorry, but I can't talk to you when you're being like this. It's late, I'm tired and we both have an early start tomorrow. I'm going to sleep in the spare room and maybe in the morning we'll both feel more calm and rational.'

'You can't talk to me when I'm like what? When I'm defending myself against your spiteful comments? Fine, go and sleep in the spare room – I'm sure you can't bear to sleep next to such a bad mother anyway!'

Tears stung her eyes but she refused to give Tom the satisfaction of seeing them fall.

'Jess, darling, look, I didn't say that—'

'Tom, don't. Go to bed, I can't talk to you when you're like this,' she parroted back at him and turned away. She didn't move her head until she'd heard the creak of the floorboards across the landing that signalled Tom had left the room. She balanced her laptop precariously on her bedside table and flung herself into the middle of the mattress and her head into the pillow, then gave into the sobs choking the back of her throat. Tom had no idea how much she wanted to be 'present' and 'there for the kids', but it was nigh-on impossible to juggle being a mum, making sure they all had clean clothes to wear and food on the table as well as running the business and, you know, maybe having some kind of life outside work and home. She loved the very bones of Tom, but sometimes she couldn't help thinking she didn't *like* him that much. Tonight was one of those sometimes.

What was most frustrating was she knew he had a point – she was always tapping away on her laptop or phone when she should have been listening to the twins do their reading or helping them with their maths, but it was only because she had no other choice. It was that or drown in the continuous storm of emails and demands for money and people asking her to make decisions, whether it was about what after-school clubs the kids wanted to go to, the colour the hallway should be painted, or what design the Save The Date app logo should be. And she knew that it wasn't the same for Tom. There was an expectation that because she was a woman, she was the one who would remember that Charlie's birthday party started at 2 p.m. not 3 p.m., that the twins both needed a costume for 'dress as a country day' next week, and that the bananas in the fruit bowl were 'too mushy' for anyone but her to possibly eat. Never mind that she ran her own business just like Tom did, and she had to make it a success – because making things happen, being in control, being successful, that was what she did; it was her *raison d'être*. At the risk of sounding like one of the kids, it just wasn't fair.

Sometimes she fantasised about running away from it all and checking into a five-star resort in Barbados. Of course, she'd never really do it – that's what fantasies were for, right? – but that hadn't stopped her Googling hotels and daydreaming about hot waiters handing her all the food and drink she could manage while she lay on a sunbed and read the book that had been beside her bed for the last six months.

Jess glanced at the alarm clock and sighed. She had less than six hours until she needed to get up – not getting the required eight hours of sleep a night was just another way in which she was failing, she supposed. She scrubbed her eyes on the edge of the duvet, reached across for the pot on her bedside table and smeared on the night cream that promised to banish wrinkles, plump skin and leave it glowing come morning. She may not have had the recommended two litres of water that day (fail number 347) but there was no way her skin could be 'thirsty' the amount of product she plastered on it, she thought ruefully. Never mind about the state of her business or her marriage (though she had already decided to filter out Tom's comments about their lack of sex life), her skin would be fully hydrated if it was the last thing she ever did.

She tossed and turned for the rest of the night, before finally giving up and throwing off the duvet. She pulled on her comfy oversized sweatshirt from the floor next to the bed and made her way downstairs towards the kettle and a hot caffeine-laden drink. 'Oh. You're awake,' she said, surprised by Tom's presence in their kitchen before the children.

'I couldn't sleep,' he said. 'I hate arguing, Jess, especially with you, you know that. And I feel awful. You're a brilliant mum and I'm in awe of everything you're doing with Save The Date. But I worry you're trying to do too much. I just want you to be happy; for us all to be happy together.'

Jess had been busying herself with teabags and hot water, but hearing Tom's voice break, she turned round to face him, cupping her hands round her warm mug. 'I hate arguing too – I barely slept last night. And I know I'm often distracted at the moment, but it is a really important time for the business and I'd be stupid not to make the most of the opportunities coming our way. I shouldn't have said those things either, but if you could help me out with the kids and dinner and everything, that would really make a difference.' She hated herself for falling back into a 'housewife' stereotype – there was no earthly reason why she should automatically take on that care-giver role and be the one who was in charge of meals and shopping – but she also recognised it was seven o'clock in the morning, she was only one sip into her first cup of tea, and actually she just wanted things to be easier around the house, not start another argument about whose job it was to feed the kids (although she already knew the answer: both of theirs, and she'd stick a fork in the eye of anyone who told her otherwise).

'I'm sorry, I will make sure I take on my share of childcare and chores,' Tom replied, sipping his own drink and looking chastened. 'I just know that you have certain ways of doing things and you've never liked me doing them differently.'

'Well, you'll just have to do them properly − i.e., my way − the first time then!' Jess risked a smile. 'And I'll try to leave work at work and be in the present more.' She saw Tom wince at her reuse of his phrase, but he quickly rearranged his face into a smile. 'We're okay then? I can sleep in my own bed this evening?'

'I'm not the one who said you couldn't!' Jess protested, but allowed herself to be swept up into a Tom hug, or 'tommug' as they'd both called it for as long as they could remember.

As she relaxed into his arms, she breathed in the smell of his skin. Ever since they'd met as teenagers she'd wanted to inhale his familiar, safe scent. He'd worn the same after-shave for ever (it was also the same aftershave as his father, which Jess tried and failed not to find a little disconcerting when they visited his parents), but whether he'd been for a workout down the gym or was fresh out of the shower, she could always detect his musky, earthy, natural smell. Despite not having thought about sex for weeks − or perhaps months, according to Tom − she realised a small ball of fizz had woken up in her stomach, and she nuzzled further into his neck.

'*Muuuuuummy*, can I have some Rice Krispies?' came a sleepy voice behind them.

The moment was broken.

*

A few weeks later, her fragile truce with Tom was still holding, thanks largely to his sudden enthusiasm for giving the twins their tea following their various after-school activities, which in turn gave Jess the extra time she needed to handle Save The Date's ever-growing inbox. She came into the kitchen with a huge smile on her face, despite it looking like a bomb had hit it, and after kissing the twins on the tops of their heads as they hungrily forked pesto pasta into their mouths and left the broccoli florets in the bottom of their bowls, she padded round the table to Tom and gave him a kiss smack on his lips.

'What was that in aid of?' he smiled. 'Not that I'm complaining, obviously!'

'How do you fancy dinner à *deux* tomorrow evening, Mr T?'

'I very much fancy that, but there's the small problem of *les deux enfants. Je suis désolé.*'

'Ooh-la-la, I love it when you go all Gallic on me! And actually Hannah has suggested she babysit tomorrow night so we can go out. She said she wanted to say thank you for finding her a husband!'

'Really? Well, if she's sure, that would be lovely,' he replied, grinning. 'I know it's not French, but I could book Rio's in town maybe?'

'Ah *si, non importa*! We get to have a grown-up night out and that's what matters. And on a Friday night too! We could go mad and go for a drink in the pub first and everything.'

'Woah! Now you're living life on the edge. But, yes, why not?'

*

Jess found herself counting down the hours till she and Hannah could knock off work and head into the house for a pre-night-out (or night-in for Hannah) drink, despite having tons of calls to make and emails to send.

'Right, I think that's quite enough excitement for one day!' she declared, throwing her mouse aside dramatically. 'Fancy a nice cold glass of rosé?'

'Always!' Hannah grinned. 'And although today has been very exciting – I mean, who'd have thought I'd have people clamouring to shower me with free flowers on my wedding day, for god's sake? – the excitement isn't over for you, Jess, surely? You've got a lovely romantic evening ahead with your one and only, filled with pasta and Montepulciano. And if that's not exciting, I don't know what is!'

'Thank you again for suggesting you babysit, Han, we both really appreciate it,' Jess said as they gathered up their numerous belongings and made their way into the house.

'Any time, you know how much I love the twins, oh and your huge wine rack! Seriously, you are so grown-up – having more than two bottles of wine in the house at any one time is definitely adulting. The only time I have more than one bottle in my cupboard is when I've saved the dregs at the end for "cooking" and then spend the next two weeks heating ready meals or making beans on toast, none of which require a splash of red wine to add flavour. And then at the weekend when I suddenly realise I have no alcohol in the house other than the very dodgy ouzo I acquired during my Greek-island-hopping phase nearly ten years ago,

I inevitably end up drinking the "cooking Shiraz" straight from the bottle.'

Jess burst into loud laughter as she handed her friend a large glass of pink liquid. 'Han, has anyone ever told you how ludicrous you are?'

'You have. Often,' she replied, clinking her glass against Jess's.

With the kids happily scoffing their sausages and vegetables in front of the iPad with the promise of chocolate cake for pudding if they ate every single carrot and pea on their plates, Tom topped up Hannah and Jess's now-empty glasses and poured himself one too.

'Cheers to the weekend and lots of wine!' he smiled.

'God, I'm going to be pi— I mean drunk, before we leave the house if I'm not careful!' Jess laughed. 'Do you mind if I go and have a quick shower and get ready while they're eating?' she asked.

'Of course not; in fact, both of you feel free to get ready. I think I can cope with these two terrors,' Hannah laughed, glancing at the twins, who were transfixed by the cartoon they were watching.

'I'm not sure screens at mealtimes are exactly top of the parenting manual, but it is Friday night after all,' Tom smiled. 'Jess, why don't you jump in the shower and shout me when it's free and I'll keep Hannah company until then.'

Jess was halfway out the room before he'd finished speaking, even forgetting to take her wine with her. 'I'll bring up your glass when I come,' Tom called.

Fifteen minutes later she was sipping her drink as she watched Tom get undressed. She knew every inch of her husband's body and neither of them batted an eyelid at the other's naked figure these days, which was both a good thing and a bad thing, she mused as she blasted her hair into submission and applied her usual tinted moisturiser swipe of brown eyeshadow and slick of barely-there lip colour. She added dangly earrings and spritzed herself liberally with the one expensive perfume she owned and had so far made last for two years, not wanting to waste it on mundane moments. Although she did wonder if it smelled a bit mustier than it had the last time she'd released it from its still-pristine box, but as it was so long ago she couldn't be sure.

Tom reappeared, his damp hair sticking to his head, but within five minutes, he'd dressed, smoothed down his locks then ruffed them up with a bit of wax and was ready to go.

'Shall we?' He smiled at Jess and strode out of the room and down the stairs.

They were greeted by both the children and Hannah licking their plates clean of chocolate cake and giggling.

'Right, we'll leave you to it, Han,' Jess laughed. 'No, don't get up to kiss me, any of you, I don't want chocolatey fingers all over me. I'll just blow kisses from here. Twins, be good for Hannah, please.'

'We always are, we love Hannah,' Lily replied, placing sticky arms round Hannah's neck. 'What is that funny smell?' She sniffed, wrinkling her nose. 'Anyway, byeeeee!'

'Glad they can't wait to get rid of us,' Jess laughed as she and Tom made for the door.

'Eight going on eighteen,' he nodded. 'Oh well, I'd rather they couldn't wait for us to leave than have them throwing themselves screaming at our legs like they used to do when they were little.'

By the time they got to Rio's via the pub an hour and a half later, Jess was feeling decidedly tipsy. 'Bagsy having the carbonara,' she said before they'd even opened their menus.

'How many times do I have to say, we *can* both have the same thing!' Tom laughed.

'And how many times do I have to say that's just not true. It's such a waste when couples do that. If you have the chilli prawn linguine I'll swap you a bit, but don't even think I'm going half and half with you.'

'God, it's so long since we've been here, isn't it? Back in the day I'd eat that linguine about once a week.'

'Back in the day before kids, mortgage payments and the joys of being self-employed, you mean? True, but although we may not have spicy king prawns anymore, we do have two smart, funny children, several hundred thousand pounds of debt and all the worry that goes with owning a business – what's not to love!'

'Cheers to that!' Tom smiled. 'Although let's hope that some of those worries around Save The Date are starting to diminish now.'

'Yep, fingers crossed, although we're not out of the woods

yet. I still can't believe how much free stuff we're being given for the wedding. So far we've had brands offering flowers, shoes, a cake, cheese, wedding favours, table decorations, even a photo booth, for god's sake. I'm beginning to wish I'd not booked the bloody venue already and Hannah hadn't forked out for her dress. Brands are literally showering us with stuff, and all they want in return is a mention on social media – it's crazy-amazing!'

'Or just crazy,' Tom grimaced. 'What's wrong with a simple but low-cost wedding where you're not beholden to anyone for social media posts or mentions?'

'But we'd be ridiculous not to cash in when we're being offered everything for free,' Jess argued. 'As I said to Hannah, it costs nothing for us to put up a quick Instagram post mentioning the beautiful flowers – we would be shouting about the wedding across our social channels anyway, so adding a #gifted isn't going to make any difference.'

'So Hannah was worried about all the extras too?' Tom raised an eyebrow.

'Not after I'd reassured her, no. God, Tom, you could be more supportive! This is my best friend getting married and I want to make her day as special as possible.'

'Special? Well, I guess marrying a stranger is pretty "special",' he replied.

Jess chose not to rise to the bait. 'It's my job to make it special in every way for her, and if that means taking a few freebies then I'm more than up for that. A balloon company has even suggested they create an archway in our colour scheme, which is amazing, although I'm not quite sure what the colour scheme is yet. I was thinking pale pink and baby blue, maybe?'

'Won't that look like one of those baby showers where they reveal the sex of the baby? I've been talking to a woman in Boston about a commission and she said she needed to move our Skype chat to next week because she had to go to a baby shower yesterday. I had no idea what she was talking about – I had to look it up online. There was me picturing she was having some kind of baby-friendly bathroom installed, and it turned out to be a party for a very pregnant woman who would probably rather be lying down than entertaining a load of squawking guests high on cupcakes. Of course I had to be polite, though, because she's high up in a big US conglomerate who are thinking about commissioning me to paint some artwork for the reception of their new building in Boston. I mean if I got that, it could be the start of something really big, you know, Jess?'

She smiled. 'That's great. But I do know what you mean about pink and blue. Maybe we should say red and white for the balloons just to be safe?'

'Did you even listen to what I just said? And shouldn't it be Hannah deciding the colour scheme – it's her wedding, after all?' Tom stared at her and Jess shook herself back to the moment.

'Of course I listened to what you were saying, I'm just a bit distracted at the moment. But that commission would be amazing, and if they're a big US company they'll pay good money. When will they let you know whether you've got it?'

'God, it really is all about money with you, Jess, isn't it? Between that and the wedding, there's no room for me or the kids. It's like you're trying to live through Hannah and make sure she has the perfect wedding because you didn't get the chance to do that for your own big day.'

'Tom! No, that's not true—'

'Isn't it? Well, that's what it feels like. We were so young and didn't have much cash so we had to make do with what our parents could pay for. So now you're living out your dream on Hannah's day.'

'There's nothing wrong with trying to give Hannah the perfect day,' she protested.

'What, because our wedding day wasn't perfect?'

'I didn't say that, and I don't know where you've got that idea from at all. Though I'm sure both of us would have wanted less "input" from our parents and more of someone actually asking us for our opinions.'

'No, not really. Because it never mattered to me about the details, Jess, it was all about wanting us to say our vows in front of our friends and family. I couldn't have cared less if there were no flowers or cake or seating plan. That was enough for me. You were enough for me. I'm sorry if that wasn't the case for you. I know you've always thought my mother was too demanding about what she wanted at our wedding, but she could see how much there was to do and was just trying to help.'

'You're turning this all around and twisting what I was

saying,' Jess protested. 'But give me one woman who doesn't dream of the perfect wedding day.'

'Hannah didn't seem to care that much before you planted the idea of freebies in her head.'

'You don't understand, Tom! I can see how much there is to do and I'm helping. I just want what's best for Hannah.'

'No, you don't, you just want what's best for your company,' Tom replied quietly.

Jess opened her mouth and then shut it again. She took a glug of her wine and twirled a large forkful of pasta into her mouth. Her carbonara had cooled and the sauce now had a glue-like consistency that at least prevented her from speaking for several minutes. It didn't stop tears from smarting her eyes, but she blinked them back and stared determinedly at her plate and concentrated on chewing.

Soon after, Tom signalled to their waiter for the bill and within minutes they were back out on the pavement. It had started to spit with rain and the light breeze had gathered momentum into uncomfortable gusts.

'Jess, I'm sorry. Let's just forget that conversation, yeah? We were having such a nice evening before then.'

'No, it's good to know what you really think,' she said tonelessly.

'Jess, I— Come on, let's grab this black cab and get out of the rain.'

Jess didn't allow herself to speak during the journey home. She was worried that if she opened her mouth, she wouldn't be able to control what came out of it and all her jumbled thoughts about Tom, their family and their jobs might come spilling out. He kept glancing at her as if he was about to speak himself but then thought better of it. She knew that he'd be kicking himself for souring the evening, but would be glad, deep down, that he'd said his piece. Tom was principled like that.

If only he was as principled when it came to helping round the house, looking after the kids and bringing in half the household's finances, Jess thought bitterly.

She could read his thoughts without him speaking, but she hoped to god he couldn't discern hers right now.

'Jess, Tank, did you have a lovely time? You're back earlier than I thought you would be; you should have stayed for another drink!' Hannah said when they walked in the front door a few minutes later. 'And don't worry, the kids were as good as gold. They taught me the dance moves to that Little Mix song, and in return I showed them the Macarena, so a good time was had by all.'

'Thanks so much, Han,' Tom smiled. 'You're a star.'

'My pleasure, really, plus I've opened a bottle of that Shiraz of yours I like so much. It's still early, why don't you help me drink it before I order a taxi in a bit? Unless you want an early night both of you?' She grinned. 'In which case, I'll just get an Uber now . . .'

'No, it's fine,' both Jess and Tom said immediately. 'Although I might go and check on the twins. You both have some more wine though,' Tom added. He headed upstairs and Jess immediately made a beeline for the cupboard, located another glass and poured herself a generous serving of Shiraz.

'Is he okay?' Hannah asked as they made their way into the lounge.

'Yeah, he's just a bit tired. And not used to drinking so much on a Friday night.' Jess forced a smile.

'That's what happens when you're happily settled down with gorgeous kids, a gorgeous house – and, of course, a gorgeous wife!' Hannah laughed. 'I can't believe it will be not just your tenth wedding anniversary, but your twentieth anniversary of being together next year,' she added dreamily.

'It's not all rose petals on the bed, Han, believe me,' Jess replied.

'Yeah, but you know each other inside out and have grown up together. There are no terrible surprises waiting round the corner. I'm marrying someone I've never even met, for god's sake!'

'But think of all the things you're going to learn about your Toby-to-be; all that discovering what you both like – and not just in the bedroom! – all that possibility and excitement that's to come.'

'What if I don't like what I learn? You and Tom know each other, like *really* know each other, and make the other happy every day *because* you know each other.'

'I wouldn't say every day. Also, don't forget that, because we do know each other so well, there are no surprises, no spontaneity. Back when we were teenagers it was all sneaking into bedrooms when our parents were asleep, and all the firsts. But now we've done it all – marriage, kids, jobs, house; all the things you're supposed to do – it can all be a bit, well, boring.' Jess suddenly wondered if she'd been a little too honest, although the way she was feeling at the moment, what she'd said was pretty tame all things considered.

'Ah, J, that's the wine talking! You always did get a bit maudlin on red wine. Seriously, you and Tom are #couplegoals and I won't hear anything to the contrary. Especially when I'm about to embark on my own romantic adventure, I need to know that happily ever afters can come true.'

'Don't listen to me going on, of course you'll get your happy ending with Toby. He's a good sort and he's as much up for this adventure as you are, I promise.'

'That's more like the Jess I know and love.' Hannah smiled. 'Although, to be fair, you're usually telling me to be careful, asking whether I should really be jumping out of a plane into the unknown or consoling me that no man is worth getting so upset over!'

'How times have changed. In just a few weeks you're going to make me so proud when you walk down that aisle, Han. And that will be just the start of your romantic adventure! But before that we have your hen night next weekend, and boy am I looking forward to that!'

'So am I, I think!' Hannah laughed. 'And at least I know there's one hen party game we won't be playing.'

'What's that?'

'Mr and Mrs – you're hardly going to ask poor Toby what my favourite sex position is when the most he knows about me is that I like chip shop sausages!'

SAVE THE DATE

Find out more about our blind-daters with a difference . . .

It's been a few weeks since we last posted the letters from our bride and groom to be, but we've been hard at work getting everything in place for their wedding – which is in just a few weeks' time #excited! So are Hannah and Toby, our Save The Date #marriedatfirstswipe daters, feeling just as excited? Read on to find out. And if you want to have your own romantic adventure, subscribe to Save The Date and download our app to meet hundreds of people looking for long-term love.

Over to Hannah and Toby . . .

Dear Hannah

I enjoyed reading your last letter – do you think the geniuses at Save The Date matched us on our love of fried English foods? Hopefully, we're compatible in lots of other ways, too, but at least we know we're never going to disagree on what takeaway we should have on a Friday night. Here are my answers to this week's fiendishly difficult questions . . .

When were you last drunk?
At my stag do last weekend. I'm guessing you

want to know what happened, but not what HAPPENED? Well, that's fine by me (though stag dos in your mid-thirties are definitely different from those you go on in your mid-twenties, believe me). Having already visited many of the major European stag destinations, my mates decided we should go somewhere a bit different, so we went to ... Scotland! Despite living in the north of England, it seemed to take us just as long to reach our destination of Perth as it would have Prague. However, though Prague may have the Charles Bridge and the Staropramen Brewery, what it doesn't have is a mini Highland Games course and a whisky-tasting tour. Or my dad, my sister (who wasn't letting the fact she is a woman rule her out of an opportunity to humiliate me with her many anecdotes about when we were kids) and twelve of my best mates. Everyone was determined to beat me at tossing the caber, hurling the haggis and welly wangin', as I believe the various races were called. Suffice it to say that despite it being my party, I wasn't allowed to win anything.

What's the most awkward question anyone's ever asked you?
This one?! And there was THAT question that my mates asked on my stag do (although they did at least wait till my dad had gone to bed), but I told

them that what happens at the end of our wedding day is between us, and that it's just another thing for us to figure out together. I guess I just wanted you to know that I'm nervous too, in case you are? Anyway, moving on ...

What are you most looking forward to about married life?
The thing I'm most looking forward to is learning a little more about you every day. You sound like one of the most interesting people I've never met, if that isn't weird to say. You seem to have lots of stories and anecdotes, and I can't wait to hear more of these and find out not only who you are, but what actually makes you who you are. Oh god, that sounds a bit pretentious doesn't it?

I think what I'm trying to say is that I'm excited for us to get to know each other properly.

Not long now.

Toby x

Dear Toby

I loved finding out from your last letter that I am the sausage to your chips (is it just me or does that sound rude?). I'm still finding it hard to know exactly what to say in my letters, as I want to say everything and nothing at the same time! Everything, because I want you to have a good picture of what makes me 'me' before you stand in front of all the people you care about and declare that you will marry me. And nothing because I want us to get to know each other more naturally when we do meet. But as there's no rule book for a blind-date marriage, let's just be glad that Save The Date have given us questions we have to answer (although they are definitely getting harder each week!).

When were you last drunk?
I had my hen do at the weekend, so then! It was good fun. I invited my mum, but thankfully she politely declined – although she did secretly tell my best friend she would pick up the tab for our drinks, which was very nice of her. However, my friend had to halve the actual total then halve it again so Mum didn't think we were all complete alcoholics! Eight of us spent the weekend in a cottage in the Lake District where we drank lots of wine, ate lots of food, went for some gorgeous walks to blow away those hangovers, and even went climbing inside a mine, which was amazing – think rope bridges, rock climbing and a spectacular view at the end, and you get the picture. My bezzie organised it, even though there was no way she was going to put on a harness and start clambering around underground herself – which is just another reason why I love her! Between everything else going on at the

moment, spending time with a group of women who constantly inspire me and support me was exactly what I needed. Lying on the sofa in our pyjamas reminiscing about all my different adventures with each of them really brought it home how much I need these women around me. I might not see some of them that often as they live in different counties or even countries, but that's what social media and WhatsApp are for, right?

What's the most awkward question anyone's ever asked you?
Oh god, cringe! The actual answer is not for public consumption, but don't worry, I have plenty of other awkward moments to draw on. Most recently, there was the time a lovely old lady gave up her seat on the bus for me because she thought I was pregnant. I had to spend the rest of the journey making up answers to her questions about when my baby was due because I was too British to tell her I'd just eaten a large bowl of pasta and my tummy was in fact a food baby not a human baby.

What are you most looking forward to about married life?
Having the kind of relationship my best friend has with her husband. They've known each other for a long time, so I know it will never be quite the same

*for us, but I hope that twenty years down the line
we both still love and respect each other as much
as they do. They've taught me how important it is
to support each other in a partnership and that you
can each bring something different to the marriage
to make it a success. The other thing I'm most
looking forward to is having another excuse to go to
the chippy for sausage and chips all the time – yay!*
   Hannah x

Chapter 12

Hannah

'Toby's definitely coming out of his shell a bit, isn't he?' Hannah smiled a few days later as they both sat at their desks in the Save The Date office. 'I was surprised he was so brave in his answer about the awkward question.'

'Yeah, I noticed you ducked out of that one a bit.' Her friend rolled her eyes.

'Well, you shouldn't have asked us such difficult questions, then! Don't forget that the world and his wife are reading our answers. I was trying to be amusing, although I think Toby is probably funnier than I am if his blogs are anything to go by, which hopefully they are. Are you all right?'

'What. The. Actual . . . Han, you are not going to believe this email,' Jess replied.

'What, Elton John has offered us sole use of his LA mansion as well as his private jet so we can fly our friends and family out to California and have our reception there?' Hannah deadpanned.

'Not quite, but almost as good.'

'What, George Clooney has offered us sole use of his country pad in Berkshire and said we can even use the swimming pool and private cinema if we want?'

'Han! Your knowledge of celebrity homes is worrying – you haven't got any restraining orders I need to know about, have you? No, this email is actually better than that. And before you take another guess about some other A-lister's private residence, it's nothing to do with celebrities, well, not really.'

'Not really? What do you mean not really? It either is an invite to hobnob with the rich and famous or it isn't. Come on, tell me, I'm about to burst here. And this better be good now you've built it up so much.'

'Oh, don't you worry, it is,' Jess replied smugly. 'How about an all-expenses-paid honeymoon to St Lucia?'

'You're not serious? Really, Jess, that's really what that email says? I don't believe you, let me see.' Jess turned her laptop round and Hannah stared at the screen. 'Oh my god, it really does say that! But do you think this Esmeralda person who sent the email is real? Esmeralda Miller sounds like a made-up name to me.'

'Well, she seems kosher enough, and she has a St Lucia Tourism Agency email. But I'll give her a call and check it all out if it makes you happy. Did you read the bit where she said she'd read your blogs and thought St Lucia would be right up both your and Toby's alley because, as well as all its amazing beaches and bars, you can drive into volcanoes, go ziplining and do diving and snorkelling; well, in any time you have left when you're not "getting to know each other better"!'

'Jess, she most certainly didn't say that last bit, only you and your dirty mind felt the need to add that on!'

'All right, Little Miss Pure And Innocent! Although as Toby brought up the question, so to speak, in his letter, how are you feeling about the wedding night itself? You managed to dodge the question when Sara asked you in the Lakes and I tried to get you to answer it in your blog, but I'm not letting you off the hook that easily.'

'Toby has made me feel better about things actually. And as we get closer to the wedding, I'm more and more convinced that I'm going to "just know" like G-ma always says she did with Gramps. We've called this whole project #marriedatfirstswipe after all, and I'm *so* here for the fire-works. And if I feel the fireworks, then who knows what might happen on our wedding night!' She grinned. 'But before you ask, I won't be texting you with an update as soon as I wake up, no. God, I've never known anyone quite so interested in my sex life! Anyway, back to the free holiday thing – and in fact, free everything thing. Are you sure we should be saying yes to all of these offers? I love a freebie as much as the next person, but it does feel a bit weird when it's my wedding we're talking about.'

'Of course we should be saying yes. You would love to

go to St Lucia and unless you have a stash of cash you've been keeping *very* quiet about for the past few years then I'm guessing you can't afford to go to St Lucia. This gives you the chance to do it – and, more importantly, the chance to do it with your brand-new husband. All you have to do is put out a few posts on the Save The Date social channels and then write a blog about it when you're back, and bob's your uncle, fanny's your aunt – fnah fnah! – and bingo, you're chilling out in the St Lucian sunshine with your beloved!'

'Well, when you put it like that . . .'

'I'm almost tempted to ditch dear Toby and marry you myself if it means a week on a Caribbean island, Han!'

'As much as I love you, Jess, I think I'll stick with Toby,' Hannah laughed. 'God, I don't know what's got into you but you've gone all hyper about the wedding. Here's me trying to be all chill despite crapping myself when I think too deeply about it, and here's you all crazy and overexcited!'

'I'm just overexcited for you two to actually meet,' Jess said, tapping her feet against her chair. 'I keep picturing both of your faces when you finally see each other on your wedding day.'

'And what does my face look like in these daydreams?'

'Happy. Very happy.' Jess nodded hard.

'And Tobes?'

'He is gazing in wonder at the beautiful woman walking towards him and can't stop himself from smiling!'

This made Hannah smile too. 'Do you think he'll mind me calling him Tobes? I like the sound of it,' she added.

'I'm sure you can call him anything you like when you're "getting to know each other", my friend! All right, I'll stop with the inverted commas.'

'I still feel weird about the fact we're engaged without actually being "engaged". I don't even have a ring,' Hannah said a little sadly, glancing at her empty left hand.

'You'll have a beautiful wedding band in a few weeks, don't you worry! And hopefully he'll have a good eye for jewellery for birthday and Christmas presents and just-because gifts for the next thirty years. It's a man's job to buy the woman gifts all the time, I think.'

'Er, Jess, the 1950s called and asked for their outdated views back! Come on, you buy Tom presents.'

'Well, only to make sure he buys me something in return.' Jess shrugged. 'After twenty years and a shared bank account, we don't really do surprises anymore, sadly.'

'God, you make it sound like romance has shrivelled up and died!' Hannah laughed.

Jess's smile didn't reach her eyes. 'Are we still going to your mum's for lunch tomorrow? I'd forgotten I'd said I'd come with you until I checked my calendar earlier.'

'How could you forget your lunch date with Joan of Bark?' Hannah said, using the nickname she and Jess had secretly coined in their teenage years when it seemed all her mum did was shout at Hannah. 'She texted me this morning to inform me she'd been to M&S and bought one of their expensive salmon and broccoli quiches in your honour.'

'Gosh, well, I shall make sure I am suitably gushing about

my salmon and broccoli quiche tomorrow. I don't want Joan thinking I'm ungrateful.'

'Don't worry, she'll save all of her smiles and simpers for you, as usual. God, between her and G-ma over the years, it's like you're their close relative not me!'

'I'm not sure I'm quite the golden girl anymore, now I've led you towards the dark side of getting married to a stranger.'

'Don't you worry, I told her it was all my idea and I had to practically force you to click through hundreds of photos of hot men until you found the hottest of them all and matched him with me.'

'I have to tell you, Han, there were quite a few men for whom the word hot was not really invented and I still had to click through all their photos. And some quite strange reasons why they wanted to apply to take part in a blind-date wedding.'

'Online dating is a scary place, Jess, and that's before you realise most people don't even look half as hot in real life as they do in their less-than-hot photo. Although, of course, the Save The Date app is better than the others,' she added quickly.

'Well saved, my friend. And it certainly is better than the others now we have so many new sign-ups. And anyway, you don't have to look at another dating app ever again – well, except for your job, obviously – now you have your Toby-to-be.'

'That's true,' replied Hannah, perking up immediately.

'The last few weeks have been so busy, I haven't had a second to think about the fact I'm not spending every night swiping left through hordes of tedious men until I find one who isn't quite as predictable as the rest.'

As Hannah made her way to her mum's house the following day, she wished Jess hadn't had to go to some reading assembly at the twins' school first and could have driven them over to Joan's herself, or at least made the bus ride there less depressing by sitting next to her instead of the slightly unkempt but very talkative old man currently snuggled up to her. She even got off the bus a stop before she needed to in order to get away from him, reasoning the extra exercise would do her good, especially as she was failing to curb her Chunky KitKat habit that she'd promised herself she'd get under control the day after she'd been dress-shopping with Jess. Except as the bus pulled away, the drizzle began, and it wasn't long before it had become more of an insistent soaking. Of course, Hannah didn't have an umbrella with her, even though she'd gone into Marks & Spencer the other day with the express intention of buying one. Instead she'd come out with a three-pack of black tights and some Percy Pigs. And she'd forgotten to bring her mum anything to say thank you for lunch, unless a single pink sweet shaped like a pig and covered in fluff from the bottom of her bag counted. She decided it didn't.

She made her way past the terraced houses stacked neatly in tight rows, and on through the streets slightly further out with their bigger semi-detached properties, until she reached the road where she'd grown up. She knew she was lucky to have had a mostly happy childhood in relative middle-class bliss, but she also knew her mum had been very lucky to keep the house in the divorce settlement that followed. She'd managed that mainly because her anger and bitterness at the split meant she was like a dog with a bone and Hannah's dad had no fight left in him, plus he had already moved on with his now-wife Charmaine – and in fact moved *in* with her.

Hannah closed the gate and softened a little as she saw how pretty the garden was looking. One of Joan's passions since her divorce (other than slagging off her ex-husband and his new family, obviously) had been gardening, and the sight of the bright and blooming flowerbeds round the front lawn was so joyful that Hannah couldn't help but smile. She clonked the door knocker three times and then used her key to let herself in before shouting, 'It's just me, Mum,' into the house. Immediately, she was hit by a swell of music that sounded like an orchestra was playing a concert in the hallway, and she had to wait for almost a minute in the entrance to the kitchen until the violins died down and a flute played a jaunty solo before she could shout again, 'Hello! It's me, Mum!'

'Gosh, Hannah, you gave me quite a fright there sneaking up on me!'

'Hi, Mum, lovely to see you, too,' Hannah replied, plastering a smile on her face and brushing her mum's cheek with a kiss.

'Jess is still coming, isn't she?'

'Yes, don't worry, she'll be here soon. Though don't forget it's me who's your dear daughter, not Jess!' She attempted another smile, this time through gritted teeth, then took a subtle deep breath. 'So, how have you been, Mum? I haven't seen you for a fair few weeks.'

'Yes, the last time you were here was when you dropped your little bombshell, wasn't it?' Joan replied, busying herself with the oven gloves. 'I can't say I'm happy about the situation, but your brother and even lovely Julia seem to think it's a good idea, and as he says, at least it's dear Jess who's matched you with this Toby man, and we know she has good taste in husbands – how is Tom, by the way? He's such a lamb, he really is. And your father says you're sure about what you're doing so his view is we should be supporting you, so it looks as though I'm outnumbered anyway.' Having finished her speech, Joan also finished poking at the quiche in the oven, then stood up and switched on the kettle. 'Do you want a cup of tea?'

Hannah gazed at her mum, her mouth open in astonishment, and it took her a few seconds to respond. 'Yes, thank you,' she said eventually. 'Did you say you'd spoken to Dad?'

'Yes, he called me last week and said we should have a chat about you – and Scott and gorgeous Leo, obviously – so we did. This quiche is almost ready, do you think Jess will be here soon?'

The knocker tap-tapped just as she'd finished speaking, and Hannah trotted gratefully down the hall to let her friend in. 'Mum's being a bit weirdly okay about the wedding,' she whispered as Jess closed the door behind her. 'Wonder boy and Julia are apparently all for it, and Dad called her to talk about it and she actually seems to have listened to him. It's odd.'

'But good odd, so let's just go with it,' Jess whispered back. 'Joan, so lovely to see you! Have you lost weight? That dress looks gorgeous on you. Thank you so much for having us over for lunch, it makes such a nice change from a boring old ham sandwich at our desks!'

'Oh, Jess dear, you are too kind. And we can't have you wasting away all the time on plain ham barms, especially when you have those adorable children and handsome hus- band to look after. Now, sit down, I'm just making some tea and then we'll have some quiche and salad, and I've even got some of that Victoria sponge from M&S I know you like so much.'

'You do spoil us, Joan!' Jess grinned.

'You, she spoils you,' Hannah mouthed at her friend while her mum poured them all a mug of strong tea.

'Although I expect you're watching your weight, aren't you, Hannah?' her mum continued. 'I remember I was so sick with nerves in the weeks leading up to my wedding day I could barely eat a thing, and my dress actually ended up being a bit too big on the day.'

'I don't think I'll have that problem!' Hannah laughed. 'I'll make sure I save a bit of space for cake, don't you worry. This looks lovely, Mum, thanks,' she added as they all sat down at the kitchen table. 'After we've eaten I'll show you the dress

I bought if you want. I've saved the link to the website in my favourites.'

'Has Hannah told you about all the little extras we've managed to line up for the big day?' Jess asked, turning to Joan. Hannah tried to shoot her friend a warning frown, but she had already started counting things off on her fingers. 'The flowers are being provided by this amazing boutique company in Manchester who've worked with everyone from Instagram stars to glossy magazines, the cake is going to be made by the geeky one from *Bake Off* a couple of seasons ago – you know, the one who made that amazing seven-tier mirror-glaze cake but was rubbish at the technicals so went out a few weeks before the final? No, well, believe me, he is *so* talented. And we've got a second cake made entirely from cheese that a local deli are doing. What else, oh yes, we've got favours being provided by a lovely little artisan gin company, and a massive balloon arch, which is going to look so cool. Then there's the photo booth and the small tree people can hang their messages to the bride and groom on, plus we might have a chocolate fountain!' Jess sat back in her seat looking very pleased with herself, though Hannah noticed Joan took a second to arrange her face into a smile.

'Well, you've definitely been very busy!' Joan managed to say. 'But it all sounds ever so expensive. Do you think you really need all of these favours and whatnot?'

'Well, that's the best bit.' Jess beamed at her. 'We're getting them all for free!'

Joan frowned and turned to look at her daughter. 'I don't

understand. Why would these people not want payment for things they're providing for your wedding?'

Hannah knew that frown meant more than just confusion – she could sense her mother's disapproval starting to build, which was never far from the surface when it came to her anyway, so she adopted a bright and breezy tone she definitely didn't feel. 'Don't worry, Mum, we do pay them, just not in money in their bank accounts. We'll be mentioning them on Save The Date's social media and thanking them on the blog, and that way they get loads of exposure and their perfect audience will see them being talked about on Instagram and Facebook. Believe me, that's worth far more than actual cash nowadays!' she ended with a light laugh. Joan continued to frown.

'I still don't think I understand. Are you saying that you're trading these "extras" for some words on Facebook and the website? So you're effectively selling your wedding day to every single one of these companies who want to give you things?'

Hannah glanced towards Jess with a pleading look, but her friend merely grimaced and said, 'I'm just nipping to the loo, won't be long!' leaving Hannah to face her mum on her own.

She tried to calm her annoyance and instead reassure Joan. 'I know it sounds weird, Mum, but that is how lots of things work now. People make whole careers out of mentioning products on their Instagram accounts and they make millions of pounds out of it.'

'But you're not some *reality star*!' her mum replied, not

hiding the distaste she clearly felt saying those two words. 'You're supposed to be a responsible professional woman, not someone who goes round marrying a complete stranger and seeing how many freebies you can get in the process! It's so cheap, Hannah. I knew I was wrong to listen to that rubbish your father was spouting about modern marriage – to think I'd almost come round to the idea and have been looking at hats on the John Lewis website! You can do whatever you want, as you have done for practically your whole life without thinking about anyone else, but don't expect me to come along and watch you selling yourself in front of everyone.'

'Mum, I—'

'I don't want to talk about it, Hannah, I'm too upset. Ah, Jess, there you are. Shall we have a slice of that cake now?'

Fifteen minutes later, Hannah and Jess were pulling out of her mum's leafy road and heading back towards Jess's house. 'Well, that didn't go as well as I would have hoped,' Jess said. Hannah continued to stare out of the window, attempting to swallow back the tears and frustration that she knew would bubble over if she opened her mouth.

'Han, are you all right?' Jess asked, placing a concerned hand on her knee as they waited for the traffic lights to change. 'Joan of Bark will come round again – she did the first time after all. You just need to get your dad to talk to her again. Who knew he'd be the one to get through to her after all this time!'

'This isn't Dad's problem.' Hannah squeezed her eyes shut so the tears gathered in their corners were locked away inside.

'*I* need to fix this.' She turned towards her friend, swiping her arm against her face to catch the drops she was still willing not to fall. 'And maybe Mum's right. I don't need all those Insta-perfect bits; we need to strip it back a little. The important thing is that I'm marrying a man who you and Save The Date have matched me with and we get to go and live our happy-ever-after for years to come. And that's it.'

'I do hear you, Han, but why not make it the best day ever at the same time?'

'Because it might mean my mum doesn't come to the wedding,' Hannah replied immediately. 'I know this has to work for the business, Jess, but it is also my life. Can you imagine if your mum hadn't come to your wedding? It would have been a completely different day, wouldn't it?' Her tears were now gone and in their place was a fierce determination to give voice to all the thoughts she'd been pushing down for the past few weeks. 'Look, Jess, I love you and I'm so grateful for everything you've done to make this a special day for me, but I think we've got a bit carried away and forgotten what this is all about. Save The Date is well on the way to global domination, or at least we've almost hit those figures the bank came up with, haven't we? And there's still so much scope for membership to grow and for the company to become massive, so I just don't think some sponsored Insta posts are going to matter.'

Jess pulled into her drive and turned the engine off. There was silence for a moment, but she reluctantly agreed. 'You're right, they're not,' she replied. 'I just want your wedding day to be amazing, Han. When I got married, of course I couldn't have done it without my mum there, but we hardly had any money to spend on the day, despite my parents giving us what they could and Tom's mum and dad helping us out too. And when I look back on it now, I just think you can see in the pictures how cheap everything was.'

'But it didn't matter!' Hannah cried. 'I was there watching two of my favourite people in the world declare how much they loved each other, and that was everything. Isn't that what you think of when you look back on it? That happiness and contentment that was spread all over your face for the world to see?'

'I suppose,' Jess said quietly, fiddling with her car keys. 'It all feels like a very long time ago now, anyway.'

'Well, it *was* what, nine, nearly ten years ago? But you could renew your vows one day and have the wedding you always wanted at that point. Especially if Save The Date actually takes over the world!' Hannah smiled.

She was more shaken by her mum's words than she cared to admit, maybe because she knew there was an element of truth to them. It made her think about all those Sunday afternoons curled up in G-ma's armchair, when she'd asked her to tell her the story of her and Gramps's wedding day, just seven days after they'd both asked their parents' permission and Robbie had asked his colonel for a few days' leave. The Second World War might have been over for a good few years, but it had changed everything and rationing was still in force. Yet the folk in the small Cornish village where

Vera and her family lived chipped in their own rations and lengths of material so Vera's mother could run her up a wedding dress and make her own mother-of-the-bride frock.

Hannah had always found the idea of the town coming together to support the bride-to-be during such a tough time unbelievably romantic, which is why she'd originally been so up for all the things companies had offered her for her own wedding day. But the make-do-and-mend wartime spirit was the antithesis of the fifteen-minutes-of-fame feel of Instagram mentions and #gifted and it had begun to sit a bit strangely with her. And her mum's outburst today had crystallised everything for her. Now she watched her friend as she continued to spin her keys in her hand and look worried.

'J, I'm sorry to spoil your plans, I really am,' she added pleadingly. 'And I'm sure there's some kind of middle ground and we just need to pare it back a little. Tell me you understand?'

Jess sighed and gathered her keys into her palm. 'I do understand, of course I do, Han. And I'm sorry if I've forced this all on you. Let's go inside and look through exactly what we've been offered and turn down anything you're not happy accepting. And then I'll call Toby and let him know. To be honest, I haven't given him any details anyway as I wanted to get everything sorted first, so he won't know any different.'

'Thank you, I appreciate it,' Hannah replied, giving her hand a squeeze. 'I'm not saying we have to say no to everything, especially if it would help Save The Date in the long term with contacts or whatever. But I need to be able to tell Mum that she was right – urgh, the very thought makes me feel sick! – and we don't need all those things. It's the only way she'll come round, I know it is. And maybe even that won't be enough to persuade her. But at least I'll have done everything I can.'

'It's fine. It's your wedding day after all. Dare I ask how you feel about St Lucia?'

'God, I'd almost forgotten about that! But maybe if we just don't mention to Mum it's a freebie and say Save The Date are paying for it, it will be fine. She's not going to look at Instagram for god's sake! The lure of sunshine and mai tais is too much even for my new-found morals. Does that make me a bad person?'

'It most certainly does not!' Jess replied immediately. 'Bring on the palm trees!'

Hannah hugged her friend before they made their way inside. 'You are the best best friend, J, you know that. And don't think I'll forget about the vow renewal thing – you should do it for your tenth wedding anniversary at the end of the year.'

Jess grimaced. 'If we make it to our tenth anniversary.'

SAVE THE DATE

Find out more about our blind-daters with a difference . . .

There are just DAYS to go until our #marriedatfirstswipe couple tie the knot, so this is our last chance to check in with them before the big day! If you've been caught up by the romance of their story and want to feel the love for yourself, subscribe to Save The Date and download our app now to meet your Mr or Mrs Perfect.

Let's find out how our bride and groom have been getting on . . .

Dear Hannah

The last few weeks have flown by in a blur of suit fittings, wedding day schedules and a growing feeling of 'Oh f***, this is really happening'! So I'm glad Save The Date only gave us one question to answer.

What's the one thing you'd like the other person to know before you get married?
In one of my letters I mentioned that I'd had one big relationship in my life, which was two years ago. What I didn't say is that two years ago I was engaged. We were so happy and we thought we had our whole lives ahead of us. We made plans to

leave our jobs and take a year off to go travelling after the wedding. Tragically, she was involved in a car accident on a country road and four days later she died in hospital surrounded by her family. We were obviously devastated. I wasn't in a great place for a while and it took me a long time to process my grief. But the thing that kept me going was knowing that she would have hated to see me so broken. So eighteen months later I finally decided I needed to get my life back on track and try to find the old me. It took time, but here I am. Although I've realised I'm not the old me, I'm just me. What happened will always be with me, it's a part of who I am now, but that's not a bad thing.

I'm telling you all this (and in a public forum, too) not to scare you away (and I really, really hope it doesn't), but to give you another little piece of me before we get married. Everyone who I care about and who cares about me knows what happened so I wanted you to know, too.

The only other thing I want you to know is that I'll be there waiting for you on our wedding day no matter what. Excited? Yes. Nervous? Probably. But I will be there.

Until then,

Toby x

Dear Toby

It is a truth universally acknowledged that a single woman about to marry a man she's never met must be in possession of nerves of steel (sorry, Jane!). So although I am crapping it – as I'm sure you are too! – I am also trying to be as calm as possible about our impending nuptials. I have never used the word nuptials before, go me! I was intrigued by Save The Date's one and only question for our final letter to each other before we become husband and wife, as I actually thought this might have been one of the questions they asked us earlier – what if whatever I'm about to tell you is a total deal-breaker and you call off the wedding?! Let's hope not for everyone's sake, eh! But hopefully my answer won't put you off.

What's the one thing you'd like the other person to know before you get married?
The thing I'd like to tell you is relevant to why I signed up to #marriedatfirstswipe in the first place. I want to find the kind of love my grandparents had. Gramps and G-ma have always been a massive part of my life. Sadly, Gramps died fifteen years ago, but I've never known two people so devoted to each other. Even in their old age they still did little romantic things for each other to show they cared. I want to grow old with someone who I'm utterly

devoted to and who's devoted to me. I haven't been able to find this person myself, so I asked Save The Date to do it for me.

Maybe it was much more simple in the 1950s when my grandparents were courting, without apps and swiping and cyber-flashing. But I'm not asking for a knight in shining armour and rose petals and chocolates. Instead I want that security of knowing the other person is at home waiting for me after a long and tiring day, and that someone is my equal, intellectually and emotionally. Is that too much to ask in the modern world do you think? Well, hopefully you don't think it is, otherwise you wouldn't be taking part in this mad plan at all, would you?!

I want to meet the right man for me – but also a man that G-ma thinks is the right man for me. And I very much hope that man is you, Toby (no pressure then!). I can't wait to find out in just a few days' time.

Love, your wife-to-be, Hannah x

Chapter 13

Hannah

'What's the word when you feel a mixture of excitement and fear?' Hannah asked as Jess perched on the edge of the bed in her and Tom's spare room and handed her a cup of tea. 'Fexcitement?'

'I think the word, or rather words, is bride-to-be on the morning of her wedding,' Jess replied gently. 'Don't worry, everyone feels like this before they get married. I can remember being almost mute with terror the whole time I was getting ready, but as soon as I saw Tom at the front of the church, I relaxed, and this incredible calmness came over me and I knew it was all going to be okay.'

'Hmm, well, you had the bonus of knowing the man standing waiting for you, remember. I know about ten things about my Toby-to-be and that's it. But actually, I do totally remember you being stressy that morning. You were trying to take your engagement ring off to put it on your other hand and it wouldn't budge, and then you got more and more worked up so you got all hot and funny and then it *definitely* wouldn't move. We spent about half an hour dunking your hand in iced water, but it was a slab of butter that finally did the trick if I remember rightly!'

'All right, no need to remind me, it's not like I've ever forgotten about it!' Jess huffed. 'Anyway, shove up and let me in this bed before I do a Lily and fall in a heap on the floor. And don't steal all the duvet.'

'God, you're so demanding. I hope Tom likes being ordered around in bed!'

'Han! We're not here to talk about me or Tom, it's *your* wedding day. Other than the "fexcitement", do you think you're ready?'

'I'm not sure I'll ever be properly ready to marry someone I've never met. But I guess? I didn't quite know how to feel when I read Toby's last letter. What a horrible thing to happen. Imagine starting the day thinking you have everything and ending it with nothing. But all power to him for picking himself up and managing to build a life afterwards. I'm just worried there's even more pressure on us to get this right. After everything he's already been through, I couldn't bear for him to get hurt because of me. You're the one who's met him in real life – is this going to be okay, Jess?' She turned to her friend with a pleading look.

Jess grabbed her free hand and squeezed it reassuringly. 'I think it is, yes. Firstly, I truly believe Toby has all the qualities you are looking for in a husband. Remember when we talked about all those things that are important to you – that he was kind, chivalrous, funny, interesting, intelligent and up for adventures? Well, when you've been reading his letters, how has he come across? If you ask me, he's already ticked all of those boxes. And while I can't promise you're going to want to tear his clothes off the minute you set eyes on him, I *think* he is your type.'

'Okay, I trust you, Jess.' Hannah took a sip of her tea and shook herself a little. 'Bring on the fireworks! But maybe you could just quickly show me a picture of Toby to put my mind at rest? I'm going to see him for real in a few hours so it doesn't matter if you let me stare at a picture for ten seconds, does it?'

'Hannah! You're like one of the twins on Christmas Eve: "Mummy, can I just have a look at my present, I won't open it or anything, but I *need* to see what shape it is!" No, you cannot just stare at a photo of Toby for ten seconds, or in fact any seconds. Now, come on, finish your tea, you'll need to start getting ready soon. But first I'll make us all eggy bread for breakfast as a special pre-wedding treat. The twins have never been so excited about a wedding in their lives. And you need to make sure you eat something before the ceremony – we don't want you collapsing before you've even walked down the aisle.'

'Thanks, *Mum*.' Hannah smiled. 'Although do you think my actual mum will make an appearance today? I keep veering between thinking she won't want to miss all the drama and remembering what she said when we went over for lunch.'

'But you've explained to her that we've turned down quite a lot of the freebies we could have had, haven't you? Then she'll have come round, I'm sure, especially with a bit of help from G-ma and your dad,' Jess said gently, stroking Hannah's hair.

'But what if she hasn't and decides she can't countenance coming? Don't forget, she'll also have to see Dad and Charmaine and Seraphina all together as one happy family, which is a tough ask for her at the best of times. She might decide she can't face the whole thing and not turn up.'

'I really believe she will come. And she'll have G-ma by her side, plus Scott, Julia and Leo to show off to people so hopefully John and Charmaine aren't going to worry her too much. And it sounds as if this whole thing has helped bring her and John a bit closer again, which can only be a good thing after all that bitterness! But if she doesn't come, there's nothing you can do. Joan knows her own mind and we aren't responsible for her decisions. She's a grown-up just like you are, Han.'

'I know, and you're right, but it's just hard. God, why is my life never simple!'

'Because you'd get bored and probably have a sulk if it was!' Jess laughed. 'Right, I can hear the sound of hungry children baiting each other, which signals it's time we got out of bed before we have a full-scale fight on our hands!'

Three hours later, everyone was fed, washed and almost dressed. Hannah's dad had arrived, along with Charmaine and Seraphina, and the children had posed for the obligatory photos and were now playing some kind of camping game beneath a duvet under the kitchen table.

'Well, at least we got a couple of shots of them before they completely ruined their outfits,' Jess said brightly. 'Although Seraphina always manages to seem clean and tidy no matter what she's been doing, whereas my two look like something the cat brought in most of the time. You'll have to let me into your secret, Charmaine.'

'She's just that type of child,' Charmaine replied breezily. 'She doesn't like getting too mucky and will take herself off to wash her hands when she needs to. She's pretty self-sufficient like that.'

'Lucky you! Please can you get her to teach Lily and Sam how to do that? Seriously, I don't know how they do it, but they always seem to look like they've been digging in mud even when they've been no further than the sofa! Right, Hannah, it's time you put your dress on and I'll start rounding up the troops. John, you're going to drop us and Charmaine at the venue, pick up G-ma and then come back for Hannah and Seraphina, aren't you?'

'That's what I've been told, so that's what I'll do,' Hannah's dad smiled. 'It's so nice seeing everyone in their posh frocks. I can't wait to see you in your dress, Hannah,' he added, his eyes tearing up immediately.

'You're not looking too bad yourself, Dad.' Hannah grinned at him. 'That suit is so smart.'

'Can you believe he was going to wear his old suit he

only digs out for funerals?' Charmaine rolled her eyes good-naturedly and patted his collar down. 'But thankfully I insisted we went on a shopping trip into town to buy a new one.'

John looked down at her, clearly besotted. 'That's why I need you by my side, to show me the error of my ways.'

Hannah felt tears prick her eyes as she watched her dad bask in Charmaine's smile. He was almost a different person from the worn-out, snappy, ageing man she remembered during her teen years, and it had been a joy to see him grow since he'd met his second wife – although Hannah instantly felt she was letting her mum down by even having those thoughts. She shook herself out of her reverie and reminded herself that today was about enjoying having everyone she loved around her and supporting her at the start of a new chapter in her life. Or at least she hoped so, anyway.

'Seraphina, do you want to come upstairs and help me get dressed?' she asked her half-sister.

'Does your dress have a zip at the back?' the little girl enquired. 'Because I always need Mummy to help me with my zip, too.'

'It has a zip *and* buttons, so I definitely need your help,' Hannah laughed. Let me just say goodbye to everyone and then you can get to work.'

'You are going to see them all again in an hour or something, so do you really need to say goodbye? I could just start helping you now.'

'Seraphina, don't be rude to your sister,' Charmaine chided.

'It's her wedding day and she'll have a lot of hellos and good-byes to say so she might as well get some practice in now. See you soon, sweetheart,' she added, giving Hannah a soft hug.

'Ah, I can't believe the next time I see you you'll be ready to walk down the aisle!' Jess squealed, folding her into her arms.

'You better believe it – you're my fairy godmother after all! God, don't start me off or I'll have make-up all down my face before we've even left the house.'

'You will not,' her friend retorted. 'That mascara promises to actually repel water and it cost as much as a small house so it better not be lying.'

After another round of goodbyes, the front door was finally shut and the house was suddenly loudly silent. Hannah grinned at Seraphina. 'Now that rabble have gone, shall we put on some music and get dressed?'

'YES! Although please can you only play "Firework" because that's the only dancing song I like?'

'Excellent choice, it's a deal.'

Half an hour later, however, after their tenth round of singing Katy Perry into a hairbrush, Hannah was definitely not feeling even brighter than the moon, moon, moon. In fact her head was starting to pound.

'Well, I've definitely felt my colours burst, but now it's time to play something else,' she said firmly. 'Let's slow it down a bit while you do me up. What about some Lewis Capaldi. Ahh, that's better. If you just pull the zip gently and then you can do the buttons, that's right.'

'Hannah?'

'Yes, sweetie?'

'Why are you marrying Toby if you've never even met him?'

'Because I think I'm going to like him,' Hannah answered a bit shakily. She checked the clock on the spare-room wall and she knew her dad would be back to pick them up and drive them to the venue very soon.

'But how do you know what's he like if you haven't talked to him?'

'Well, we've written each other letters, so that's like talking to each other.'

'So what does he look like?'

'I don't know yet. But I'm really excited to find out! I bet you are too, aren't you?'

'Yeee-s. But I'm a bit scared that he could be really ugly and not a very nice person,' Seraphina said, pulling herself round to face Hannah. 'What if he doesn't like me? Or what if he doesn't like you?' Her eyes were wide and fearful now.

'How could he not like you, sweetheart, when you're such an angel!' Hannah cried, squatting down to Seraphina's height and putting her arms around her tiny waist. 'And I have it on *very* good authority that he is one of the nicest men you could ever meet, which is even more important than what he looks like.' She hoped she sounded sincere, as, now her stomach was turning over and the nerves were kicking in big time, she didn't know what she really believed. She stood up, plastered a smile on her face and added, 'I trust Jess to have chosen the very best person for me to marry and I just know that you are going to love Toby and he is going to love you. Now, I think I just heard the front door, do you want to go and let Dad in?'

Seraphina scampered off down the stairs seemingly satisfied with Hannah's answer, even if Hannah herself wasn't. Alone in Jess's spare room, Hannah sat on the bed, being careful not to crease the lacy folds of her dress. Now, in the quiet of the room, she let out the breath she felt like she'd been holding in her body all morning.

She steadied herself on the edge of the mattress and took a large gulp of air, thinking about the people she would have around her on her wedding day. While her dad would always support her, Hannah could tell he was still worried about her marrying a man she had never met, and her mum had obviously made no secret of how she felt about the whole idea. At least G-ma had been full of excitement and positivity when she'd spoken to her the previous day.

'I'm so happy I've lived long enough to see you get married and find your happiness. Although, of course, you are doing it as only you can, dear Hannah!' she'd laughed.

Then just before they'd rung off, G-ma had gently said, 'Don't forget that love at first sight is completely possible. When I met your grandfather at that village fete when he was home on leave from the army, I knew immediately he was the one. He wasn't just the most handsome man in the room, it was his loving spirit that shone through. And he proved to be the kindest, most caring of men, and I never doubted his love for me for as long as he lived. That is what I wish for you, my darling.'

Hannah had been almost too choked to reply. Her grand-parents had had no idea how their future would play out in the years after the war and all that it had brought, but they had still made it through and spent every day of the rest of Gramps's life with the person they loved most. So perhaps that could be her and Toby's future too.

Hannah could hear her dad and Seraphina downstairs, so she gathered everything she needed, tucked her pumps into her overnight bag and slipped on her shoes.

It was time.

Chapter 14

Jess

'Can you help me tie these last few chair sashes, Charmaine? I told the twins not to pull at them but did they listen to me? Did they heck! Tom's had to take them outside and threaten no screens for a month to get them to calm down and stop causing havoc.' Jess blew her hair away from her face and stopped to fan herself with the plastic folder that had been permanently attached to her person for the last hour as she made her way through her exhaustive checklist so she knew everything was as it should be.

'Perhaps they ate too much sugar at breakfast,' Charmaine said conversationally. 'I always find my body goes a bit haywire when I have too many sweet things.'

'Perhaps, especially as they're not used to having much sugar,' Jess replied, bending down to floof a ribbon so Charmaine couldn't see her don't-you-bloody-dare-tell-me-how-to-parent expression. 'Anyway, no harm done. Right, I think we're almost there.'

She stood up and cast her eyes around her, taking in everything from the twinkling fairy lights wrapped around the wooden beams that stood proudly across the high white ceiling, to the rows of chairs with their pink sashes, and the huge 'T' and 'H' letter lights displayed at the front of the room behind the registrar's desk. The bunches of deep pink hydrangeas and green foliage that sat on small side tables looked simple but pretty and the afternoon sunshine lit the room with a golden glow. All it needed now was people.

Satisfied, Jess gave a small nod, asked Charmaine if she'd mind checking whether the registrar had arrived and if the prosecco they'd had delivered from Aldi was definitely enjoying an ice bath. She then went to find her bag so she could finally put away her folder, check her phone and get ready for the main event. Thankfully, there were no missed calls from either Toby or Hannah, so she texted Tom that he could bring the kids back (as long as they didn't start untying the chair sashes again!) then threw her phone into her bag and wandered over to the large windows at the side of the room.

Manchester had decided to play ball for the occasion and the city was at its most spectacular. The sun had lit up the iconic traditional red-brick buildings surrounding the hall and glinted off the top of the modern glass Beetham Tower beyond. The bridges spanning the waterways were reflected in the still canal and the uncharacteristically bright sky turned the water almost blue instead of its usual muddy brown.

Who said Manc was all grey and industrial. Jess smiled to herself.

She just hoped it was a sign of the bright future Hannah and Toby had together. The weight of responsibility had been lying heavy on her shoulders the last couple of weeks, and although she had been nothing but positive when talking to Hannah, in the early hours of the morning her anxiety had reached fever pitch as she lay in bed playing all of the possible – and mostly truly awful – scenarios in her head. The worst thing was she couldn't even talk to Tom about it. Outwardly, things between them were fine, but they'd shared words that could never be unsaid, and she was well aware of how he felt about Jess 'using' Hannah to save her business, so she knew she couldn't confess her concerns about the pair's long-term happiness to her husband. Which in itself was another source of anxiety for her. But today wasn't the day to be worrying about her own marriage – her focus had to be all on Hannah and Toby.

She realised the noise levels had started to build in the room from low murmurs to excited greetings, and she turned to find the photographer taking covert shots of her staring out the window.

'God, stop, Cassie! Today isn't about me. Look, people are arriving, why don't you go and get some shots of them.'

'Don't worry, I'm going!' Cassie laughed. 'And I know this is all about the bride and groom, but you did say you wanted to be able to use the pictures on the Save The Date site too, which means you as the owner of the business need to be in some of them.'

'Thank goodness Photoshop and its many clever airbrushing features exist then,' Jess said. Cassie winked at her and moved towards the large doors at the back of the room where there were small clusters of guests forming. Jess turned to look and saw a slightly awkward group of five people who were whispering quietly to each other, one of whom was the groom himself.

'Toby!' Jess cried, striding over to them. 'Gosh, you do look handsome! I'm Jess,' she explained to the other four. 'And you must be Toby's family.'

'Great to see you again.' Toby smiled, giving Jess a hug. 'And yes, this is my mum Elaine and my dad Phil, and this is my sister Melissa and her partner Michaela. Jess is the owner of Save The Date.'

'It's you we have to blame for today then is it, Jess?' Phil boomed.

For a second, Jess froze, not knowing what to say. Her heartbeat quickened and her throat tightened. 'I—'

'Or should I say *thank*,' Phil continued, his face breaking into a grin. 'We have high hopes for Toby's future with Hannah, whoever she is!'

Jess's heart seemed to quicken even more, but this time in relief. 'Not as high as mine!' she laughed. 'It's lovely to meet you all finally. I know this isn't the most conventional of weddings, but I truly believe Toby and Hannah are going to be happy together. Toby, I haven't been able to tell you this until today, but Hannah is actually my best friend. Which is how I knew you were so well suited.'

'Oh, I . . . I don't know what to say,' Toby stuttered. 'But I guess that all makes sense if I think about it.'

'Well, I think it bodes very well for your future together, Tobes,' Melissa bustled in. 'You've trusted Jess in the lead-up to this whole thing, so why stop now. Don't you think, Mum?' she cajoled.

Elaine smiled and agreed, but Jess could see she was less convinced than her daughter.

'I'll show you where you're sitting so you can make your-selves comfortable,' she said, returning Elaine's smile warmly and touching her lightly on the arm. 'And you're Toby's best woman, aren't you, Melissa, so I can just run through everything with you all now Lara the registrar is here too.'

Fifteen minutes later, Jess could feel everyone relaxing a little, especially as Toby's friends had arrived and the chairs on the right-hand side of the room were filling up with people and chatter. After his initial awkwardness, Toby seemed to be growing in confidence surrounded by his family and friends, so Jess felt able to slip away to see how the other side of the room was getting on. She'd been keeping half an eye on the door to spot Joan the minute she walked in, but there was still no sign of her and Jess was beginning to worry she'd been wrong to reassure her friend her mum would be there to support her. However, she also realised she hadn't seen Scott and Julia as yet, so maybe they'd all come together. Unless Joan had steadfastly refused to leave the house and had ordered her son not to go either. Jess shivered despite the warmth of the day and wished she'd had a sneaky slurp of the prosecco currently chilling in the next room.

'Mu-um, are we doing the wedding soon?' Lily asked, running up to her. 'Dad says he thinks most people are here now and there aren't many chairs left.'

'I think there are still a few people to arrive,' Jess said. 'Lils, can you look after Charmaine for me at least until the ceremony starts?'

'Charmaine is a grown-up so doesn't need looking after,' Lily replied scornfully. 'Anyway Granny and Grandpa are talking to her.'

Jess smiled across at her own parents who she hadn't even noticed had arrived, and gave a silent prayer for their kindness and her mum's sixth sense when it came to knowing who needed someone to chat to at social gatherings. She'd loved hosting dinner parties when Jess was growing up, and although Jess hated all the boring adult chat, she remembered adoring being allowed to stay up late and hand round tiny glasses of sherry and bowls of Bombay mix. Now her mum spent much of her time running WI meetings and organising charity afternoon teas, so she was at home chatting to anyone and everyone. And Jess's dad always managed to find someone to talk to about his two main loves: golf and DIY, so she knew she didn't need to worry about them. They were also talking to – or rather being talked at by – Hannah's grandma, and Jess walked over to give them kisses all round and check G-ma was all right getting round in her wheelchair.

Satisfied everyone seemed happy, Jess checked her watch

and realised that Hannah, her dad and Seraphina should now be arriving. She wandered to the back of the room and through the open double doors towards the main entrance to see if their car was anywhere in sight. In doing so, she almost walked slap-bang into a small, elegant figure sporting a large statement hat.

'Joan, you're here! Oh, I'm so glad you came – you look gorgeous!' Jess kissed her on both cheeks, narrowly missing taking her eye out on the feather that sat proudly atop Joan's head.

'Well, I want to meet the man who's marrying my daughter,' Joan replied with the air of the Queen. 'Scott and Julia are just parking the car and making sure they have everything they need for Leo. The bag they've brought with his things in is as big as a suitcase. In my day, as long as you had a clean nappy and a spare babygro, you were fine, but I'm sure they know what they're doing. And Mary and her husband Bill were following us here. They didn't know the way once they got into town and who can be doing with one of those sat-nav wotsits?'

'They can be very confusing,' Jess agreed, struggling not to smirk at Joan using her 'phone voice' in the manner of Hyacinth Bucket from *Keeping Up Appearances*. 'Now, Joan, do you want to go in or are you waiting for Scott and Julia? Your mother is already holding fort in the corner.'

'I'm sure she is,' Joan replied wryly. 'Why don't you introduce me to the man himself, Jess dear. And I suppose I'd better meet his family too.'

'I think you'll really like them,' Jess said, far more confidently than she felt. 'They seem so nice, especially Elaine, Toby's mum.'

Thankfully, Toby charmed Joan within seconds with his compliments about her outfit and how young she looked. Melissa caught Jess's eye and winked and Jess grinned back.

'Mum, Dad says to tell you that the eagle has landed,' Sam said a little breathlessly as he appeared beside her. 'Are we having a real-life eagle at the wedding? Can I hold it?'

'Sadly, we are not, Sammy boy,' Jess laughed. 'But it does mean that we need to get everyone into their seats and ready for the ceremony, so you go and help Dad spread the word.'

Sam ran off and Jess placed a soft hand on Toby's back. 'Hannah's arrived.'

Toby's face broke into a huge smile. 'Well, she hasn't had second thoughts then. Although she hasn't actually seen me as yet, so there's still time I suppose!'

'It's going to be fine, it really is.' Jess's stomach swirled like a tornado as she marvelled at how calm Toby seemed, on the outside at least.

'I think I'm more nervous than you,' Elaine tittered at her son.

'I'm just happy it's finally my wedding day,' he said simply. 'Joan, shall I show you to your seat? I think you should sit on the end of the row over here so you get the best view as your daughter walks down the aisle.'

Jess checked everyone was in place, signed to Melissa to check she had the rings and received a thumbs-up and a huge grin in return, and then hurried towards the small room off the entrance hall where the bridal party were waiting after their chat with the registrar. Hannah and her dad were standing close together having what looked like a deep and meaningful conversation that Jess wasn't sure she should interrupt, so she waved at Seraphina, who was skipping around in front of them. She waited a couple of seconds to make sure Hannah got the message then trotted back into the main room as fast as her heels would allow her, nodded at the staff in charge of the music, and slid into her seat breathing heavily.

The music volume increased and everyone stood up and turned in expectation. Seraphina came first, revelling in the *oohs* and *ahhs* from her audience and giving everyone a good sprinkle of glitter from her now-patchy wand. And then came John and Hannah. The top part of Hannah's dress sparkled with sequins and showed off her toned arms, while the pretty white tulle skirt swished around her calves as she carefully picked her way down the aisle in her pointed heels, grasping her dad's arm tightly. Jess watched as Hannah looked up and saw her Toby-to-be grinning at her like he couldn't believe his luck. She met his gaze and smiled shyly back.

'Okay?' Tom asked, squeezing Jess's hand. She nodded and squeezed back, grateful in that moment that whatever the future held for all of them, her husband was by her side.

Chapter 15

Hannah

Hannah felt her heels give way, and she began falling backwards towards the cold, dark floor. She tried to scream, but her throat had closed up completely. Instinctively, she knew that in just a few seconds she wouldn't be able to breathe at all, as the shadowy shapes around her stretched out their hands to smother her. Then suddenly she snapped her eyes open and found her head was cocooned in a soft, feathery pillow nest. Disorientated, her heart hammering, she tried to slow her breathing and trigger the rational side of her brain to kick into action. Her chest began to feel less tight and everything started to come back to her. She swivelled her eyes to her left and a head of dark hair came into view. Hannah reached for her ring finger and felt the cold metal of her wedding band.

Yep, it really had happened. She was a married woman!

She sat upright in the bed and quickly realised that she was a married woman with a hangover. Her head throbbed and the room swam a little around her. She saw a glass of water on the bedside table and glugged half of it back in one go as she looked around her. Jess, or rather her company, had treated them to a room at The Midland, one of Manchester's swankiest hotels, for their wedding night. Hannah's heart quickened again.

Their wedding night.

She looked down and was glad to discover she was wearing her knickers and a vest top, which she vaguely recalled chucking into her overnight bag the previous morning in case she decided against the cute but revealing short pyjamas she'd also brought with her. So maybe she hadn't been too drunk to make sensible decisions, she thought. However, her recall didn't stretch as far as her actually remembering what had happened when they reached the hotel. She'd been dancing – *everyone* had been dancing – and she remembered taking off her heels to make the short walk to the hotel from the wedding venue and shoving on her white pumps instead, and she had some kind of vague memory of getting the lift up to their room. But beyond that, it was a bit of a blank. She reached for her glass again and drained it, before letting out a small burp and lying back against the fluffy pillows.

'Hannah, you're awake!' a voice next to her murmured.

She looked across and Toby smiled at her. 'Happy first day of the rest of our lives!'

For a second, Hannah didn't know what to say. Her head

swirled and she could feel another burp building painfully high up in her chest, but she tried to swallow it down.

'Hi,' she managed. 'So yesterday really happened then?'

'It seems so.' He grinned. 'It was a great day – and night – wasn't it.'

'Yes?' Hannah replied, her heart still thumping. 'Although the end of it is a bit hazy, I have to say.'

'Yeah, people drank *a lot*,' Toby agreed. 'Although I have to say I'm feeling great this morning.' He sat up and plumped up his pillows, revealing his bare chest, the smile never leaving his face.

Hannah couldn't shake the unease swooshing around along with the prosecco in her stomach. She took a deep breath.

'Toby, I know this sounds weird ... but when I say that the end of the night is hazy, I mean it's *really* hazy. I can't remember much about when we got back here. I just need to know if we, you know ...' She tailed off awkwardly.

'If ... ? *Oh*, if we ... No, don't worry, nothing happened. Well, a bit of kissing happened.' He grinned again. 'But you got changed in the bathroom and told me you definitely didn't think we should sleep together, other than in the same bed, obviously – you took great pains to say you weren't expecting me to sleep on the sofa or anything, which was nice of you. But no, we didn't ... do anything, don't worry.'

'Okay, great,' Hannah breathed. 'I mean, I'm sure it would have been great if we had, you know, but ...'

'Hannah, it's fine, it really is. Right, do you want the first shower or shall I jump in quickly? We don't want to miss breakfast, do we? One of the best things about staying in a nice hotel is the cooked breakfast the next morning, I always think.'

'You go first, that's okay,' she replied. She waited for the bathroom door to shut behind him, heard him whistling an indistinguishable tune, and threw herself back against the pillows. If there was one thing Hannah really wasn't, it was a morning person. Unfortunately, it seemed that Toby was very much a lark. Although it also appeared he had drunk quite a bit less prosecco than she had, unless he was one of those annoying people who never got hangovers no matter how drunk they were the night before. She would take a lark over a non-hangover-sufferer any day, she mused.

Her phone lit up on the table beside her and she saw she had a whole screenful of notifications, most of which appeared to be from Jess. She pressed call and before she'd even heard the ringing noise, Jess's voice was in her ear.

'Hannah? You're alive then? So, how was your first night together? Tell me everything!'

'I'm not sure there's that much to tell,' Hannah replied, her voice barely above a whisper in case Toby was a super-quick showerer and her conversation suddenly became less private. 'To be honest, I can't remember much after us screaming our way through "Livin' On A Prayer" using a prosecco bottle as a microphone.'

'God, yes, Lily kindly reminded me about that at six o'clock this morning. She even demonstrated exactly my level of out-of-tune singing and embarrassing dancing, which was kind of her. God, I'm glad the paracetamol has kicked in a bit. Tom promised to take the kids to the park for as long as possible to give me a bit of time to myself. Anyway, so you can't remember much after that, fine. But, shit, Hannah, does that mean you can't even remember whether you had sex with him?'

'Don't worry, it's the first thing I asked him this morning,' she replied, massaging her head and wishing she'd asked Toby to refill her glass before he got in the shower. 'And, no, before you ask, we didn't have sex, and yes, asking him was the most embarrassing start to an arranged marriage I can think of.' She heard Jess cackling in her ear and found herself smiling despite herself. 'God, the whole thing is ridiculous. Oh well, it's done now. But the rest of the day was fun.'

'It was *so* fun,' her friend agreed. 'You looked beautiful, Han, you really did. And Toby managed to charm the pants off Joan of Bark, which is quite the achievement.'

'She didn't stop singing his praises to me all day!' Hannah laughed. 'Poor Scott was well pissed off. It's usually him or little Leo she's showing off to everyone about. Although he seemed to have cheered up a bit by the time he hit the dance floor with some of Toby's mates. Thanks for sorting everything out yesterday, J, it was really amazing.'

'It was totally my pleasure, you know that, and I'd do it again for you in a heartbeat. Although let's hope it was the one and only wedding I organise for you now you have your happy-ever-after with Toby!'

'Fingers crossed,' Hannah said, glad Jess couldn't see her

oh-my-god-is-this-for-ever-I-barely-know-him face. 'Right, I'd better go and get ready for breakfast.'

'Okay, love you, Han. Call me later, all right?'

'Will do. Love you, J.' She ended the call just as Toby emerged from the bathroom, a large towel wrapped around his waist.

'All yours. Take your time – I'll see if I can work the coffee maker.'

Hannah grabbed her bag and scuttled into the bathroom. The mirror was pretty steamed up and she was grateful she couldn't see her bleary, smudged eyes and pillow-lined face, until she realised that was exactly what poor Toby had had to see staring back at him this morning.

After a restorative ten minutes under the hot-enough-to-make-her-skin-red shower, she felt infinitely better and almost ready to munch her way through bacon and eggs. But first she decided she needed a layer of make-up between her and her new husband – she didn't want to put him off his breakfast.

'God, can you imagine a world without toast and jam?' she said through a mouthful of just that half an hour later. 'I think I'd rather die than not have a thick layer of strawberry jam on a thick slice of white bread ever again.'

'I'm not sure I've thought about it before!' Toby laughed. 'Although if someone put a gun to my head, I think I'd have to choose peanut butter on toast over jam. Except with a fry-up, though, that would just be too much. But surely damson is the king of jams, not boring old strawberry?'

'Excuse me, "boring old strawberry"? Damson jam is tasty, I grant you, but the pure Englishness of strawberry means it wins the top trumps of jam prize every time.'

'I'm still unconvinced. But the real question when it comes to strawberry jam is whether you spread it on a scone before or after cream. And choose wisely because this could make or break our marriage, Hannah!'

'It is definitely an important question, you're right. But everyone knows the only way to do it is to put the jam on first, followed by as much clotted cream as you can get your hands on.'

'Phew! We don't have to get divorced after all,' Toby laughed. 'That is, indeed, the correct answer. Although even the thought of scones is making me feel a bit queasy after all that food.'

'Well, as you say, breakfast is a big part of any hotel stay, and it was our duty to make sure we got value for Save The Date's money. Jess would never forgive me if I told her I had a bowl of yoghurt and granola, followed by an apple to really push the boat out. Not that she'd believe me – she knows I can't resist a posh fry-up. Or any fry-up really.'

'I still can't believe Jess is your best friend and she didn't tell me until yesterday,' Toby said, shaking his head.

'But if she had, you'd have been able to find me on the internet super-easily – I'm pretty much the only person who likes every single picture she puts on social media. And I had no way of finding out anything about you, so it wouldn't have been fair if you'd had some intel on me, would it?

And all those things you might have found out about me might have made you think twice about going through with the wedding.'

'Of course they wouldn't,' he protested. 'And we do know a little bit about each other from our letters. I know how much you like chip shop sausages and you know how much I like chip shop chips, for instance.'

'That is true,' she agreed. 'But if you think of all the things we do know about each other compared to all the things we don't know, it's a tiny number.'

'But you can't know what you don't know, if you know what I mean?' Toby said, and they both burst out laughing.

'No, I definitely don't know what you mean!' Hannah giggled. 'I'm not sure my poor little brain can cope with too many negatives today, to be honest.'

'I agree, so let's make today all about the positives instead. Oh god, does that sound cheesy? Oh well, I've said it now! I was thinking that we could take a walk around town this morning, maybe go to the art gallery and have a wander round the Northern Quarter and then the marina. What do you think? And remember we're all about the positives.'

'So I have to say yes, you mean? Well, it just so happens that I think that sounds like a great idea.'

'Excellent! Let's go and walk off some of this black pudding then.'

A couple of hours later, they'd checked out several Lowry paintings, marvelled at an intricate Victorian dress made entirely out of lace, pretended to be impressed by some unintelligible modern art and were having fun deciding what jobs all the hip millennials out for brunch in the Northern Quarter did during the week.

'I bet you that guy with the huge beard is a graphic designer and brews unique IPAs in his spare time,' Toby said.

'Good guess – that or he's a barista in a coffee shop and plays banjo in a band at gigs that only his friends go to. Whereas it's clear that the girl with blonde hair he's talking to is a social media influencer. Or at least thinks she is. I've watched her take about twenty photos of her breakfast but not even one forkful of avocado has reached her mouth.'

'If I weren't still so full from my own breakfast I'd go in there and offer to eat it for her. I hate seeing food go to waste and I love avocado on toast, even though I'm probably too old to be a millennial.'

'You're definitely not too old,' Hannah said, shaking her head. 'Because if you are, then I am too, and I refuse to admit that. Although the media seem to have got bored and moved on to Generation Z now anyway, so perhaps I shouldn't care so much. Shall we walk over to this marina you've promised me? I can't believe I grew up in Manchester and have never even heard of it, never mind been to it!'

They began walking past a row of large red-brick buildings, some of which were covered with huge murals. Toby took her hand and threaded his fingers through hers. He smiled at her and Hannah smiled back a little shyly.

She was surprised how relaxed she felt in the company of

a man she had only met twenty-four hours before, though as soon as she started consciously thinking about their relationship, her heart began thumping more heavily in her chest again and she could feel her hand turn clammy in Toby's grip. Despite having travelled all around the world on her own and done everything from sky-diving to jet-skiing, this was by far the scariest thing she'd ever done.

She wished Jess was by her side, holding her other hand to steady her.

Instead she tried to use some of the CBT techniques she'd learned over the years. Her friend Dee had taught them all when they'd lived together in Argentina. Dee had struggled with mental health issues when she was younger, and so was a huge proponent of therapy and counselling and decided to pass on some of what she had learned. It had been no surprise to Hannah when Dee had messaged her on Facebook to tell her she was training to be a counsellor herself while she was out in Australia.

Hannah tried her best to block out her racing heart and instead concentrate on the here and now. She really looked around her and noticed they'd reached a truly pretty stretch of the river full of colourful canal boats. There were groups of people soaking up the sunshine on the grass, and a few couples strolling along the walkways with dogs on leads. There was a family of swans on the water who every so often ducked underneath the surface to retrieve a piece of bread or plant. The sun glinted off the water and the sides of the canal boats. She felt her heart rate slow again and a feeling of calm seemed to wash over her as she turned her face up to the sun and felt its heat on her cheeks.

'You're very quiet – are you okay?' Toby asked, shattering her visualisation.

Hannah blinked and smiled. 'I'm fine, thanks, I was just thinking how I don't really know this part of the city at all. It's beautiful here.'

'Yes, it's one of my favourite spots, especially when the sun is shining. There are loads of new flats round here and I even thought of buying one last year, but I ended up going further out to West Didsbury.'

'Very nice! I don't even really know what you do for a job. All you said is that you work with figures on a computer screen?'

'I'm not sure you really want to know that much more about it, to be honest! I work for a big accountancy firm and look after the software for a couple of large clients.'

'Sounds, erm, techy! Do you like it?' Hannah asked.

'Yes, I do. I know it doesn't sound that interesting, but I spend a lot of time trying to think of ways round problems and how to improve apps and software tools and make them work even better. It definitely is quite techy – and geeky – but I work with a good bunch of people. There were only a couple of them there yesterday as it's a bit of a weird thing to say to your colleagues: "Do you want come to my blind-date wedding next weekend?" But I think you met Eva and Marie, as well as Mike and his partner?'

'Yes, I did, and they seemed nice. I think it might have

been Mike my brother was chatting to later on, poor guy!'

'I'm sure he coped, he's a real good'un. Anyway, do you enjoy working with Jess at Save The Date?'

'I actually enjoy it more than I thought I would,' she said. 'At first I think Jess felt sorry for me. I'd just come over for Scott's wedding and had used the last of my savings to buy the flights, so she got me to do little bits of work for her and paid me over the odds for them. Then when I flew back after Leo was born and said I was going to stay in Manchester, she offered me a full-time job that meant I could afford a flat on my own. It's not the nicest place in the world, but it's mine. Well, it's my landlord's, but you know what I mean. And working with Jess has been really cool. I think we were both a bit worried about her being the boss and me being the employee, but she tends to let me just get on with things, and I like to do stuff properly, so we're both happy. Well, I am – you'd better ask her for her side of things!'

'It sounds like a great set-up, and working with your best mate is very cool. My old boss was awful and wanted to micro-manage everyone the whole time, which was horrible and made you start questioning everything you were doing. He left last summer, thank god, and the whole team is so much happier now. Anyway, no more talk of work, especially as tomorrow we're jetting off on our honeymoon! I still can't believe Jess has sorted us a week in St Lucia for free, it's mad.'

'It is,' Hannah agreed. 'Although, seriously, you won't believe how much free stuff people tried to give us, it was crazy. And while there was a lot of stuff we turned down, a free holiday to St Lucia was never going to be one of them! I guess we'd better head back? I still need to go home and pack before our flight tomorrow night.'

'I know, me too,' Toby nodded and gave her hand a small squeeze, before leaning down towards her and kissing her softly on the lips.

Hannah was a little taken aback, but before she could process what was happening, her body seemed to take over and she was responding to Toby's kiss. It was tender and gentle, rather than rip-your-clothes-off passionate, but as they were standing in the middle of a marina surrounded by other people, Hannah decided tender was perfectly fine. And they had a week in St Lucia for passion, after all.

SAVE THE DATE

Our blind-daters with a difference got married!

Yes, FINALLY our blind-daters have met – and got married! It was a beautiful day and you can check out the photos (yes, you can finally see who they are!) on our social media channels, and by searching the hashtag #marriedatfirstswipe. Don't forget to subscribe to Save The Date and download our app now if you haven't already, and you could meet hundreds of people looking for long-term love, just like our newlyweds Hannah and Toby.

Talking about the happy couple, let's find out how their first week of married life has been . . .

Dear Hannah

What a week! Our wedding day was extraordinary, surprising, nerve-racking and amazing. But as much as I enjoyed introducing everyone in my life to everyone in yours, in some ways it felt like a distraction from the real thing, the main event: me and you. So waking up with you the following morning and spending the day wandering through Manchester showing each other our favourite haunts was exactly what I needed. It meant we could put all the husband and wife stuff aside for a bit and just concentrate on getting to know each other as people. When I was writing these letters before we met, I found it hard to know what to say, but answering our final set of questions from Save The Date has been so much easier.

How did it feel to be going on honeymoon with someone you'd only just met?
It actually felt quite normal to be going on holiday with you the next morning. And once we'd smiled our way through all the questions about how long we'd known each other, we managed to score an upgrade, so I don't think either of us were complaining! I always think that a long-haul flight is the ultimate test of any relationship – and I'm happy to say you passed the test with flying colours (although, as I'm writing this you're sat snoring next to me, so I'm not sure you passed the train test quite so well!). I've never known a ten-hour flight go so quickly, though you're obviously a pro when it comes to travelling and took the mick out of me for my 'amateur' blow-up pillow and plane attire – so rude!

How was your time in St Lucia?
When we arrived at our hotel many (many) hours later, the journey was all worth it. Waking up the next morning to that view (I'm talking about the sea 😊) was incredible and made the whole holiday feel

extra-special. St Lucia is the most beautiful place I have ever been. The beaches, the waterfalls, the food – I think I'll be dreaming of those lobster rolls for evermore. I may have moaned just a little when we were climbing Gros Piton (I'm sure I remember you saying it was just a little hike up a hill, but it definitely turned out to be more of a mountain scramble!), but it was totally worth it when we got to the top.

I will never forget our afternoon snorkelling in the sea in front of our hotel, moving among the coral reef and tropical fish. Holding your hand as we swam beneath the water together was truly magical. And watching the sun set on Reduit Beach with you, sipping the strongest cocktail I've ever had, was one of the most romantic things I've ever done.

I hope you enjoyed those moments as much as I did.

How do you feel about being back home and starting married life together?
That's a tough one! I feel lucky to be married to such an exciting woman. You are gorgeous inside and out. I didn't really have many expectations on our wedding day – I guess I was more worried about whether you'd actually come than what you looked like, and I already knew from your letters that you were funny and interesting. But when I saw you

walking towards me, I was speechless. You looked absolutely amazing and I was extremely proud to be your groom. I was worried your family would be suspicious and wary of me, but they couldn't have been more welcoming and friendly.

I can't wait to see what the future holds for us.

Love, your husband Toby xx

Dear Tobes

I'm currently sitting on my bed in my flat in Manchester, wondering whether the last ten days have been a dream. It's hard to comprehend that just over a week ago I saw you for the first time as I walked down the aisle towards you and the registrar. Half an hour later we were legally married. I still can't get my head round that sentence, to be honest. It was amazing meeting your family and friends and hanging out with everyone I care about for the evening – even if it did end with me (and a bottle of prosecco) dancing to cheesy nineties hits and waking up with a headache of epic proportions! I'm still a bit annoyed you were hangover free. I'm sure I remember you had a drink in your hand every time I saw you that night!

How did it feel to be going on honeymoon with someone you'd only just met?
For all my jumping out of planes and signing up

for blind-date weddings, I can be quite an anxious person. Chatting to you as we walked round Manchester before we flew off to St Lucia felt natural and relaxed, and it was so nice that we got on really well. But if I'm truly honest – and I always want to be honest with you – every time I thought about the fact that we are now actually married, I felt a bit scared and anxious. It wasn't anything you did or didn't do, it was just the whole situation, and my reaction to it – it's not every day you marry a stranger, after all! I don't think the whole husband and wife thing had really sunk in the day before, despite the ceremony and speeches and cake and everything; it was almost like I was just at a really fun party and the marriage bit was happening to someone else. So I was pretty nervous about going on holiday with someone I'd just met.

How was your time in St Lucia?
Despite the way I was feeling, once we were on the plane and heading off on our adventure, I began to be excited about the week ahead of us. And what a week we had! I literally peed my pants laughing watching you scream your way down that zipline through the trees. I have never heard another human being make that noise before – it was amazing! I will treasure the photos I took of you that day for ever (and sell them to the papers for huge amounts

of money if you ever become a super-famous IT person, obviously!). I had such a fun time climbing a beautiful mountain, being massaged with chocolate (two of my fave things in one – #winning!) and lying on a postcard-perfect white sandy beach.

How do you feel about being back home and starting married life together?
Weird! But excited. Snorkelling with you among the coral reefs at Anse Chastanet and seeing all the ridiculously beautiful fish around Pigeon Island made me realise I want to learn to scuba dive and get my PADI certificate. I can't believe I've travelled all over the world and swum in the sea in every place I can, but have never actually learned to dive properly. Maybe we could learn together if you're up for it? As for real life, well I'm not sure what that is right now! We've got a TV interview lined up and we're very much still figuring out the logistics of how our lives will work with friends, family, jobs and everything, aren't we? But I wanted an adventure, and getting married to a man I didn't know and had never met has been one hell of an adventure so far!

Here's to more adventures for many years to come.

Love, Han x

Chapter 16

Jess

'Well, hello Mrs Sutton!' Jess grinned at Hannah on her first day back in the office.

'I think you'll find I'm still Ms Edwards, thank you very much. I've been Hannah Laura Edwards for thirty-five years and getting married doesn't change who I am, so why would I change my name? And before you ask, Toby is completely fine with it, not that it's his decision to make anyway.'

'Okay, keep your hair on!' Jess held up her hands in surrender. 'I'm as much of a feminist as the next person and I shouldn't have assumed you'd be changing your name. Although you know how desperate I was to get rid of Shufflebottom and the second Tom and I said "I do" I definitely became a Taylor.'

Hannah's mouth twitched and her face broke into a smile. 'Sorry for snapping, J, I'm just knackered. I think the jet lag is catching up with me. I thought I'd escaped it, but apparently not.'

'Don't worry, it's the worst, I know. Anyway, tell me *everything*. How are things going between you? How was the honeymoon? Did you "get to know" each other properly?'

'Jess! I thought we'd agreed no more inverted commas! Yes, things are good. St Lucia was just insanely beautiful – I mean literally beyond my wildest dreams beautiful. God, it already feels like a dream, it was just brilliant.'

'Aww, I'm so pleased you had a good time – and hugely jealous you got to lie on a white sandy beach in blazing sunshine. The weather's been horrible here, all rainy and grey.'

'It is Manchester in mid-September though!' Hannah laughed. 'If it was Caribbean hot then I'd be worried.'

'I know, but still, especially as it was so gorgeous less than two weeks ago for the wedding. Anyway, I want to hear all about your amazing adventures in St Lucia in detail later.' She took a breath. 'I read your blog. I'm so proud of you writing about your anxiety.'

'Thanks,' Hannah said quietly. 'I was worried what Toby would think when I told him how scared and anxious I'd been feeling, but he called me this morning to ask me to go for dinner on Friday and he said how glad he was I'd written about how it affected me.'

'That's brilliant,' Jess said. 'But had you not talked to him about it while you were away?'

'No, there wasn't ever really a good time. And I didn't want to make a big thing about it.'

'But you have just written about it in a blog that thousands of people are going to read and share? The unique views are already huge for that page and it only went live a few hours ago.'

'Sometimes it's easier to write things down, especially when it's so personal,' Hannah shrugged. 'I'd have felt too embarrassed and weird telling him how I was feeling face to face. Although I didn't put too much detail in there.'

Jess looked at her friend, but decided not to press the point that it was weirder to tell her husband how she was feeling via a blog rather than in person. She supposed it was still early days and it was easy to forget Hannah and Toby had actually only met less than two weeks ago. 'Well, he seemed *very* effusive about you in his blog!'

'What can I say, I have that effect on people, ha!'

Jess laughed along with her, but inside she couldn't help worrying that Hannah was not as happy as she was making out. 'So . . . did anything else happen?' she probed.

'All right, Mum! Yes, we had a couple of snogs, and maybe a bit of other stuff too.'

'And . . . ?'

'And, it was nice. Really nice.'

'But?'

'Why do you think there's a but?'

'Because, Hannah Edwards, I know you.'

'It's just weird, that's all. It's not like he ever said any of that stuff he put in his blog to me when we were in St Lucia.'

'In the same way you didn't tell him how anxious you were feeling!' Jess said. 'Han, of course it's going to be weird trying to work each other out to start with, but you've got all the time in the world. I bet if he had been as emotional with you in real life you'd have freaked out even more.'

'Probably. One part of me wants him to declare how much he loves me and the other part wants him to stop at the holding hands part! God, I'm so confused! And poor Toby can't win.'

'But the good thing is that he's in exactly the same situation as you,' Jess said gently. 'Talk to him, encourage him to talk to you and only do what you feel comfortable with, both physically and mentally.'

'I know and you're definitely right, oh wise one.' Hannah smiled at her and Jess was glad to see she looked less like she had the weight of the world on her shoulders than she had half an hour before. 'And I've probably got a bit of that downer feeling you get immediately after a big event you've been building up to, and I'll feel a million times better in a few days. Plus, we have that TV interview tomorrow, don't we, although I'm trying not to think about appearing on screen – urgh! Anyway, how are *you*? What's happened while I've been away?'

Jess's eyes unconsciously flicked to the heap of material in the corner of the small summerhouse and she hoped her friend didn't notice. 'I'm good! And you know, same old, same old, sorting out TV interviews for my best friend and her new husband, that kind of thing!'

'*Are* you good? What are these doing here then?' Hannah demanded, pulling at the pile and producing the sleeping bag and camping mat Jess knew full well were there.

'The kids were "camping" in here the other day,' Jess fudged.

'In the Save The Date office? Really?'

Jess felt her cheeks go pink. She'd never been a good liar. 'No,' she sighed. 'Not really. I've slept in here the last couple of nights.'

'*Why?*' Hannah asked, clearly shocked. 'I hope you haven't been working yourself into the ground while I've been away. God, I feel so guilty for leaving you to cope on your own for that long when everything is so busy and—'

'It wasn't that,' Jess broke in. 'None of this is your fault, Han, I promise.'

'None of what? I don't understand, I thought you said before the wedding that Save The Date was doing all right now and the bank had called off the hounds?'

'It is and they have.' She swallowed. 'Look, it's Tom. Or rather me and Tom. We haven't been getting on that well these last few months, arguing and not being that nice to each other. I just needed some space.'

If Hannah's face showed she was shocked earlier, it was nothing compared to her incredulous expression now. 'But you and Tom ... you're, you're okay?' she stuttered.

'Yes. No. I don't really know. Look I don't want you to worry, Han, and I'm sure everything will be fine, so—'

'But I still don't get why you've been sleeping in here. Why not just sleep in the spare room if you really don't want to share a bed for a few nights?'

'Because I needed to escape, to have a break, to not be the

one who has to deal with Lily falling out of bed at two a.m. or telling Sam that he can't have cereal for his tea and to take his hand out of his pants. It's just all too much sometimes.'

Jess's phone began to ring, saving her from whatever difficult question Hannah was going to ask her next, and she snatched it up with relief. It was another hour before she was free to talk to again. Subscription figures had gone through the roof when she'd shared the wedding photos on social media and had posted a short blog on the site. The public reaction had blown her away and already she was fielding requests from various magazines asking to interview both Hannah and Toby, plus it was likely there would be more when the local news ran a feature on them in a few days. She knew they were going to have to carefully choose what press they did, especially as neither Hannah nor Toby were that up for putting themselves out there now the realities of the situation had begun to sink in. There had already been some comments on the new blog about Hannah not seeming to be as into the marriage as Toby, which was just another thing for Jess to worry about. And then there was the situation with Tom.

She sighed and snuck a couple of covert glances at her friend while she was on the phone. She could see that Hannah was scrolling through her email but had a permanent frown on her face. Jess was annoyed at herself for burdening Hannah with her problems when she had enough of her own already, but she knew she couldn't successfully lie to her oldest friend, and she hated herself for even contemplating being dishonest in the first place. Nor could she hide behind her phone for ever, although that didn't mean she wasn't going to take the cowards' way out and leave the office for the rest of the day.

'I've got a few errands to run and then Tom forgot it was his day to pick the kids up from school so I've got to do it and I've promised I'll take them swimming afterwards. So, I'm not going to be around for the rest of the day, Han. Sorry to leave you on your own on your first day back, but I'm sure you've got a million emails to wade through anyway, and make sure you knock off a bit early and get an early night. You need to get on top of that jet lag before the interview tomorrow,' she said brightly.

Hannah gave her a long look before she replied. 'No worries. But can we maybe go for lunch on Friday to catch up properly? We don't have to go into town, but what about trying out that new coffee place near the station?'

'Sorry, I've got the twins' sports day – you remember they had to cancel it back in July when it wouldn't stop raining? Well, they've rescheduled it for midday on Friday in the September rain instead, and I don't want to miss Lily beating all the boys in her class yet again!'

'You give her a big cheer from me.' Hannah smiled. 'What about dinner on Friday? Can Tom not give the kids their tea after sports day and we'll go and get a pizza somewhere, or even order a Chinese and eat it here? You are half-living in here after all.'

It was a low blow, but Jess knew Hannah had only said

it to hammer home the point that they needed to talk after her revelation earlier. 'Fine, yep, why not,' she said. 'I'd like that. Though aren't you supposed to be having dinner with Toby on Friday?' She watched the realisation that she was going to have to choose between her best friend and her new husband register on Hannah's face, but was surprised by how quickly she replied.

'Don't worry, I'll rearrange with him. We have just spent a week in each other's pockets so I'm sure he'll understand I need to spend some time with you. I'll book us a table, shall I?'

'Great,' she said with as much enthusiasm as she could muster. As she grabbed her jacket and her car keys, it struck her how sad it was that the strongest emotion she had about having dinner with her best friend was dread, when a few weeks ago she would have been counting down the hours. Just another thing to add to her growing list of grudges against Tom.

On Friday evening, after wine and garlic bread had been ordered at the local pizza restaurant and she'd reassured Hannah for the hundredth time that she hadn't said anything embarrassing on live TV the previous day, Jess decided to get the conversation about her marriage out of the way.

'I'm sorry if I upset you on Wednesday, Han. There's nothing to worry about with me and Tom, believe me; I just needed a bit of space. I think everything with the business and having to be the one everyone looks to for answers to everything just got a bit much. Sometimes it's just knackering being the one in charge, you know?'

Hannah nodded. 'I know, it's hard enough being a grown-up in my own little life, never mind having to think about kids and a house and a husband. Although I guess I do now have to think about the husband bit, but you know what I mean. It's not the same for me; we're not living together for one thing. Having to be on top of the bills, food shopping, appointments and everything else for a whole family must be exhausting, especially with all of the Save The Date stuff that's been going on recently. But Tom knows that and must be doing his bit, surely?'

Jess grimaced. 'Look, he's great with the kids and he has his own business to sort out, and he does try, kind of. But it's all the things that, as women, seem to naturally fall to us. So it's me the school will contact first if one of the twins is sick; it's me who has to remember when it's dress up as a Roman day; it's me who it's assumed will make sure they have a box of food to take into school for harvest festival. And that's before we get to things like bin day – sure, Tom will do his bit and take the rubbish out, but only once I've told him which colour bin week it is and reminded him another three times to do it. And even though he might do the supermarket shop, I'll have to write him a list of what we need; and even though he might cook tea a few nights a week, it'll be me he asks what we're having. I know they're all small things, but you're right, it *is* exhausting. And so boring. And with all the exciting things happening with the business and your wedding, he just doesn't understand why I've been so invested in it all.'

'You have lived and breathed it with me, that's for sure.' Hannah smiled. 'But Tom seemed excited about it all when we initially talked about it back in January, and he was involved with choosing Toby in the first place, wasn't he?'

'He was, and he's really pleased Toby has turned out to be such a good guy. He just seems to think I've been prioritising the company over him and the kids. But then he doesn't realise all the things that go on in the background, like the dress-up days and the harvest festival boxes,' she added bitterly.

Hannah's expression was one of shock, though she immediately tried to look sympathetic, which made Jess quickly backtrack. 'As I said, I'm just tired and now things are calming down with the app, I'm sure it will all be fine.'

'Maybe you need to take some time out and spend a week with just Tom and the twins,' Hannah suggested. 'I'm back now and can look after everything with Save The Date after this week. Things are bound to calm down, so you don't need to worry. And maybe Tom can take the week off, too,' she added, warming to her theme. 'Then you can have some days out together when the kids are at school. Maybe go into town, see a film and have a posh lunch. I can always babysit one night too.'

'I don't know. It's my business, I need to be looking after it, at least for now. And we can't really afford to spend money on days out at the moment. We've only just got STD back on track after all.'

Hannah gave her a long look. 'If I ask you something, Jess, will you promise to give me an honest answer?'

'Depends what it is,' Jess replied, nervously. The waiter appeared with their pizzas at that moment and they were both briefly distracted by the delicious food in front of them. Jess dived in and was already chewing her first mouthful when she noticed Hannah was still looking at her. 'What? Okay, I'll answer you honestly. You know I'm rubbish at fibbing anyway.'

'Do you think there's another reason you were prioritising my wedding over everything at home?'

'Other than the fact it affected both my best friend's happiness and the perilous state of my business – which we rely on to pay the mortgage and buy the kids' school uniform, let me remind you?'

'I agree they're two big reasons, yes,' Hannah nodded. 'But do you think you've also been looking for that excitement? And by putting all your efforts into my marriage to Toby, you're kind of living the excitement with us? You've got tired of being that person everyone relies on for the boring answers to life admin, so you've enjoyed the spontaneity of organising the wedding and seeing Save The Date change and evolve every day?'

'And what's wrong with caring about my best friend and her new husband?' Jess asked immediately. 'I would do pretty much anything to see you happy, Han, you know that.'

'At the expense of your own happiness?' Hannah replied. 'I totally get it – you know me, I get bored with things after about five minutes and want to know what's the next new exciting thing to do or place to go. So I do understand. Which is maybe why you need some proper time out, just you and Tom, to find those new and exciting moments in your relationship. Because they will be there for the taking. You're both still young and in ten years or so, the twins will be leaving home or going to university or whatever, and you and Tom will have all that time back to spend together. Don't forget, I know what it's like when parents don't get on and are constantly arguing, and it only got worse for Mum and Dad when Scott and I left home – not that Scott really left home and stood on his own two feet, but you know what I mean. Suddenly, they didn't have us there to bridge the gap between them and they realised they didn't even like each other that much anymore. And it was horrible. Well, less horrible for Dad, obviously, as he moved seamlessly on to Charmaine, but you know that Mum has never quite recovered from it all.'

She took a breath and Jess stared at her, her mouth agape. 'Look, J, I'm not saying that's what will happen to you and Tom, of course I'm not. And I guess sometimes being married *is* boring – well, I'm about to find out, aren't I? And of course, he has to want to change things too, but what you and Tom have is so much more than arguing about taking the bins out, even I can see that. I'll never forget when we were sixteen and I thought the two of you together were the cutest. But then when I saw you on your wedding day, I realised what proper love looked like. And then when I met the twins for the first time and you were holding Sam and Tom was cuddling Lily, I realised what family really means. You and Tom are like pizza and melted cheese – one without the other is a bit rubbish.'

Jess was embarrassed to feel her eyes brimming with tears, and she wiped the sleeve of her jumper over her face and attempted a smile. 'I happen to like melted cheese on its own!' she hiccupped.

'I know, me too, that was a pretty crap comparison, you're right,' Hannah agreed, reaching for her friend's hand. 'But pizza without cheese is definitely rubbish. And you without Tom wouldn't be the Jess I know and love. I don't have all the answers, J, and I'm sure things aren't as black and white as I've made them sound, but I mean it about taking some time out. It doesn't have to be immediately, which means you can make sure certain things are sorted out first, but you do need to step away and spend time with your family.'

Jess nodded, not really trusting herself to speak, and instead took a huge bite of melted-cheese-laden pizza and a large slug of wine. They ate in silence for a few moments, before she replied. 'I'll think about it.' She saw Hannah's face break into a grin and couldn't help smiling herself. 'But there is one condition.'

'What's that?' Hannah asked eagerly.

'That you tell me everything about St Lucia. I need my excitement fix after all!'

Chapter 17

Hannah

After dinner, Hannah made her way home with mixed feelings. She hoped she'd got through to Jess and reassured her that all was definitely not lost when it came to her relationship with Tom, but the very fact she was having to do so had shaken her whole belief in not only their marriage, but in her own brand-new one, too. If Jess, who succeeded at everything, was having problems, what did that mean for Hannah? In fact, she had been married for just two weeks and she had already pissed off her husband big time.

Toby had been less than pleased when she'd told him – over text, as clearly she was a bit of a coward when it came to cancelling her first proper date with her husband – that she was going for dinner with Jess instead of him. She hadn't felt like she could tell him that Jess was having problems with her marriage, so she'd merely said she needed to catch up with her best friend after being away. Which she knew sounded a bit lame, but it was the truth, pretty much, so she refused to feel too guilty despite his slightly passive-aggressive reply:

> Oh, that's a real shame. I was looking
> forward to it and had booked us a nice
> restaurant in town. I'll need to cancel that
> ASAP so I don't get charged.

She'd tried to appease him by suggesting they go out the following evening to the same restaurant instead; however, he'd replied that it was booked up. In desperation, she messaged him to invite him round to her place, promising she'd cook for him, even though that would mean she'd have to spend all morning cleaning and hoovering to get her flat looking halfway presentable, and all afternoon cooking something delicious in her tiny kitchen so she didn't have to stress out about doing it all when he arrived. Thankfully, his reply had saved her the trouble:

> Great idea, though why don't you come over
> to mine and I'll cook for you instead, save
> you having to slave over a hot stove all day –
> especially if you and Jess have a few bottles
> of wine tonight!

She had readily agreed, though she was convinced the wine comment was another dig at her going out with Jess and not him. She hoped she was just reading too much into it.

It wasn't as if she really knew Toby at all, and although he seemed like a really nice guy, it had definitely helped that they'd so far spent most of their time together in an idyllic St Lucian bubble, where the hardest decision they had to make was choosing between a fish restaurant and a barbecue joint for dinner. Who knew how they'd get along back in the cold, grey reality of Manchester and their actual lives? Shit had very much got real, as her brother used to say.

Lying in bed that night, she idly played with the wedding band on her finger.

Two weeks. Fourteen days. Three hundred and thirty-six hours. Too many seconds for her to work out in her head.

That's how long they had known each other.

Suffice to say it felt like both a long time and a ridiculously short time. A lot had happened in those two weeks, but equally, she knew it was just the start of potentially forty or fifty years together. Forty or fifty *years*.

Unsettled, she got up for a drink of water. She could barely imagine being married for fifty *days*, never mind years. It wasn't that she didn't like Toby – what she had learned of him so far had been positive, and she was well on her way to really liking him as a person (other than his slightly sulky texts) – but the thought of being with him for fifty years was just, well, crazy! She realised now that, although she'd been the one to suggest the blind-date wedding in the first place, she hadn't really thought about what would happen after. Once the excitement and anticipation and craziness of the situation had died down. Of course, her intention was to find the 'forever' love her grandparents had shared, she just wasn't sure what that meant day to day, now she was actually married. How much did she really know about her grandparents' life together, anyway? Only what they had chosen to tell her when she was growing up. What about when Gramps had left the army, damaged but alive, how had they navigated those first difficult few months? And again, when they'd had to uproot their lives to move to Cheshire for his new job – how had they started again with a small baby?

Hannah thought about all those Sunday afternoons she had spent with her grandparents when she was younger, baking or going for what Gramps called 'an improving walk' in the park. Her parents never held hands when they were out together, but Gramps would reach for G-ma's hand as soon as they left the house, even if they were just going to the corner shop to treat Hannah and Scott to some secret sweets that they mustn't mention to their mum and dad. Looking back now, it was those small gestures between her grandparents that Hannah remembered the most – like when they'd catch each other's eyes and smile when telling stories about their courtship. Gramps was often the quieter of the two, but when he had something to say, everyone listened, including G-ma. It was he who had planted the seed of travel in Hannah's head when he talked about the places he'd been to when he'd been in the forces and how he wished he'd been able to go back to more of them when the world wasn't at war anymore, and explore new places. Although G-ma always said she was happiest staying at home with her family around her, she did agree to a few holidays to Spain and France before Gramps began to get more frail, but Hannah could tell this was more for his benefit than hers.

Seeing her grandma crumple when Gramps died devastated Hannah. For a few years, it had felt like G-ma was a shadow of her former self and the old lady found it difficult to even say her husband's name. But gradually, she had learned to live with her huge loss and had grown in confidence in being on her own, thanks in part to Joan being a dutiful daughter, Hannah had to admit. Over the years, G-ma seemed to have taken it on herself to channel her husband and become Hannah's biggest champion when it came to supporting her in her travels and offering her advice when she needed it. G-ma was more worldly-wise than Hannah had ever felt, despite having travelled everywhere from South America to Australia. Even when she FaceTimed her from their little house on the beach in Argentina, with the background sound of the other girls shrieking as they got ready for their night out and calling to Hannah to come and have another fernet and Coke, G-ma would bring her back down to earth with her sage advice.

Hannah knew she hadn't been to see her grandma as much as she should have recently, so she resolved to call her the following day and arrange for her to meet Toby properly. She fell asleep clutching her blanket and dreamt she was in her grandparents' house with the smell of their real fire and the sound of Frank Sinatra singing softly from the ancient tape player in their living room.

*

Despite having the whole day to get ready for dinner at Toby's, Hannah was in a proper flap by the time she left her flat to get the bus to West Didsbury. She'd gone for a cute vest top under a soft pink cashmere jumper she'd found in a charity shop that was too good a bargain to pass up, even though it was too big and kept slipping off her shoulder. She'd paired it with a denim skirt she'd been meaning to give to charity (her rule was one in, one out). She'd stared at herself in the mirror before deciding the skirt was definitely too short, even with thick black tights. Shaking her head, she wriggled out of it and threw on a ditzy floral dress more suited to summer, but that felt wrong too, so she went for the classic jeans-and-a-nice-top combo. But that felt far too safe, so she was back to square one with the super-short skirt option.

'Fuck it!' she swore loudly to herself as she glanced at her watch. 'Fine, this will have to do, you were going for a "maybe it's time to consummate our marriage" vibe after all.'

She and Toby hadn't talked about the physical side of their relationship at all. They'd done their interview for *North West Tonight* on Thursday and, although the presenter had asked them leading questions about that topic, they'd both steered her away. Toby had been pretty nervous around the cameras, which conversely had helped quell Hannah's own nerves as she knew one of them had to be calm and collected. Jess had been in the background, giving them the thumbs-up every so often, and afterwards she said Hannah was a natural on screen. Hannah had been worried about saying something embarrassing her mum would 'never live down', but she hadn't actually minded talking about their honeymoon and all the amazing things they'd done. However, the interview seemed to have frightened Toby away from doing any further press. They'd had a request from *Cosmo* to do a photo shoot and interview, which Jess was keen for them to do, but only if they were both onside. She'd asked Hannah to sound Toby out, but Hannah had told her not to hold out much hope.

This evening Hannah was hoping they wouldn't spend it just talking about their sex life, but actually having sex. Tonight was the night, she'd decided, despite Jess's comments that she shouldn't rush into it. So what if she didn't exactly have the fancy-the-pants-off-him feelings yet? Sleeping together would cement things between them and hopefully make everything less awkward – the more they acted like husband and wife, the more they'd feel it, surely?

She stared at herself in the mirror, before realising she'd forgotten to change her greying bra and seen-better-days knickers for the pretty (and thankfully push-up) bra and matching lacy but not scratchy knickers she'd pulled from the back of her drawer, but then finally she was ready. She barely had time to brush her hair, slather on some concealer and a layer of foundation and chuck her lipstick in her bag, before shoving her feet into ankle boots, shrugging on her coat and thundering downstairs. At the last minute, she ran back upstairs, grabbed her toothbrush and threw it into her bag, then power-walked to the bus stop, thankful her coat was longer than her skirt, which was currently skimming her butt cheeks.

Luckily, the bus driver saw her approaching and stopped for her so she didn't have to wait for twenty minutes in the cold as the breeze whipped around her thighs. She thanked him profusely.

She wriggled her skirt back down as delicately as possible, before plonking herself into a seat. As she got her breath back and added some powder to her face and colour to her lips, she decided that she just needed to relax and enjoy the evening – if the bus gods were smiling down on her then maybe the marriage gods would be too.

It was at that point she realised she'd forgotten to pick up the bottle of Waitrose wine she'd bought to impress Toby.

When she got off the bus, the only shop still open that wasn't an artisanal coffee/wine emporium (their description, not hers) was the Co-op, and so she forked out a tenner on what she hoped was a decent bottle of red, but was more likely an overpriced, vinegar-tasting keep-at-the-back-of-the-cupboard abomination, but at least she'd tried.

Eventually, her phone told her that she had reached her destination, and she looked around at the street of smart terraced houses and large trees rustling in the breeze as the evening drew in, and was immediately glad Toby had suggested she come to his house rather than him turning up at her scruffy rented flat.

She knocked on the red front door and before she'd had a chance to pat her hair down, Toby opened it and stood before her. He was dressed in well-fitting dark-blue jeans and a maroon jumper, which Hannah knew before she even touched it was cashmere. Great minds, clearly. They smiled at each other shyly for a beat, then Toby quickly ushered her in.

'Hey, good to see you, Hannah.'

'And you, Tobes, or should I say "husband"?'

'God, it still feels weird doesn't it,' he laughed. 'I'm not sure when it'll properly sink in. Come in, let me take your coat. You look lovely tonight.'

'Thanks!' she replied, tugging her skirt down as he relieved her of the only thing protecting her modesty. 'You're not looking too bad yourself. That colour really suits you.'

'So my sister told me when she forced me to go shopping with her a few months ago. Seriously, I'm not sure why she seemed to think just because I was single I had no idea how to dress myself.'

'Well, she was right about the jumper, so I'm definitely not dissing her – and from what I've seen, she isn't someone who should ever be dissed, to be honest!'

'Ha! You're so right. Melissa may have a heart of gold but she doesn't take kindly to being argued with, believe me. Can I get you a drink before the grand tour? There's prosecco? Or I have wine, beer . . .'

'Prosecco would be great, thanks. Oh, and I have this for you. It's probably rubbish as there wasn't much to choose from, so apologies in advance.'

'It looks good to me.' He smiled politely.

'You know a bit more about wine than me, I can tell.'

'What makes you think that? I mean, I'm not complaining, I've always wanted to at least look like I know something about wine.'

'I just think you seem like a person who's thoughtful and erudite when it comes to vino. You studied the wine list in St Lucia pretty carefully before ordering us a bottle when we had some with dinner.'

'That may have been because I was trying to impress you and not quite so obviously order the second or third cheapest on the menu – and it seems to have worked! Here you go, and before you ask, I have no idea of this prosecco's provenance beyond the fact it's Italian and costs eight quid from Lidl. Anyway, cheers.'

'To us!' Hannah added, clinking her glass against Toby's and taking a delicious glug that fizzed and popped in her mouth. 'Hurrah for Lidl is what I say.' She smiled at him and was touched by how much effort he'd clearly gone to and how nervous he was about her being in his home. 'Now, are you going to show me round this establishment?'

'Sorry, yes of course. Right, so this is fairly obviously the kitchen. Small but perfectly formed is how the estate agent described it when I came to view it, and I can confirm it is definitely small and definitely formed.'

Hannah laughed, earning a smile in return from Toby.

'And then through here is the living room,' he continued.

'This is nice.' Hannah nodded, taking in the bay window

and period fireplace, as well as the large sofa, big telly and shelves groaning under the weight of books. 'And not nearly as bachelor pad-ish as I thought it might be. You've even got fairy lights round the fireplace!'

Toby coloured slightly and looked sheepish. 'If I'm being honest, they are a new addition, and again I'll blame Melissa. When I WhatsApped my mates to ask them how to make the place look a little cosier, every single one of them messaged back with "cushions", so I went out and bought a couple, as you'll see. But when I asked Melissa, she immediately replied "fairy lights". I didn't know if she was actually being serious, but I took her at her word, and it seems John Lewis even sell Christmas tree lights in September, so they are now adorning my fireplace.'

'They're cute!' Hannah laughed. 'And the cushions are nice too. But I feel bad you felt you had to add these things just for me.'

'I have actually become weirdly attached to the fairy lights now,' Toby chuckled back. 'God, this prosecco has gone straight to my head. Obviously it's nothing to do with me being a bit nervous about showing you my house.'

'Christ, don't be nervous, you should see my flat!' Hannah said. 'Although, on second thoughts, let's not mention my flat for now. Shall I pour us some more prosecco and then you can show me upstairs? I mean, not in that way, obviously.' It was her turn to blush, and they both burst out laughing.

'Let's be honest, this is a bit of a weird situation and we're both likely to embarrass ourselves at every opportunity so we should just go with it,' Toby said, leading the way to the bedroom.

The upstairs was compact but practical, and Hannah smiled at the pile of cushions arranged on the bed both in Toby's room and in the spare room next door.

'There was a three-for-two offer, so obviously I got six!' Toby explained. 'And this is the bathroom, which thankfully doesn't have cushions in it.'

'It looks nice and clean,' Hannah commented, at a slight loss what else to say about the perfectly nice white bath, basin and loo.

'I cleaned it specially. Although that's not to say I only clean it when people come round,' he added awkwardly. 'Anyway, I hope you're hungry as I've got an app full of takeaway options. I didn't think I'd inflict dinner à la Toby on you – or me – so early on in the relationship,' he added, leading her back down the stairs. 'We could have Indian or pizza, or there's a great Thai place?'

'Ooh, yes, I'm a sucker for gaeng keow wan kai.'

'I'm afraid you're going to have to explain what that is. My knowledge doesn't go further than green curry!'

'Sorry, I was being a knob trying to sound impressive!' Hannah grimaced at how ridiculous she sounded. 'Gaeng keow wan kai is actually plain old green curry with chicken, but for wankers who've spent time in Thailand and want to show off about the fact. So, yes, I'm a sucker for green curry.'

'Well, we seem to have established that I don't know much about wine, you know a bit more about Thai food and we both have a tendency to get rather pretentious from time to time.'

They both laughed and Hannah felt herself relax a bit more, although that might have been the prosecco they were both glugging pretty fast. Toby filled their glasses and Hannah examined the pictures on the wall of the living room.

'Is this the Blue Mountains?' she asked, pointing to a photo of a gaggle of twenty-somethings all with their arms round each other and grinning.

'Good Oz knowledge,' Toby nodded. 'That was a boiling hot day and a big group of us decided to do a long walk along the paths, only it was further than we had anticipated and by the time we got back we were all sweaty, sunburned and ridiculously thirsty. But it was pretty cool anyway.'

'You look like you're having fun.' Hannah smiled, then stared more closely at the picture and the dark-haired girl leaning into Toby's chest. Could she be his fiancée who had tragically died? She pulled her gaze away. 'And this is a nice photo of you and your family.' She pointed at another shot.

'Yeah, I like it, despite never really loving pictures of myself,' Toby answered quickly. 'Weirdly, we were at my great-aunt's funeral a few years ago and although it was sad, it was really nice to catch up with extended family and listen to amazing stories about my aunt and all her siblings growing up. She was pretty eccentric and her funeral was definitely not all black and sombre, which is why Melissa is wearing that bright blue dress and Mum made Dad wear a pink tie, which he hated. Whenever they come round and he sees that photo, he's off again about how wrong it is to wear fuchsia to a funeral. So never mention it to him or else you'll set him off! Actually, and I should have asked you before as Melissa definitely told me to, but I'm going over to Warrington tomorrow to see Melissa and Michaela and they invited you to come, too.' He stopped talking and looked at Hannah awkwardly. 'Sorry, I should have given you more notice and you've probably got other plans, I just thought—'

'No, it's fine, I'm pretty free tomorrow, so yes, I'll come. It will be lovely to see Melissa again, and Michaela. I feel like I hardly spoke to them at the wedding.'

Toby beamed. 'Oh, great. They'll be pleased, let me text them now. Michaela's an amazing cook, she was talking about making something from the Dishoom cookbook. They went to the one in town so much they felt they ought to just buy the book and save some money!'

As they waited for their takeaway to arrive, they chatted about adjusting to the Manchester weather after a week of Caribbean bliss, and returning to work.

'It's going to be so weird being in the office again after everything that's happened, including *that* TV interview,' Toby said. 'I know you went back immediately, which must have been tough.'

'Yeah, but at least I'm working with Jess, so I haven't had to keep things a secret like you – although that secret is well and truly out now anyway! Although the flip side of that is Jess wants to know *everything* and has been questioning me non-stop about St Lucia. I think she wished she was there herself, to be honest!'

'You're lucky to work with your best mate. My team at work are great, and we go out for a few drinks every so often, but most of them are more colleagues than proper friends, you know. Although at least that means they probably won't ask me too many questions! I'm their boss, anyway, so they're not likely to say anything too awful to my face.'

'I didn't know you were one of the top bods,' Hannah said. 'If your underlings are too annoying I'd just give them a really horrible piece of work to do as punishment!'

Later when they were full of pad Thai and green curry, Toby changed his Spotify playlist from guitar bands to a more mellow soundtrack.

'Good choice, I love Michael Kiwanuka.' Hannah smiled. 'I've just thought, I don't even know your favourite band, which is a bit rubbish since you're my husband.'

'Is it a cop-out to say I don't really have a favourite?' Toby said.

'Well, it's marginally better than saying you like Ed Sheeran and Coldplay, I s'pose!'

'I know it sounds crap but I like loads of different music. I grew up listening to The Beatles and quite folky stuff my parents liked, and then I got really into indie in my teens and have just always liked guitar bands. Then as I've got older I've listened to more of a variety of stuff, from jazz to classical to Billie Eilish.'

'Eclectic,' Hannah laughed. 'I feel like I missed out on

loads of music that was around when I was in my twenties because I was travelling so much, so I spend half my life listening to the atrocious early noughties dance music I liked at uni, and the other half trying to get my head round what all the kids are listening to these days so I don't feel so out of touch. Although I realise that even by saying that sentence, I prove how out of touch and grandma-ish I sound! My stepsister Seraphina seems to play Katy Perry and Ariana Grande on repeat, and she's always trying to get me to floss or do whatever ridiculous dance is the new craze. I tried to teach her Whigfield's 'Saturday Night' dance a few weeks ago, but she was having none of it because, and I quote, she would "look like she was in the olden days".'

'I guess the nineties are the equivalent of the olden days to kids today,' Toby said, earning himself a pretend glare from Hannah.

'Ha! Well, you're even older than me, so that makes you ancient in Seraphina's eyes.'

'I'm only, what, three years older than you? Which means if I'm ancient, you're peri-ancient, so there!'

'Rude!' Hannah snorted. 'That's not how husbands should behave to their wives.'

'How should husbands behave then?' Toby said, and Hannah felt the air around them become heavier. He moved towards her and she tilted her head. The feel of his lips on hers was soft and still unfamiliar. They'd barely had any physical contact since St Lucia; the only time they'd seen each other since was at the TV interview. Now she let herself melt into his touch and felt his lips and tongue explore her own until he slowly pulled away and grinned at her.

'Is *that* how husbands should behave?'

'I'm not sure; maybe you should show me again,' she teased. It was Toby who pulled away a second time.

'I think I'm starting to get a hang of this husband thing. What do you think?'

'I'd agree, though you can always have more practice.' This time their kiss lost its soft, exploratory feel and instead became hotter and more urgent. Hannah pulled her jumper off and Toby's eyes widened a little when he saw her strappy vest top and enhanced cleavage. Hannah gave thanks to the creator of the push-up bra, and they resumed their exploring, this time in a little more depth. Her heartbeat increased as his hands moved across her chest and found her bare skin. Soon she was pushing at his jumper and reaching for his belt, but suddenly she felt his hand pull hers away and the rest of his body freeze.

Hannah stopped immediately. 'Are you okay?' she asked as her breathing began to slow.

'Yes. No. I'm sorry,' Toby whispered. 'I just . . .'

'What is it?' she replied quickly, searching Toby's eyes for an explanation.

'I . . . I want you to know that I haven't been with anyone since . . . since Emma died.'

Hannah froze, unsure of what to say to that and very aware that, without her jumper, she had a lot on display.

Toby took a deep breath and continued: 'I guess I've

just been waiting for the right person; for it to really mean something. So I wouldn't feel like I was dishonouring her, you know? But I don't want to stop, Han. I just wanted you to know the truth.'

Hannah tried to reply, but couldn't find the words. 'Toby, I . . .' She shuffled along to the end of the sofa and reached for her jumper. She forced her mouth into a smile and tried not to notice his look of confusion at her sudden change in demeanour. 'We don't have to rush things. We have the rest of our lives together, after all,' she added, in an attempt to convey a certainty she definitely wasn't feeling. 'Look, it's late, I'll order an Uber.'

'You're leaving? I didn't mean for you to go, I just thought I should be honest. I really do want to carry on, I was just—'

'Toby, it's fine, really. You don't have to explain yourself.'

She fiddled with the app on her phone, and there was an awkward silence as she waited for her taxi to appear. Hannah got up off the sofa to check out of the window then found herself staring at the pictures on the living-room wall again.

She was shaken out of her thoughts by Toby coming to stand next to her. 'Will you still come to Melissa's tomorrow?' he asked, biting his lip.

'Of course. Look, Toby, I know tonight has ended up being a bit weird, but I guess this whole thing is a bit weird, isn't it? I think we just need to feel our way through things as best we can and see what happens.'

'Okay,' he replied, but his attempt at a reassuring smile didn't reach his eyes.

Chapter 18

Jess

'So, yeah, when your husband adds a ton of pressure by saying he's essentially been saving himself for the right person, which he thinks is you, it kind of kills the mood.' Hannah grimaced as she finished explaining to Jess that, no, her date night with Toby hadn't been the biggest success.

'But of course he thinks you're the right person,' Jess protested. 'You're married! I don't think he meant to put all this pressure on you; he probably just wanted you to know that sleeping together is a big step for him because of what happened to his fiancée, which is kind of understandable, right?'

'Yes,' Hannah sighed. 'But also, I don't want to be compared to her, you know? It's strange knowing he's wishing she could be there with him instead of me. Way to make someone feel rubbish.'

'Hannah, stop! I'm sure that's not what he was thinking.

It must be awkward for him, too. Have you spoken to him about it? Maybe you need to get him to open up.'

'Awkward is the word, you're right. Anyway, did you talk to Tom about how *you're* feeling? Have you booked that time off yet?'

'He was working on a commission all day Saturday and then Sam spent most of yesterday vomiting, which wasn't fun for anyone, and although he's better today we couldn't send him into school so Tom's keeping half an eye on him this morning and I've said he can come and do some reading in here this afternoon if you don't mind?'

'Of course I don't mind, poor little mite,' Hannah replied immediately. 'God, that does not sound like a good weekend.'

'It wasn't the best,' Jess sighed. 'So apart from the weirdness with Toby, how was the rest of your weekend? I need cheering up!'

'It was fine. We went to see Melissa and Michaela the next day. Toby didn't even mention what had happened.'

'Maybe he didn't want to talk about his sex life in front of his sister!'

'Yeah, but he had the whole drive there and back to talk to me about it, but it was as if it had never happened; like he thought that if he didn't mention it then maybe it would mean it wasn't real.'

'That is a bit weird,' Jess conceded. 'What was Melissa like? She seemed really fun when I met her at the wedding.'

'She's great, actually, and Michaela too. They cooked this absolute feast of spiced lamb and cuminy, fennely potatoes.'

'God, I'm practically salivating just listening to you!'

'I'll bring you a doggy bag next time. Dare I mention we had profiteroles for pudding?'

Jess let out a moan.

'Christ, J, you sound like you're having an orgasm for god's sake!'

'Chance would be a fine thing,' Jess murmured. 'Go on, other than scoffing your way through all of my favourite foods, what else happened?'

'Well, their adorable pugs took the spotlight off me a bit, so I'm forever in their doggy debt. And Melissa has a wicked sense of humour. She and Toby are pretty different.'

'Does he not have a wicked sense of humour then?' Jess looked at her friend worriedly. When she'd plucked Toby from all of the men who had applied to be a part of the blind-date wedding, his ability to make her laugh had been high on the list of things she'd liked about him.

'Sometimes. I think I just couldn't get past the way he seemed to be putting on a show yesterday. I can understand it more in front of his sister, as you said, but he was doing it in front of me, too, and I didn't know what to do. I should have called him out on it, I know. Though I think Melissa realised things weren't as rosy as Toby was making out – she took me to one side later on.'

'Not in a scary way, I hope? I can imagine Melissa isn't someone to get on the wrong side of!'

'No, she was nice. She told Toby and Michaela we were going to have a sisterly chat while they washed up. I think she saw my face because she added that no one was to worry and she promised to be gentle. Anyway, she asked how much Toby had told me about Emma, and explained how broken he was for eighteen months after she died. She said it's been a long way back for him and that she feels responsible for pushing Toby into the Save The Date thing.'

'He could have said no, though,' Jess reasoned. 'And from the start he was one of the most responsive and seemed open to the blind-date wedding idea.'

Hannah nodded. 'Yes, Melissa said he's determined to make it work, but it's been a long time since he was in a relationship and he might be a bit, well, rusty – and this isn't just any relationship, so it's always going to be harder. She also said he isn't great at opening up about things, so I might need to be the one who leads any big conversations, at least to start with. Though it's not as if that's my forte either! Anyway, Melissa gave me her number in case I ever need some non-judgemental advice.'

'I'm not sure how non-judgemental Melissa can be when it comes to her brother!'

'I know, but she was being nice. And I did take what she said on board – you would have been proud of me, J. On the way home I tried to start a conversation about what had happened the previous night, but Toby completely shut it down and changed the subject.'

'I'm proud of you, Han.' Jess smiled. 'And all you can do is try to chip away at the wall he's put up. It's going to take you both a bit of time to get your heads round your relationship.'

'Yep, I know,' Hannah sighed. 'Although, on the other hand, Toby started going on about settling down and having babies at one point – which was even weirder given the awkwardness of the night before. Seriously, I didn't know what to say at all!'

'What *did* you say? I mean, have the two of you spoken about the children thing yet?' Jess probed.

'Well . . . insofar as we both quite like kids. But give us a chance, we've only known each other two seconds!'

'I know when I had my initial chat with Toby when I was going through the selection process, I asked him whether kids were a definite yes or no for him and he said he thought he'd quite like children but only with the right person, which seemed a very sensible thing to say.'

'It does, though we both still have a long way to go before we can categorically say we're with the right person to have kids with,' Hannah said. 'I saw a picture of her, you know.'

'Of who?'

'Emma. His fiancée.'

'Oh. And?'

'She was beautiful, and so smiley. And he looked so happy next to her.'

'Well, of course he was happy, he was in love with her,' Jess replied gently. 'But she died, which was terrible for everyone involved, but he's not in love with her now, he's moved on, which is why he wanted to be part of this whole project in the first place.'

'What if he hasn't moved on though? What if he is still in

love with her?' Hannah said quietly. 'Oh, don't listen to me, I'm just feeling a bit tired and emotional, it's probably still the jet-lag. Despite how many long-haul flights I've been on, it still always takes me ages to get over it. And to make matters worse I've got a massive dose of PMT today. Just ignore me.'

Jess glanced at her friend and felt a gnaw of worry in her stomach; maybe she should have stuck to her guns in the first place and told Hannah the whole blind-date wedding thing was ridiculous.

'Jess, stop it!'

'Stop what?'

'That look. I know that look – it's you worrying you've ruined my life by setting me up with Toby. You haven't, I promise, it's just going to take a bit of time for us both to get used to the situation, as you said. And, in fact, everyone around us. His family seem pretty on board with everything, but I've had to promise Mum that Toby and I will go round at the weekend. I was just going to take him to see G-ma, but when Mum found out she went a bit crazy and immediately called me to say she would collect G-ma from her flat and we all had to go to hers for Sunday lunch. I managed to negotiate her down to a cup of tea on Saturday afternoon, which means we only have to stay an hour, ninety minutes max, which is enough to inflict on Toby, especially as we'll also have to go and see Dad and Charmaine at some point. Although at least they should be a bit easier because we can take Seraphina out somewhere to take the heat off if Dad starts getting intense. You know what he's like.'

Jess laughed. 'Yep, but his heart's in the right place. Do you think your mum will ask Scott and Julia and Leo to be there on Saturday, too?'

'I'm not sure. I think she'll want to have Toby to herself as much as possible – although she'll have G-ma to contend with too! I guess I'll have to take him round to Scott's at some point, but at least Leo will be a cute distraction. And I'm so overdue a proper night out with the girls. I know some of them were at the wedding, but I hardly got time to chat, and then there's Dee and Johanna who are in God knows where now. *Hmph*, it's exhausting this parading your new spouse round everyone, isn't it!'

'Well, it is when you marry someone nobody has met before!' Jess said. 'Oh, I've got something exciting to tell you about Save The Date – I can't believe I haven't told you already this morning.'

'That would be my fault,' grinned Hannah.

'Well, anyway, I haven't been able to tell you before now as nothing was concrete, but I've had an offer to buy the business!'

'To buy it? Is that a good thing?' Hannah looked at her, confused.

'It is when it's the kind of money they're talking about! It's big bucks, Han!'

'Right, well then, that's great,' she replied, still frowning. 'It's a bit out of the blue, isn't it?'

'Yes and no. Since the business has been doing so well, I've been thinking about selling it. You know I only started the app in the first place because I could see a gap in the market, and although loads of good things have come out of it – you and Toby for starters! – the whole reason for working so hard was to make it a success financially, which thankfully it now is. And then at the end of last week, I got a call from an investment company saying they had a client who was thinking about making an offer for the business. He named a figure that frankly made my eyes water, so I'd be mad not to at least follow it up.'

'What would selling the app mean day to day?' Hannah asked carefully.

'It would depend, I think. I could negotiate to still be CEO and nothing much would change, I guess, other than the fact we'd be owned by someone else. Or I could sell the whole thing and walk away completely and do something else, especially with that kind of money.'

She noticed Hannah's expression and realised how insensitive she'd been. 'Shit, Hannah, I didn't mean to worry you, I should have explained properly. Obviously, if I stayed as CEO, you would stay in your job if you wanted to. And if I stepped away then I would of course negotiate a position in the new team for you. Without you, none of this would have happened and Save The Date would have disappeared completely. You're integral to everything, you know that, but I should have made that clear before I even told you about the buyout.' Seeing her friend nod in understanding and look less freaked out, she decided to say what had been on her mind for the last few weeks.

'Han, I hope you don't mind me saying this and don't take it the wrong way, but have you thought about what you might want to do career-wise? As I said, there'll always be a job for you here, but if I'm honest, I'm a bit surprised you've stayed this long. I've never known you last more than six months in one country before, never mind in one workplace! I love working with you, but I also know that, when it's just you and me, I'm the one who does all the more exciting things and you end up having to do loads of admin, which isn't really challenging you, is it?'

Hannah's frown had been becoming more and more pronounced as Jess spoke, but she knew she had to get to the end of what she was trying to say. Although looking at Hannah's expression, she did wonder whether she'd have been better off saving her motivational speech for another day.

Hannah huffed so hard, her hair blew in the breeze. 'I haven't really thought about it, to be honest.' She shrugged. 'I mean, I have had other things on my mind recently, you know, like getting married! I guess I need to think about long-term stuff at some point, especially if you're selling the app, but there's no rush, is there? The sale isn't going to happen overnight?'

'No, it definitely isn't, these things take time.' Jess nodded. 'But even if I wasn't thinking about selling up, I'd probably be having this conversation with you, Han. I s'pose what I'm saying is if you're putting down roots and maybe thinking about having a family—' At that, Hannah's eyes went wide. 'All right, I did say maybe! It's just that if you were, then you probably want to also think about your career, that's all. And maybe this is the push you need to start that process.'

Hannah sighed once more. 'You're right, J. Again. But I'm not sure I've got space in my brain with everything else going on at the moment.'

'I know the feeling, I do! And I'm not saying you need to make any decisions now, just maybe start having a little think, that's all.'

'Okay, *Mum*!' Hannah said, her grin back on her face.

'Damn, that reminds me, I'd better go and take Sam off Tom's hands before he gets square eyes from playing too many games on the Xbox.'

'Tom or Sam?' Hannah laughed.

'Ha, probably both of them! Though Tom's eyes can get as square as he likes. Poor old Sam has a reading and spelling test tomorrow, his sister reminded me, and I don't think FIFA counts as reading practice.'

Jess pulled on her jacket and made her way up the garden towards the house. The temperature had dropped significantly in the last few weeks and it felt almost wintry with the wind whipping around the trees. She noticed that the lawn needed cutting too, before it became waterlogged with a carpet of autumnal leaves, as well as the rose bushes that they were already late pruning and the pond full of dead irises that needed chopping out to enable green shoots to grow come spring. It all filled her with despair, and she added them to the ever-growing to-do list in her head – the tasks that only she would ever notice needed doing.

She walked through the back door into the kitchen and then on into the living room, where she was met with a scene that wouldn't have been out of place in nineties sitcom *Men Behaving Badly*. Tom was spark out on the sofa, mouth open and snoring lightly, while Sam was half a metre from their flatscreen TV, headphones on, playing a violent-looking shooting game that Jess swore she'd banned him from ever turning on again. Strewn across the floor were empty crisp packets, satsuma peel and plates of crumbs.

Her first thought was to turn round and walk straight back to the summerhouse away from all the chaos. She knew that what she should do was wake Tom up, remove Sam's headphones and tell them both to clear things up immediately. But looking round at the room that she'd made sure was tidy just a few hours before, she didn't even know where to start.

Chapter 19

Hannah

Hannah was very aware that Toby hadn't yet been to her flat, but she decided the following Saturday before they drove to see G-ma and Joan was not the day for that. Okay, Toby's house hadn't been as grand and grown-up as she'd worried it might be, but there was still no getting away from the fact that he owned a two-bedroom period property in a nice area and she rented a one-bed flat that had definitely seen better days, in an area that wasn't quite so nice, and she wasn't feeling strong enough to manage his reaction to that as well as deal with a visit to her mum. She supposed it was fairly clear from the outside that her flat wasn't Buckingham Palace, and this would be the second time Toby had come to pick her up so it couldn't be that much of a surprise, but even so, in the same way she made sure she went to visit her mum and not the other way round, it was clear it would always be easier if she went round to Toby's.

She fiddled with her bag as she waited for the doorbell to

ring, and tried to distract herself from the butterflies in her stomach by texting Jess to ask how things were. Her friend had been almost scarily angry when she'd found out Tom hadn't been supervising Sam like he should have, so Hannah hadn't wanted to broach the subject of Tom since. She couldn't quite see why Jess was so pissed off. Sure, Tom had been pretty crap, and Sam had been naughtily opportunistic to take the chance to play the horrible violent game he'd been banned from even mentioning, but Tom was presumably knackered after working for much of the weekend and she kind of had to applaud Sam for his ingenuity. Not that Hannah would ever say that to her friend, of course – and she wasn't a parent herself, so what did she know?

Even so, she was worried that Jess looked permanently on edge, and if Hannah so much as mentioned Tom, her face would immediately scrunch into a scowl. With the news of the potential sale of Save The Date, she should be putting her feet up a bit, but if anything she was spending longer days in the office than ever before. It was like she was almost willing her marriage to fail. What upset Hannah the most was that Jess would barely even talk to her about it.

Jess's reply came back blandly:

All good, thanks, give Joan my love! x

The doorbell finally gave its feeble call and Hannah grabbed her bag and made for the door, quickly shutting it behind her before she'd even said hello to Toby.

'Hi, sorry about that.' She smiled. 'That coat is nice, very cool.'

'Another Melissa purchase,' he said ruefully. He scooped her into a warm hug. 'It's nice to see you, Han; I've missed you this week. Going back to work has been exhausting and I was wiped out by the time I got home last night.'

As they reached the car Hannah saw two large definitely-not-supermarket bouquets on the back seat of his BMW. 'Oh, Tobes, you shouldn't have!'

'I didn't, I mean they're not for—'

'Don't worry, I was only joking,' she laughed. 'But they are beautiful and Mum and G-ma will love them – and you.'

'Ha! Okay, but next time I will buy *you* flowers. What did you get up to last night?'

'I texted Dee quite a bit. She seems to be having the best time in Queensland where she's working part-time as a counsellor, as well as being a tour guide on boats going out to the reef so she gets to snorkel or dive every day. Which reminds me, I had a look into PADI courses and there's one near Stockport that looks pretty good and you do it across a couple of weekends. Though it's not cheap, sadly, so I'll have to see.'

'Do it! I might even join you.'

'Really? That would be brilliant, Tobes! We'll have to book somewhere with amazing diving to go on holiday next year.'

Toby smiled at Hannah's mention of the future. 'Has Jess said any more about the buyout?'

'No, I don't think anything's definite. They need to check out the offer in detail, so it's unlikely to happen quite yet. Which at least gives me some time to think about what I want to do. Maybe this is the push I need to start that process anyway,' she said, echoing Jess's words in an attempt to sound grown-up. 'Although all Dee's talk about the reef and the sunshine in Cairns has kind of made me want to go back to Oz,' she added dreamily.

'That would be a long commute from Manchester.' Toby smiled tightly.

'True, but I could totally see myself living out there again at some point. I'd hate to think I've done all the travelling I'm ever going to do. In fact, I can't even imagine that! What about you, do you think you're settled in Manchester for good?'

'Well, it makes sense when my parents and Melissa live nearby. And obviously my job is here. But I'd love to live near the sea at some point. There's something so calming about it, I think.'

'Totally. Right, let's move down to Cornwall and instead of doing my PADI I'll learn to surf well enough to become an instructor, and you can sort out all the iPad problems the wealthy people who live in Padstow and Rock have, and we'll go and visit Dee in Oz on holiday and invite all our families down to our picture-perfect whitewashed house overlooking the sea. Deal?'

'Deal!' Toby laughed, his eyes crinkling as he glanced at her. 'Sounds like my idea of bliss, other than the fixing iPads part, but I'm sure we can tweak that bit. Oh, and we'll need to get a dog. You can't live in Cornwall and not have a dog – it's basically the law.'

'And it's a law that I'm very much on board with. What about a collie? Or even a Weimaraner?'

'Are they the big ones that need loads of exercise but then come and put their head on your feet? Then I'm in! I think we're nearly at your mum's, do I turn right here?'

'Yep, and then she's just a couple of hundred metres down the road on the left. Perfect.' Hannah felt almost giddy after their conversation in the car. She'd decided to put that awkward night at Toby's behind them and try to just enjoy things more. She grinned at Toby. 'Right, you grab the flower garden and I'll put on my best dutiful daughter face and I'm sure we'll be fine!'

They walked up the path and Hannah's energy immediately began to sag, but she forced herself to smile at Joan when she opened the door.

'Hi, Mum, nice to see you. Mmm, something smells yummy! This is Toby,' she said, stepping aside to give him some space and almost clocking herself over the head with the flowers he was holding. 'Though obviously you know that as you met him at the wedding,' she added awkwardly.

'Mrs Edwards, lovely to see you again,' Toby said enthusiastically. 'And these are for you.' He handed over the impressive bouquet and Hannah watched as her mum beamed and actually simpered.

'Toby, they are gorgeous. Oh you shouldn't be spending

all your money on me. But they are so beautiful, thank you. And I've told you, do call me Joan.'

Hannah let Toby follow her mum inside before she brought up the rear. She laughed to herself as her mum continued to titter and simper away in an unnaturally high voice and Toby complimented her about everything from her hair to her house.

'And you remember Vera, don't you. Mum, this is Toby,' Joan announced grandly, while Hannah rolled her eyes at her mum's obvious attempt to pretend to G-ma she already knew her son-in-law better than she did.

'Of course, Joan, I'm old, not senile. I'm hardly likely to forget Hannah's new husband, am I? Toby, it's lovely to see you again, and these flowers are gorgeous, thank you.' She smiled as she clutched the bouquet he had presented her with.

'What kind of tea would you like?' Joan asked Toby as she gestured for him to sit down. 'I've got English Breakfast, Earl Grey or camomile.'

'Camomile? Earl Grey? Who are you and what have you done with my mum?' Hannah sniggered as she gave G-ma a kiss on the cheek and squeezed her hand.

'I'm quite partial to Earl Grey, actually, and Mary can only have camomile now as the doctor says caffeine does something funny to her insides, so I have it to keep her company when she comes round,' Joan sniffed.

G-ma winked at Hannah and she stifled another giggle.

'I'm happy with just normal tea, thanks, Joan.' Toby smiled. 'Would you like any help at all?'

'No, no, you sit down. I was doing a bit of baking for Mary's church sale so I thought I'd knock up a little Victoria sponge to have with your tea. You do like cake, don't you, Toby dear?'

He grinned. 'I do. It's like you read my mind, Joan.'

This time Hannah couldn't stop herself from giggling as her mum busied herself in the kitchen.

'This special treatment is all for you, Toby my lad!' G-ma whispered loudly. 'I don't usually get the home-made cake treatment.'

'And I never do!' Hannah laughed. 'Not even Jess does, and Mum never stops telling me how great she is, so she must really love you already.'

Hannah was surprised how much she enjoyed the next hour, the four of them chatting and laughing together. Joan was definitely on her best behaviour and seemed to flourish in Toby's praise of her baking. Seeing her mum's eyes shining as she nattered away about going to the theatre with a group of women from Mary's church, Hannah felt a deep guilt that she didn't try harder with her. It wasn't that they didn't get on exactly, more that Hannah always felt her mum was judging her for her life choices, and that she didn't live up to the daughter she wanted her to be. And Joan had never really lost the bitterness and anger she had felt at the breakdown of her marriage, even though it had happened almost a decade before and the relationship had been unhappy for many years prior to that. Hannah looked at her mum's smiling face now and vowed to see her more often and maybe even suggest a day out somewhere together.

She also noticed her grandma had been a little quieter than normal, so as Toby and her mum were chatting, she squeezed her arm and whispered, 'Are you okay, G-ma?'

'Yes, lovey, I'm fine, I'm just watching your delectable husband charm the three of us women. He is quite a chap!'

'Ha! Glad you think so.' Hannah smiled.

'Well, it doesn't really matter if *I* think so – it's what you think that counts, darling.'

'Would I be able to use your bathroom, Joan?' Toby asked at that point.

'Of course, Toby dear. Upstairs, first on the left.'

Joan barely waited for him to leave the room before she said loudly, 'You've done okay for yourself there, Hannah! As you know, I was less than happy about your and Jess's ridiculous scheme, but she seems to have come up trumps for you with Toby there.'

'I'm really glad you like him, Mum,' Hannah replied warmly. 'It's important to me that you both do.'

'As I said, Hannah, it's not about what we think,' G-ma piped up.

'How are things going on the marriage front?' Joan asked, giving her an all too familiar piercing stare.

'Good. They're good,' Hannah reassured her. 'It's early days, obviously, but it's nice to get to know each other properly.'

'Nice? Good? Talk about damning with faint praise, Hannah!'

'Mum! What do you want me to say?'

'Well, I don't know what expressions young people use nowadays, but do you fancy him?'

'Mum, shh!' But she couldn't help but giggle, especially when she caught G-ma's eye and saw her face starting to twitch too.

'Come on, Hannah, I may be getting on a bit, but I do remember what being in love feels like, you know. The butterflies, the tingling, the passion . . .'

'Mum, stop, please!' she laughed. 'Enough about the tingling, okay? Look, we're just sussing this whole marriage thing out and I don't want us to rush. We've potentially got the rest of our lives together for those butterflies and, um, tinglings to grow.'

'I suppose you're right.' Joan's smile faded and she fixed her with another piercing stare before saying quietly, 'Don't forget, if it's not right, there's always a way out, Hannah. Don't settle for second best if you don't feel the way you think you should.' She leaned forward and touched Hannah's arm. 'Believe me, it will only lead to unhappiness for you both. Ah, Toby, there you are, what about another slice of cake? And Mum, you'll have one too, won't you?'

Half an hour later, when Hannah was putting her coat on and watching G-ma say something she couldn't hear to Toby, she turned to Joan.

'Thanks for this afternoon, Mum. It was lovely to see you.' She hugged her that little bit harder than she would normally. 'And, G-ma, I'll pop round to see you during the week.'

'You'd better!' Her grandma wagged her finger at her.

'Thanks so much for the tea and delicious cake, Joan,' Toby added, also giving her a hug. 'You'll be applying for *Bake Off* next!'

'Well, I hardly think so, but that's kind of you to say,' she replied, touching her hair self-consciously.

'You are *such* a suck-up!' Hannah laughed once they were both in the car and the box of her stuff from the loft her mum had left out for her was on her knee.

'No, I think you'll find I'm just a model son-in-law,' Toby said, smirking.

'Otherwise known as a suck-up,' Hannah said. 'Anyway, what were you whispering to G-ma about before we left?'

'If you must know, I was just reassuring her that I would take good care of you,' he replied.

'I'm not sure I need taking care of, but you definitely managed to charm the pants off the pair of them, so you're doing something right. Which means you're definitely a suck-up.'

Back home, she managed to shoo Toby away with a quick peck on the cheek and the promise of a late brunch the following day and a walk round Tatton Park if the rain held off for long enough.

She poured herself a glass of wine, turned on *Strictly* and settled down on the sofa to look at her phone. WhatsApp groups had a lot to answer for, she thought as she surveyed the 145 messages she knew would largely be irrelevant. Although she also knew that to delete herself from the lists would be making a huge statement and she couldn't bear the individual messages that would follow asking her why 'Hannah has left the group'.

Finally, she was able to put her phone down and rifle through the box of bits and bobs her mum had given her when she left. Sometimes it felt like Joan was trying to erase all evidence of Hannah from her childhood home – even though her bookshelves were filled with photos of both Hannah and Scott when they were kids, and more recent ones that also included Julia and Leo. Hannah still remembered the strange feeling when she'd returned from travelling and found that her mum had cleared out her old bedroom and asked her to take her stuff with her. But as Toby was apparently such a hit with Joan, Hannah decided she'd get a couple of their wedding pictures framed for her to at least bring the photos up to date.

The box seemed to mostly contain Hannah's old schoolbooks, and while she instantly threw away the maths and science ones, she pored over the creative writing notepads she found, laughing at the stories ten-year-old Hannah had written. There were a few old pens, including one of those with four colours that you click down at the top, which she put to one side as she recalled Jess had been obsessed with them when they were younger. There was also an old homework diary, which she flicked through, before doubling over laughing when she saw the inside back cover, which was covered in bubble writing declaring 'Hannah Edwards luvs Kiran Jones', whoever he was.

At the bottom of the box was a small pamphlet with a large

title written in different coloured pencil: *What We Can Learn From The Older Generation by Hannah Laura Edwards, aged eight and a half.* She opened it and began to read.

Interview with Vera Watkins, AkA G-ma

Hannah: Hi, G-ma, thank you for being part
of my project on what it's like to be old.
What do you think is the biggest thing
you've learned in your long life?

Vera: Well, that's quite some question, young
Hannah. I thought you were going to give
me some easy ones first!

H: I know, but I couldn't think of any easy
ones that would be interesting for my
project so I fibbed a little. Sorry G-ma,
though Dad says it's only a white lie, I
think.

V: White lies are sometimes okay, that's
true, that is actually one of the things
I've learned during my very long life!
Right, what else? I suppose another thing
I've learned is that if you're a good
person then generally good things will
happen for you.

H: Does that mean if you're a bad person then bad things will happen?

V: Maybe. But I've always focused on the good side of things. Sometimes it's hard to choose to do the thing you know is right, but it pretty much always turns out to be the best thing in the end.

H: What else do you think you learn when you get as old as you?

V: Well, I think you learn that it doesn't matter what anyone else says, if you want to achieve something then you can, or you can certainly give it a very good go. But it takes hard work, dedication and passion. I suppose the same could be said for a long and happy marriage!

H: You and Gramps got married a VERY long time ago and you both always look happy, except when I eat too much of the cake mixture before it goes in the oven, but you don't look like you're working that hard?

V: We might not look like we are, but underneath the surface we've both been working hard at our marriage every day since our wedding day all those years ago. And it's not always easy, believe me.

H: What kind of work do you and Gramps have to do?

V: Well, we have to talk all our problems through with each other and try to solve any big issues with each other's help. Like any couple, sometimes we fall out over something, but we always try to find a compromise that both of us agree on. There are a few rules we have that we both try to live by.

H: Rules? Like what?

V: Rules like always being kind to each other, remembering you can afford to lose an argument, always talking to each other even about the difficult things, remembering you're a team and one half of a whole. And finally, which is the one I think is the most important, remembering to say I love you every day. When you care so deeply about someone it's important that you tell them how much they mean to you as often as possible.

H: Wow, that's a lot of rules, maybe even more than we have at school! How do you remember them all, G-ma?

V: I suppose once you know someone really well and care about them you WANT to follow the rules so they become a positive thing in your mind and you never forget them.

H: I don't get it . . .

V: You will one day, Hannah, sweetheart. You know, the Ancient Greeks believed that humans were originally spherical creatures and one day the gods were so angry with them that they hit them all with thunderbolts and separated each human into two beings. They believed that's why grown-ups always want to find their 'other half' to make them whole again. And when they find that other half, they never want to be separated from them, just like Gramps and I never want to be separated from each other. One day, Hannah, you'll meet someone who makes you realise you were only ever half of a person before you met. And I can't wait to be here to see that happen.

H: Me too. Thank you for being a very good interviewee, G-ma!

At the bottom of the page the teacher had written:

What a brilliant interview, Hannah! Maybe you should think about being a journalist when you grow up! 10/10.

Hannah gazed at the pamphlet in her hands. Reading G-ma's words about her love for Gramps was amazing, but it also served to highlight just how paper-thin Hannah's own relationship with Toby clearly was. Her grandparents had both known immediately how they felt about each other and had been able to build a marriage based on pure love. Hannah still had no idea how she felt about her husband – so where did that leave the foundations of their relationship?

Chapter 20

Jess

As she stamped her wellies into the grass in an attempt to get some feeling back into her frozen feet, Jess wondered for the millionth time what drove people to jog round a muddy field at nine o'clock on a Sunday morning. If it wasn't for her vivid memories of lugging the twins round in her belly for nine long months, she'd think they couldn't possibly be related to her. But apparently her children delighted in taking part in ParkRun with their dad, come rain or shine – although only if Jess promised to come along and give them an encouraging *whoop* from the sidelines. She supposed she should be pleased they were fit and full of energy; she only wished they were less inclined to show it off on one of the few precious mornings she didn't have to work.

She risked removing her gloves briefly to sneakily send a couple of urgent emails while she waited at her agreed cheering-on point. It had been quite a couple of weeks, especially with the potential sale of the business moving quicker than she'd expected. And Hannah had definitely been distracted, though Jess couldn't pinpoint why. Toby seemed to have effortlessly won over Joan of Bark and G-ma a few weeks ago, and although she knew her friend was apprehensive about seeing Toby's parents for lunch today, she had no reason to think they wouldn't be just as enamoured with her. Jess had so many plates to keep spinning at the moment that it was impossible for her to be fully on top of any one part of her life.

She looked up just as Lily and Tom flew past.

'Woo, keep going, Lily, you're doing brilliantly!' she shouted, then she scanned the crowd for Sam, who appeared a minute and a half later. He would not be pleased if Lily beat him again and she wished Tom had chosen to run with him and encourage him on, rather than prioritising being at the front.

'Go, Sam! You can do it, you're nearly there!' she screeched, clapping her hands violently as if that would somehow make his legs go faster. After checking he was safely on his way, she began to trot as quickly as possible over to the finish line to cheer them all over. She squelched through the park as best she could, but quickly the mud became stickier and her right welly stuck to it like glue. As she took her next step, she completely left her boot behind. Her pink and yellow stripy sock with a large hole in the heel dug deep into the mud and she only just managed to save herself from falling face-first into the quagmire by grinding her surviving welly into the ground for dear life.

'For fuck's sake!' she shouted and tears pricked at her eyes. She wasn't hurt, but neither was she seemingly able to put one foot in front of the other. Just another thing she was failing at.

She could see that the finishing area was starting to fill up – and she wasn't there. 'Fucking, fucking hell!'

She no longer cared that everyone from small children to huge Labradoodles was staring at her, and fumbled in her pocket for a tissue. She pulled out a handful that had probably been in very close proximity to an eight-year-old's snotty nose, but wiped her dank, mud-covered sock with them anyway, before shoving it back into her welly, where it squelched wetly. Finally she was able to yank the boot out of the mud and gingerly make her way onto a less muddy patch. Still holding the dirty tissues, she hobbled towards the finish area, where she summoned up the energy to whoop Sam over the line. Lily and Tom had already completed the run and were lining up to get their finish number.

'Well done, Lily!' she called as they made their way over to her shortly after. Tom's arm was round their daughter's shoulders and she appeared to be crying. 'What's wrong, darling?'

'I got a personal best,' Lily sobbed.

'Oh my goodness, that's amazing, sweetheart!'

'But you weren't there to see it!' Lily continued, and burst into fresh tears. Jess reached out to give her a cuddle.

'But I saw you when you were nearly at the finish and you looked so fresh, even though you'd just run up that hill.'

'It's not the same as you seeing me cross the line though,'

she hiccupped, and Jess's heart almost broke. 'Eurgh, what is that smell? Have you just wiped dog poo on my top?'

Jess stared down at the tissues still in her hands. 'No, no, darling, it's just a bit of mud, I was wiping my foot, and—'

'I'm *never* doing ParkRun again,' shouted Sam as he joined the little group. 'I'm never going to get any better and I can't believe Lily nearly tripped me up at the start, did you see? Tell her off, Mum, it's not fair.'

'I'm sure Lily didn't mean to trip you up, and you did really well, darling, so don't worry about not beating your time.'

'I got a personal best anyway so you'll never be as good as me!' foghorned Lily through her tears, which made Sam promptly start crying too. Jess looked to Tom for help, but he was chatting to someone, seemingly unaware his children were both having major public meltdowns.

Jess desperately tried to shepherd the weeping and squabbling twins through the park, every step of her right foot squidging the mud further into her sock, while Tom stopped to chat to every second person, all of whom he seemed to know. After another five minutes of arguing and sobbing, Jess was close to tears herself, and with Tom still laughing and joking with some other dads, she realised she'd have to break her no sugary snack rule *again*.

The promise of a treat from the sweet shop seemed to brighten up the twins, though they were still able to produce more tears when she told them they could only choose one bar each. Embarrassed at the commotion they were causing, she quickly relented and said they could also share a twenty-pence mix and added a dark chocolate Bounty for herself.

All their previous hysterics and spitefulness were forgotten as the twins walked ahead of their parents sharing strawberry laces and chatting about how big the spot on their teacher's nose had been on Friday, and Jess breathed a sigh of relief, stuffing the Bounty into her mouth, barely chewing it on the way down. She turned to smile up at Tom, who had finally caught up with them, but was met by a frown.

'I can't believe you weren't there for Lily when she crossed the finishing line,' he chided.

Jess nearly choked on her chocolate. 'I did try, but my welly fell off in the mud and it went all through my sock and I had to sort myself out.'

'She was really upset, you know.'

'I know she was, thanks, Tom, I was there for that bit! I didn't do it on purpose, *obviously*.'

'Getting a personal best is a big thing for her. You know how much she likes running. I think we just need to make sure we're supporting her properly.'

'Thanks for the lecture, Tom, I'll bear that in mind next time I'm trying to make sure everyone has a clean sports kit, has eaten a proper breakfast and the wet-weather stuff is in a bag ready, all before half past eight on a Sunday morning,' Jess hissed, aware the children were well within shouting distance. 'God, are you just having a go at me because I was pissed off when you let Sam play that horrible video game? Are we really doing that point-scoring thing?'

'No, of course not, I was just saying that it's good to encourage the kids when they really excel at something, and Lily seems to have a proper talent for running. And Sam's pretty good, too.'

'I do encourage them! What do you think I do every evening when I'm helping them with their art projects or homework? And every morning when I'm listening to them read and testing them on their spellings? All while making their packed lunches and finding missing shoes and cleaning up the breakfast things. And then going to work and trying to make a success of my business so we can pay the bills?'

'Jess, I know you do a lot around the house, but if you only let me—'

'Let you *what*, Tom? Let you fall asleep on the sofa while the house – and our children – go to rack and ruin?'

'Now you're just being silly.'

'Silly? Right, okay, well, thanks for that, Tom! I'll tell you what's silly – you in those ridiculous shorts trying to beat your eight-year-old daughter in a fun run and leaving your son behind to get upset on his own. What are you trying to prove for god's sake?'

'What am *I* trying to prove? I'm not the one who spends the entire weekend making their child's art project them-selves just so you can show off to the other parents about what a good mum you are. I'm not the one who barely lets the kids put their paintbrushes down before you start tidying up around them in case they get a speck of paint on the table.

I'm not the one who insists they have extra French lessons instead of letting them enjoy being kids, even though we can't afford them, just so you can show off about how they can count to a hundred and order a coffee and croissant! It sounds very much like you're trying to control their lives and prove something to the world, Jess, but at what cost to your children? And at what cost to me?'

Jess stopped outside the house and stared at her husband. The air rushed around her head and she felt as if she were far away and might faint, but at the same time his words sped through her brain. It felt like she was looking down on the scene from outside her body and it was all happening to someone else.

It started to drizzle, and she opened her mouth but couldn't find any words to say. Then she turned and caught the twins staring at them both, their eyes wide and mouths slightly open, a look of fear imprinted on their faces. The sight of her children instantly snapped her to attention and she dug in her bag for her keys. 'Right, kids, muddy trainers off, please, and go and wash your hands properly and brush your teeth again after all those sweets. And then you can maybe watch an episode of something on the iPad – but only if you promise not to argue about what it is. Off you go.'

She didn't stop to notice if Tom followed her and the twins inside, instead she focused on chivvying them out of their trainers and up the stairs.

She and Tom didn't utter another word to each other the

rest of the day, and picking up on the strained atmosphere, the twins were both far quieter than normal, despite being cooped up in the house as the rain set in.

Jess refused to let herself think about what Tom had said and filled her mind with cleaning trainers, putting the washing machine on multiple times and making a perfect Sunday lunch for them all. Lily didn't even comment on the hated broccoli on her plate as Jess prattled on to them about school, play dates and their class assembly the following week. Sam didn't make his usual lame joke about getting his just desserts, either. Instead, he practically inhaled his apple crumble so that he didn't have to sit at the table under the heavy cloud of his parents' fury for a second longer than necessary.

After lunch, Tom retreated into his work room, leaving Jess to play Junior Monopoly with the twins, though Lily couldn't even be bothered to demand *she* was the dog, and immediately settled for the hat when Sam reached for the little silver canine piece. He chose not to crow when she landed on his hotel-laden expensive properties and had to pay him hundreds of pounds when usually he would be goading her with laughter at her misfortune.

Saddened by her children's realisation they shouldn't be having too much fun given their parents' mood, Jess tried even harder to make them happy. She suggested they bake fairy cakes, and allowed them to not only scrape out the batter from the bowl, but then to eat two each when they'd come out of the oven and had a chance to cool. The twins couldn't believe their luck after their sweets and apple crumble earlier, and so even their sugar highs were more muted than normal. Inevitably, they both then crashed hard and began to squabble, but Jess merely plastered on her Mary Poppins smile and sat them in front of the TV with *Junior Bake Off*.

She was just as exhausted as the kids, but when she finally had time to sit down with a mug of tea for more than two minutes, she pulled her laptop towards her and opened a new window on Google. Her meeting with the prospective buyer on Tuesday was in Cumbria, which was an easy drive from where they lived, but she suddenly couldn't get Hannah's suggestion of a break away from everything out of her head. She typed the words 'B&B Lake District' into the search engine, and scrolled through the results until eventually she landed on a 'boutique' bed and breakfast in Windermere that had everything she was looking for – a huge double bed, a roll-top bath, views of rolling hills, a pub within staggering distance, and a delicious-sounding breakfast cooked by the owner each day. She couldn't help but be seduced by the romance of it. If ever there was a place to get away from it all with your beloved, this was it.

As she clicked through to the payment page, she could already feel some of the stress leaving her hunched shoulders. She didn't even flinch at the ridiculously high final total and merely tapped her card details into her computer, knowing this was exactly what she needed. She checked her email, and nestled at the top of her inbox was her confirmation:

Thank you for your booking at The Lakeside
Nook for four nights from Monday October
11 in the Ambleside Suite. Single person
supplement has been applied.

She shut the laptop and opened WhatsApp on her phone.

Hi Han, hope you've had a fab weekend.
How did it go with Toby's parents? I want
to know everything! You'll be pleased to
know I've taken your advice and booked
a few days away in the Lakes either side
of my meeting on Tuesday so I won't be
in all week. I'll check my emails now and
forward anything you'll need, and you can
just WhatsApp me if there's anything super-
urgent you can't sort on your own or need to
ask me about. Hope that's okay x

Hannah's reply came back super speedily:

Yay, that's fab news, J! You deserve it, and
I'll be fine keeping STD ticking along in the
meantime. Are your parents looking after
the kids? What did Tank say? I bet he's so
happy to be spending a whole week just you
and him! Xxx

Jess replied quickly, before she could overthink what Hannah's reaction would be.

> Actually, it's just me going. Tom will be
> looking after the kids. Bring on the wine! xx

As her phone lit up with multiple messages from Hannah almost immediately, Jess turned it face down on the table and went upstairs to pack.

Chapter 21

Hannah

So far, Hannah's weekend had been exactly what she needed. She'd spent most of Saturday pottering around in her flat, and actually going to the gym instead of just talking about it. Then, that evening, she'd FaceTimed Dee in Australia and they'd had a proper catch-up. Dee still couldn't quite believe Hannah now had an actual husband, and she'd made Hannah tell her all about the wedding and honeymoon in detail. She'd been so enthusiastic that Hannah had found herself embellishing her feelings a little without even meaning to, leaving Dee with the impression she and Toby were Mr and Mrs Right and more loved-up with each passing day. Dee, meanwhile, regaled her with stories of Queensland and her job taking tourists out to the reef to snorkel among the fish.

'Oh my god, I am so jealous!' Hannah had groaned. 'I miss everything about Oz.'

'You should come out and see me!' Dee had shrieked.

'What about at Christmas? Imagine having a barbie and then going down to the beach instead of being stuck in freezing cold Manchester. You know you want to!'

'I so want to!'

'Then come! I mean it, Han. I'm housesitting for a mate in Sydney over Christmas and there's loads of space. Then you could come back up the coast with me and chill out at mine for as long as you want. Oh, please say yes, we'll have such an amazing time!'

'Hell, yes!' Hannah had laughed. 'Oh my god, I'm so excited. I know it's only October now, but I already can't wait! I'm going to start looking at flights right now!'

Even the thought of lunch the following day with Toby's parents couldn't dampen her spirits. Toby had texted her every day the previous week, but Hannah couldn't help feeling like there was a growing barrier between them – all those things that hadn't been said after that night at his flat – and the most contact they'd had since was a chaste kiss when they were saying goodbye. It felt like somehow their relationship was going backwards not forwards. Melissa was definitely right in saying Toby wasn't good at being open about his feelings, and after being shut down the first time, Hannah didn't really feel able to bring it up again.

She tried not to overthink her outfit to see her in-laws, but she did want to look like she'd made an effort, so she reached for the ditsy floral midi-dress she'd discarded on their date night. She couldn't remember the last time she'd actually worn it – it was one of those things she'd bought in Topshop on a whim before jetting off to South America, thinking she could be an 'English rose' while she was away. Unsurprisingly, she'd spent the whole time in her denim cut-offs and the dress had stayed scrunched up in the bottom of her backpack. It had never completely recovered and now looked a bit more boho than beautiful rose, but she decided it would have to do, especially as Toby was due to arrive at any minute. She remembered to pick up the semi-decent bottle of red she'd left out ready as she heard the knock on her door and pulled her Converse on.

'Hannah, you look so pretty!' Toby exclaimed when he saw her. He was dressed in a rather formal, crisply ironed pale-pink shirt that seemed to wash out his skin rather than enhance it. Hannah guessed it hadn't been bought on his shopping trip with Melissa. 'I don't think I've ever seen you wear a dress before. Other than on our wedding day, I mean, and you always look lovely, but—' He stopped, clearly not quite sure where he should go with the rest of the sentence.

Hannah smiled. 'Thanks. I hope your parents like red?' she asked, holding up the bottle.

'They do, and they'll love you, too,' he reassured her as they got into the car.

'We'll see who's the suck-up today, won't we!' Hannah added.

Neither of them said much on the drive over to Knutsford, and instead let Classic FM provide them with a dramatic soundtrack to their journey. Several times Hannah thought about saying, 'Shall we use the drive to talk about some of the obstacles we're clearly both struggling with?' but she always chickened out and swallowed the words back down. Toby, on the other hand, didn't seem to be preoccupied with worries about their relationship at all, and hummed happily away to himself. All too soon they pulled up outside a large detached house and the opportunity had passed.

'Right, bring on the Yorkshire puddings!' Toby laughed. Hannah smiled awkwardly.

'Toby, darling, don't you look dapper in that new shirt!' his mum cried when she opened the door. 'I knew that colour would suit you. How are you? I hope you haven't been working too hard?'

'Hi, Mum,' he greeted her, kissing her on both cheeks, then turning back to push Hannah forward. 'I'd like to properly introduce you and Dad to Hannah, my wife!'

His pronouncement was met with a lot of cooing, more kisses and shaking of hands, until finally they were both invited inside out of the sharp northern breeze and into a very neat sitting room.

'I'm just putting the final touches to the vegetables,' Phil, Toby's dad, boomed. 'I hope you're hungry!'

'He's made enough to feed an army, as always,' Elaine tittered.

Hannah smiled. 'Don't worry, I have a big appetite.'

'That's my girl!' Phil grinned at her. 'Extra Yorkshires for you!'

The roast turned out to be absolutely delicious, so Hannah busied herself with tucking into as many roast potatoes as she could without looking too greedy, while Toby's parents questioned him about work, whether he was getting enough sleep and whether he was still taking those zinc supplements their friend Doctor Adrian had recommended. Satisfied their son was in as good health as possible, talk turned to Hannah and Toby's relationship.

'So, how are you finding married life, Hannah? We're so excited that you're now part of the family!'

'Thank you, Elaine, I'm excited to be part of it too,' Hannah said. 'Obviously, it's been a bit strange since the wedding. I don't think anybody ever expects to meet their husband for the first time at the altar! But hopefully we'll have time to really get to know each other over the coming weeks and months.'

She'd been pretty pleased with her answer, but she noticed Elaine's face had become quite intense. 'Oh, I do hope so. Phil and I are looking forward to all that the future brings, aren't we, Phil? Of course, we love Melissa's Michaela to distraction, but when they told us those dogs are the only babies they were ever going to have, well, your heart sinks, doesn't it?'

Hannah smiled politely, but her internal monologue went into overdrive. Was Toby's mum really pushing for grandchildren during their first Sunday lunch together? Not even Joan would be so insensitive and unthinking as to say that. Her thoughts were interrupted by Elaine continuing her speech.

'And how are your plans for moving in together coming

along? Have you discussed what area you're going to live in yet? Obviously it needs to be somewhere close to your work, Toby. I always worry about how tired you must be from all that commuting.'

Hannah was well aware it only took him around half an hour to get into the office, but she bit her tongue and looked at Toby for a reply.

'There's no hurry, Mum,' he said after a short silence. 'You know how full-on things are for me at work, and Hannah has a lot on too, so we just need to find some time when we're both not quite so busy.'

'Of course, Toby, of course,' his mum replied. 'I don't know how you do it, I really don't. Now, I know you're probably not thinking about Christmas yet, but as you're both so busy I want you to know that nobody expects you to host the big day just because you're married, so we wanted to invite you here for the festivities. You could come on Christmas Eve and then stay as long as you like!'

'Thanks, Mum, that's really kind,' Toby replied, reaching for Elaine's hand. Hannah presumed he would follow up with something along the lines of 'But we haven't had a chat about what we're doing over Christmas as yet, so let us come back to you once we know our plans.'

But no. Instead, he said, 'We would love to come here for Christmas, wouldn't we, Hannah? Dad always does the best turkey and trimmings.'

'Well, I don't like to blow my own trumpet, but—'

'Phil, you know you make the best Christmas dinner this

side of the Pennines!' Elaine tittered. 'Hannah, we'll have to get you your own stocking to hang next to Toby's – we've still got his from when he was a boy, you know. And, who knows, in a year's time, we might even need another wee stocking!'

Hannah smiled along then excused herself to go to the bathroom. She locked the door firmly and stared at her flushed face in the mirror. How could Toby sit there and let his parents say those things? The way they were going, it would have to be a bloody immaculate conception for Phil and Elaine to end up with any grandchildren running round the Christmas tree. Never mind the fact she was hoping to spend Christmas soaking up the Aussie sun. What had Toby been thinking agreeing to it all there and then? She gritted her teeth and tried not to let the tears of frustration fall.

A few minutes later, although she could barely bring herself to go back to the table, she knew she'd been in her in-laws' bathroom a suspiciously long time. Taking a deep breath, she made her way downstairs again. Phil's large form emerged from the kitchen just as she was passing.

'There you are, Hannah!' he boomed. 'I was just getting us a top-up of wine. It's so great to have you here.' His volume dropped a little as he continued. 'I'm sure you know, Toby has had a tough time of it the last few years, and to see him so happy with you is brilliant. That's all you want as parents: to see your kids happy and healthy. So we're over the moon that you two have found each other – even if it was all a bit unorthodox! But we're pleased he's now settling down and getting the chance to have the future he always wanted. Welcome to the family, Hannah!' He enveloped her in a hug, and she had no choice but to pat his back and smile as he led her into the dining room again.

She endured another two hours of talk about Toby's childhood prowess on the guitar and how it was a shame he'd not played in so long, before she was able to get Toby to notice her 'don't we need to be getting back?' signs, and another half an hour before they were able to extract themselves with promises to come for dinner in a couple of weeks.

'Well, it's safe to say Mum and Dad loved you!' Toby grinned when they were back in the car and had safely pulled away from his waving parents.

'They're nice,' Hannah said, because the truth was they *were* nice – but just far too full-on, given the situation. 'They obviously care about you so much.'

'And you too, now.' He beamed. 'It was kind of them to invite us for Christmas. Especially when they said that we don't need to lift a finger.'

'Yes,' Hannah agreed. 'But I wish you'd not accepted their invitation without asking me first. Dee has asked me to go to Australia for Christmas and it's going to be amazing!'

'Well, that does sound great, but maybe we can do it next year. It's important for us to put down roots here like Mum and Dad said, and we can be near both our parents if we stay local.'

'I see my parents all the time, but I haven't seen Dee in

years. Christmas in the sunshine will be so relaxing and exactly what I need after such a stressful few months.'

'But Mum and Dad are expecting us now,' Toby said, his tone implying he thought that was the end of the discussion.

'No, they're expecting *you*,' Hannah said, shaking her head. 'I can't be cooped up in this country all the time. Other than the honeymoon, which doesn't really count, I haven't been anywhere all year. It's crazy and it's not like me at all.'

'But don't you want to spend Christmas together? What do you mean our honeymoon doesn't really count?' Toby signalled left off the roundabout and accelerated hard onto the motorway.

'I just mean it wasn't like proper travelling, that's all, don't twist my words.'

'I wasn't, I was just trying to understand.'

'And I'm trying to understand why you let your parents sit there and say all those things about us having their grand-children when we've never even had sex, let alone discussed having kids, for god's sake!'

Toby looked confused. 'Well, you always talk about how much you adore Leo and love spending time with him, so I presumed that's what you'd want too. Is that wrong?'

It wasn't lost on Hannah that he failed to address her mention of nothing happening in the bedroom. 'It's wrong that we've never actually discussed it and your parents sat there and practically ordered us to get reproducing!'

'Hannah, that's not very fair, they're just excited, that's all.'

'At the moment they seem more excited about our relationship than we do, that's for sure.'

'No one's saying we need to have kids right this minute. Just calm down.'

'Don't tell me to calm down!' Hannah could feel all her frustration rising into her chest. 'You're the one who won't talk about anything. We haven't even discussed what happened at your place, never mind talked about how we're both feeling about our marriage.'

'Look, it's hard for me, Hannah.'

'It's hard for me too. We all have baggage, Toby,' she exploded. 'You don't get to do the poor bereaved fiancé act for ever.'

Toby visibly recoiled and shrank into his seat, but although Hannah immediately regretted what she'd said, the red mist had descended.

'It's not like you'll even speak to me about it. Neither of us are perfect, Toby, but at the moment it feels like you're living in make-believe land where everything is shiny and rosy between us. And it's just not the case. It really isn't. I'm starting to think I might have made the biggest mistake of my life saying "I do".'

Toby flicked his head to stare at her, before returning his eyes to the road, and didn't utter a word. Hannah had shocked herself into silence too, but her last sentence continued to choke the air in the car like a noxious gas. They pulled up outside her flat and not knowing what else to do, Hannah reached for her bag and the door handle. 'Look, Toby, I—'

'Save it, Hannah.'

She looked across at him, saw the set of his mouth and got out of the car. As she fumbled in her bag for her key, she half-thought he might open his door and come after her, but instead he performed a perfect three-point turn and drove back down the road away from her flat and away from her.

Chapter 22

Jess

Tom's reaction to the news Jess was going away on her own for a week had been pretty much what she had predicted: disbelief, followed by the realisation he would have to look after the twins on his own, followed closely by anger that she was actually serious.

However, she'd found it much harder to tell the twins. As they were snuggling down into their duvets, she'd gently mentioned that she was going away for a few days.

'Is it for work?' Sam had asked, wide-eyed.

'Yes, some of it,' she'd fudged, which seemed to satisfy her son and she'd given him a soft kiss on his cheek and stroked the top of his head.

'But who will make us our packed lunches?' Lily had demanded.

'Dad is still going to be here – I'm not leaving you on your own, darling, don't worry,' she'd said, smiling.

'Dad doesn't know how to make sandwiches properly. Last time he put too much butter on them,' she'd complained. 'And he is rubbish at French plaits. You're nowhere near as good as Chloe's mum at them, but Dad is another level of rubbish.'

'I'm sure he'll learn,' Jess had soothed. 'It's time for sleep now, Lils. Sweet dreams, my darling, and see you in a few days.'

That night she'd hardly slept, tossing and turning, wondering whether she was doing the right thing. She still hadn't allowed her mind to replay Tom's furious speech to her in the rain, but that hadn't stopped her from worrying what might happen while she was away. The house would likely go to rack and ruin, the kids would probably end up malnourished, and who knew what Tom might get up to. Perhaps he would get a babysitter – probably some sixteen-year-old neither of them had ever met – and go out for a night on the lash. He could bring anyone back to their bed and if she wasn't there she'd never know. A small part of her brain had known that 3 a.m. catastrophising was unhealthy, but she hadn't been able to stop herself.

She'd still been awake when her alarm went off three hours later. She'd told Tom she'd leave early to catch the train to the Lakes so she didn't disrupt the twins getting ready for school. As quietly as she could, she'd had a shower, got dressed and packed her remaining toiletries into her bag. She'd looked in on both the kids, blew them silent kisses and tiptoed downstairs. The sun was just starting to rise as she'd made her way to the train station, and, despite the freezing air, the sight of the trees shedding their jewel-coloured leaves with the golden glow of the rising sun behind them had unexpectedly made Jess's heart soar. Her spirits had continued to lift as she'd walked away from her house and daylight had filtered ever more strongly through the branches. Even her train being delayed for fifteen minutes hadn't shaken the strange new sense of optimism she'd felt as she sat on the platform bench visualising herself lying in a huge bath full of bubbles reading a book without any interruption from shrieking kids, or sitting in a teashop sipping Earl Grey and slathering clotted cream onto jam-laden scones, without even a whimper of *'M-um, my hot chocolate is too hot!'*.

In that moment, she'd wondered what she'd been worried about last night. Tom would be far too exhausted from looking after the twins to even contemplate going out for a pint, never mind a whole night down the pub. After making their breakfast, school lunch and tea, plus copious snacks to combat the seemingly continuous plaintive *'but I'm hu-ungry!'* moans, one drink would likely knock him straight out and he'd be asleep on the sofa by 9 p.m., rather than having a lock-in down the pub.

Now, sitting on the train from Manchester Piccadilly to Oxenholme, coffee in hand, she wondered if it was horrible of her to feel pleased that Tom was about to experience what she felt twenty-four/seven. She decided it was nothing less than he deserved.

Finally, in the safety of the almost-empty train carriage,

she felt calm enough to examine Tom's accusations from the day before. How dare he say she was more interested in showing off about the kids than she was in actually appreciating their abilities; how dare he say that she valued a tidy home over their happiness; and how dare he say that she cared about herself more than she did about the twins, and just wanted to control them all. She knew she would never forget the vitriol with which he'd spoken to her and the utter derision that had flashed across his face when he'd torn into her. The intensity had reminded her of their argument in the restaurant when Tom had said she was putting the business before her family. Now he was saying she was putting her desire for her children to succeed ahead of him. She just couldn't win.

She and Tom had argued in the past – Jess knew it was impossible to be with someone for twenty years and not disagree on things. But the last ten months had felt different. Even when they'd disagreed, it had always felt like she and Tom were on the same side, no matter what. Now, she wasn't so sure. A tiny voice in her head told her that there might not be a way back from everything they'd said to each other. But a future without Tom was unthinkable. Wasn't it?

As the train trundled through Preston, she couldn't help but remember what Hannah had always said about how miserable she and Scott had been hearing their parents argue constantly throughout their teens. John and Joan had stayed together out of a sense of duty to their children, but in doing so had been the cause of their unhappiness.

Even thinking about Sam and Lily's little faces crumpled in horror at the sight of her and Tom shouting at each other made Jess scrunch up her eyes to stop the tears from falling. She'd been gone less than two hours and already she missed them.

As her mind whirred with visions of shared custody and maintenance payments, and her heart raced with fear and anxiety about what the future might hold, she looked out of the window and noticed the hard, industrial cityscapes give way to soft green fields and lush hills, and her brain seemed to calm. She began to push away the negative thoughts and concentrate on the next few days. Soon she would arrive at the beautiful B&B and be able to hear the lapping of the water on the lake shore, the gentle sounds of animals in the fields and the light tap of walking poles on the uneven paths.

A few hours later, and after leaving her suitcase at the B&B, she'd filled up her water bottle, shoved her waterproof into her small rucksack and jumped on a steamer that took her on a glorious trip around the huge lake. As she gazed out across the vast expanse of water, she wondered why she and Tom didn't bring the kids here more often. Back in the earlier, pre-children days of their relationship, they'd loved spending whole weekends in the summer climbing the peaks around Derwent Water or scaling the heights of Scafell Pike, then coming straight back and settling into a pub for the evening, muddy walking boots and all. It had felt like they didn't have a care in the world and that they had their whole lives ahead of them – together. Since having the twins, they'd been caught up in a whirl of play dates and parties, and even during the long, long summer holidays, they had rarely ventured the ninety minutes up the M6 to introduce Sam and Lily to some of their favourite places.

Jess's heart ached for those simpler times, and deep in her chest she felt a stab of pain for what she and Tom had been then compared to what they were now. She pulled out her phone to send him a text, but there was no signal in the middle of the lake. Part of her was pleased she wasn't able to cave and tell him she was missing him; the other part of her looked at the Insta-perfect photo of him with his arms round the twins on the lock screen of her phone, and longed to be part of their embrace.

That evening, she installed herself and her book in a cosy corner of the pub just down the road from her B&B, and after staring hungrily at the smiling couple's food on the next table, ordered herself chicken pie and chips, as well as a large glass of red wine. She had just finished her epic meal and was wiping red cabbage from around her mouth when a shadow loomed across her table and uttered the dreaded words,

'Is anyone sitting here – do you mind if I join you?'

She minded very much, but was obviously too British to say so. 'Erm, sure, if there's nowhere else.' She cursed herself for not having invented a friend to be waiting for. All she wanted was to leisurely enjoy her second glass of wine while reading her book – was that really too much to ask?

Apparently so.

'I'm Simon, by the way,' the man said, plonking his beer on the table and holding out his hand. 'But everyone calls me Si.'

'Hi,' Jess said, shaking his hand for as short a time as she could get away with. Then seeing he was still standing and was obviously waiting for her to return the introduction, she reluctantly added, 'I'm Jess,' before smiling briefly and looking down pointedly at her book.

'I'm working for a client up here for the week,' Simon said, settling himself into his chair and glancing at not one, but two phones, and placing them both screen-up on their table. 'Are you here for business or pleasure?'

'Both. I have a meeting up here and I needed a few days away in the fresh air,' she said, then cursed herself for volunteering information that could invite more conversation. Not that Simon seemed to need an invitation anyway.

'A relaxing trip to the Lakes. Perfect.' He grinned. 'Well, you seem to have brought the good weather with you – it didn't actually rain at all today, which must be some kind of record up here, I think.'

'Do you come here often then?' she asked, before realising how her comment sounded and laughing. 'I mean, are you up here on business a lot?'

'I've been speaking to you for two minutes and already you're propositioning me!' He smirked. 'But to answer your question, yes, I'm up this way a fair amount. I'm an accountant and I've been doing some work for a small chain of outdoor shops based in the Lakeland area. It's not the most exciting of jobs, granted, but it does mean my company put me up in a nice hotel and I get to spend some time in the fresh air, as you put it.'

Jess nodded politely, tuning out as quickly as she could. As she sipped her drink, she took a second to study the man she was now reluctantly sharing a table with. He was a little older than her and his dark hair was greying seductively around his temples and down into his beard. His startlingly green eyes seemed to twinkle at her and she reached for her wine, feeling her face flush beneath his gaze.

'As I said,' he continued, clearly not put off by her lack of response, 'it's not the most dynamic of jobs, but it pays the bills. What about you? What do you do, Jess?'

'I run a dating app. For people who want to get married.'

Simon opened his mouth and roared with laughter. 'No one on dating apps wants to get married, they just want a shag, surely! Most of them are married already and not getting any at home so they swipe right on someone who looks like they might be up for it. Isn't that what Tinder and Grindr and all that are about – find someone halfway good-looking who happens to be in the pub down the road, meet them for a drink, go to their place and shag. Job done!'

Jess smiled tightly. 'Well, not on my app they don't.'

'Really? Is it full of a load of freaks then? I should look it up and try it out next time I need the services of a devoted wife.' He continued to laugh at his own wit.

'No, actually, it's full of respectable men and women who just want to find The One,' Jess said primly, feeling her cheeks grow hot as she tried to control the anger bubbling beneath the surface.

'Well, good for you.' He raised his glass to her then nodded at the rings on her left hand. 'What does your husband do while you're running your little app?'

Jess stared at him. She was embarrassed that she had allowed herself to find those evil piercing eyes and scraggy beard in any way handsome just minutes before. She knew if she stayed a moment longer she would end up lamping Simon, so draining her wine, she grabbed her coat and bag before saying haughtily, 'It's not a "little" app as you put it, and what my husband does or doesn't do has nothing to do with you!' and swept out of the pub.

It was only when she was several metres down the road that she realised she'd left her book on the table. She was two-thirds of the way through *Wolf Hall* – she'd tried and failed to finish it many times, but it took so long when she could only read in five-minute bursts as and when the twins decided to behave – and she was determined this time she would get to the end. So she summoned up her courage and marched back into the pub to retrieve it.

It seemed Simon-but-everyone-calls-me-Si had already moved on, having wormed his way into a group of women near the bar. He gave her a sneering grin as she came back into the pub, so she hurried over, grabbed her book and raced out again. Despite him making no move to follow her, she didn't stop looking over her shoulder until she was safely inside her room at the B&B.

The next day, Jess felt oddly out of place in her smart trouser suit as she went to catch the bus to her meeting with Save The Date's potential buyer. The roads were full of people dressed in walking boots, fleeces and bobble hats, and the more adventurous even had professional-looking poles. As she wriggled around in her uncomfortable jacket and looked out of the window at the crisp autumnal day, Jess longed to be out walking the 'non-challenging' looping trail through the fells the tourist information assistant had suggested the previous day. But Save The Date was at least one of the reasons she was here, and she knew she couldn't back out of the meeting now.

Thankfully, two hours later she was on the same bus, threading its way along the narrow roads back towards the B&B. The meeting had been far more successful than she could ever have imagined, and the company involved had been so excited about her 'little dating app' that she had started to wonder why on earth she was selling it. And then she'd remembered everything that was going on back home and all her feelings of being overwhelmed. Plus as soon as the finance people had started talking money, Jess had realised it was a complete no-brainer; there was no way she could turn down that kind of cash.

Once she'd got back to the B&B and changed into her comfy trousers and fleece, she set off on the walk she'd promised herself that morning, only stopping to raise her face towards the gentle sun that shone down into the valley. The de-stressing power of the great outdoors propelled her round the trails, and she was slightly out of breath when she arrived back in the town. Keen to avoid any sight of odious Simon, she had an early tea in a pizza restaurant, before treating her now-aching limbs to the bubble bath she'd been fantasising about all day.

It was amazing how quickly she'd got used to spending time on her own, she mused later as she snuggled into a double bed all to herself. She'd actually finished *Wolf Hall* and had decided she'd make a trip to the independent bookshop nearby tomorrow and pick up a copy of the latest Marian Keyes. She was proud of the fact she'd barely looked at her emails, and as the B&B had Netflix, she'd caught up on the new series of *Queer Eye* without any of the eye-rolling and tutting she'd usually get from Tom if she watched it at home.

Speaking of Tom, the only contact she'd had with the world outside her lakeside bubble had been a daily text from him telling her the kids were fine but missing her, and she'd replied earlier saying she'd FaceTime the twins the following afternoon. She'd also received a WhatsApp from Hannah reassuring her that everything was fine with Save The Date and she hoped she wasn't too lonely on her own. Jess felt a gnaw of guilt in her stomach that actually the opposite was true, but being away had already made her realise how little time she ever had to herself, and she couldn't help but lux-uriate in the feeling of no one asking for a snack, or what was for tea or how she was going to make enough money to keep her business afloat.

It was total bliss.

The next morning marked the third day she'd been away from home and she woke to grey skies and the kind of constant drizzle that left you cold, wet and miserable after anything more than ten minutes outside. So she contented herself with a late breakfast and a mooch around Ambleside's shops. She was just sipping a caramel latte and enjoying huge forkfuls of lemon drizzle cake in one of the many coffee shops on the high street when her mobile buzzed with a FaceTime call.

'MUMMY!' a loud voice screeched out of her phone, before she could plug in her headphones and turn the volume down. 'Me and Sam just heard some boys swearing really loudly in the street, but Dad says if we're good he'll take us to McDonald's for tea and—'

'Lil-yyyy, you weren't supposed to tell Mum that! Dad said we'll have to have the fruit bag instead of chips if you tell Mum and I really want chips! Mum, pleeeeeeeease can we have chips?'

Jess watched her children on the screen talking nineteen to the dozen in her ears and couldn't help a huge smile spreading across her face, despite the imminent trip to McDonald's she wasn't supposed to know about. 'It's fine, Sam, you can both have chips this once, if Dad says you can, and I hope you just ignored those boys being silly in the street. Have you both had good days at school? Is Dad there with you now?'

Lily raised the phone above her head so Jess could see

Tom weighed down with lunchboxes and bags but waving at her in the background as they walked through the park. Suddenly, the picture went fuzzy and all Jess could hear was 'Sam, stop it! Get off me, Lily! Dad, tell him to stop!'

'Sam and Lily Taylor, if you don't behave, you won't be going to McDonald's and I won't be bringing either of you a present home from my trip,' Jess boomed, much to the surprise of her children and the rest of the coffee shop. She flashed a quick apologetic smile at the elderly-looking woman on the next table, who smiled back at her in return and raised her hand in a 'don't worry about it' gesture.

'Sorry, Mum,' chorused the twins in her ear, and their little faces appeared back on her screen. 'Have you really got us a present?' asked Lily. 'What is it?'

'You'll have to wait and see when I'm back later in the week,' Jess laughed. 'Now, how did you both do in your spelling test yesterday?'

She listened to them both chatter on about making insect hotels, how Lily's friend Clara was getting a Hermione costume for her birthday and that the teacher who had taught their class last year had brought in some slices of her wedding cake, but the greedy Year Three children had eaten it all before they could get some themselves. They never seemed to mention doing any actual work at school, but Jess loved hearing all their stories – especially when she could sit back in a coffee shop and listen rather than having to clean lunchboxes, make the tea and supervise their maths at the same time.

'When are you coming home, Mum?' Lily suddenly asked

amid the background noise of Tom telling Sam to stop dragging his jumper sleeve along a dirty wall.

'Not too long now, sweetheart,' she promised, feeling the guilt stir in the bottom of her stomach.

'Old Ted misses you at bedtime,' she said quietly, before Sam loomed back into view and foghorned, 'Dad said to tell you that I miss you too, and even though he told me to say it, I actually do think it's true. We've run out of proper Weetabix and Dad bought the Tesco ones that taste like cardboard that you said we'd never have to have again. So please can you come home soon?'

Jess laughed but felt her eyes fill with tears. After promising both children she would be home as soon as she could and watching as they made Tom bend down so he was on the screen so they could all blow her kisses, she eventually ended the call. Her face ached from smiling so much, but her eyes stung as tears streamed down her cheeks.

The elderly lady on the next table looked across in concern and shuffled her chair closer to Jess.

'Are you okay, lovey? I couldn't help overhearing some of your conversation and it sounds like you have a couple of livewires there! Here, have a tissue.'

'Thank you,' Jess sniffed. 'And you're right, they are very much livewires, bless them! They definitely keep me on my toes when I'm at home. And they're probably running rings round their dad right now.'

The woman smiled gently. 'It must be hard being away from them.'

'Yes, I didn't think I was really missing them until seeing them on my phone just then. Technology, eh!'

'But we're so lucky to have FaceThingy and Skypey, or whatever it's called. When my Geoffrey was away back in the day, we only got a few moments to chat while he fed his ten pences into the payphone, and all too soon the pips would sound and you'd be saying goodbye again. But still, you make the most of what you have, don't you?'

'You do,' Jess agreed. 'How long have you and Geoffrey been married?'

'We only got twenty years together before he was taken away from us, god rest his soul. Cancer, and in the days before all these new-fangled immuno-wotsit therapies and cures those clever scientists are finding now.'

'Oh, I'm so sorry,' Jess said, her eyebrows rising in sympathy and her hand instinctively moving to her chest.

'Thank you,' the woman nodded. 'But I can look back now and know I was lucky to have every one of those twenty years with the best of men. I might not have thought it every day of every week, when the girls were newborns and so demanding of our time, or when Geoffrey was working up in Scotland and I was left at home with three kiddies under five. But he was – and still is – the kindest, most gentle man I've ever met. My only regret is that it was only after he died that I realised just how kind and how gentle he was.' She stopped and looked at Jess through glassy eyes. 'All I'm saying, lovey, is that the old adage is true – you don't know what you've got until it's gone. Anyway, you don't want to listen to an old lady like me rabbiting on, I'll leave you to finish your cake. Nice to meet you, lovey.'

Before Jess could pull herself together to say any more than 'you too' through the tears that had started falling again, the lady had shuffled off to the counter, had a quiet few words with the server, paid for her drink and walked off down the street. Jess stood up, and sat down again abruptly when she realised she had gone, then started when she felt a hand on her arm.

'Sorry, I didn't mean to make you jump,' the waitress said gently. 'I wanted to tell you that the lady who just left paid your bill.'

'Oh, gosh! Thank you for letting me know,' Jess managed, before succumbing to more inevitable tears. She wished she'd stopped sniffing long enough to tell the lady what a lovely man Geoffrey sounded like he'd been, to sympathise with her about how hard it must have been bringing up three teenage children without her husband.

She instinctively reached for her phone to text Tom, but then quickly put it back on the table. She gathered up her things, gave the waitress a watery smile and went out into the street.

'Hello, you've forgotten your phone!' the waitress called from behind her a few seconds later. 'It was ringing so I noticed it on the table.'

'Thanks, you're a lifesaver!' Jess sighed. As she took it from the waitress's hand it started vibrating again. 'I'd better get this, thanks again,' she said as she hurried to answer it. 'Hannah! Is everything okay?'

'Yes. No. I mean yes,' came Hannah's voice into her ear. 'I've forgotten the password for the membership spreadsheet and thought you might know it off the top of your head?'

'Of course, it's SamAndLily2.'

'Damn, of course it is, I should have known that, sorry, J. Anyway, how are you? How was the meeting?'

'It was good, thanks. Lots to think about. How are things there?'

'Yeah, fine. I saw Tom earlier. Oh, Jess, he's not in a good way. He's missing you something chronic, I've never seen him like this.'

'Is he? He seemed fine when I FaceTimed the twins earlier.'

'He was obviously just putting on an act. Jess, believe me, he needs you. And I know you need him, too.' Jess heard Hannah's voice wobble, but she seemed to catch herself before launching into an impassioned speech. 'Look, you've both probably said things in the heat of the moment that you now regret, and although you can't unsay them, you have the power to say new things that can bring new life, new happiness to your marriage. But you have to talk to Tom and tell him exactly how you're feeling, J, he can't read your mind. All those things you've been saying to me over the past few weeks, you need to say to him. And of course there's no waving a magic wand and making everything all right overnight, but the more you invest in a relationship, the more you get out of it, right? And you and Tom just need to give yours some TLC. Tell him how stressed you've been and that you need him to step up at home, but realise you have to be there for him, too; you're a team. Without you he's unbalanced, not himself. Like the Ancient Greeks said, once you find your other half, you never want to be separated from them.' Hannah's voice shook again.

'What have the Ancient Greeks got to do with anything, Han! Are you going mad down there without me?' Jess said in a vain attempt to lighten the mood.

'Yes, I am a bit. Just say you'll come back tomorrow, J, please. You and Tom need to talk and you can't do that from a hundred miles away.'

'But what if we can't work things out?' Jess whispered, fear creeping into her voice. 'What happens then?'

'You can always work things out if you both want to enough. And I know Tom does, so the question is, do you?'

Jess's breath caught in her throat and she swallowed hard. 'You know I do, Han.'

'Then come home! Promise me you'll get on the train in the morning? Promise me, J?'

'Okay, all right. I'll come back in the morning, I promise.' Jess heard her friend let out a long ragged breath and she felt tears prick her own eyes. 'Thanks for talking some sense into me.'

'Any time, J.'

'And, Hannah? You're wiser than you give yourself credit for, you know. I'm not sure what's going on with you and Toby at the moment, but it seems to me that you should listen to your own advice sometimes. And stop rolling your eyes at me – I might not be able to see you, but I know you,

Han! Fine, if you don't believe me, will you at least go and see G-ma and talk to her?'

Hannah sighed. 'Right, I will, but only because I was going to see her tomorrow anyway.'

'Great. Make a day of it and shut the office for once. Our inboxes will still be there the next day and the one after that. Your happiness is too important.'

'If you say so, boss!'

Jess could hear the slight smile in Hannah's voice. 'I do say so, yes. Now, go home, call G-ma and tell her you're coming to spend the day with her tomorrow. Go, now!'

'I'm going! Love you, Jess.'

'Love you too, Han.'

Chapter 23

Hannah

Hannah woke up on Thursday morning feeling strangely refreshed. The previous day had seemed long, what with her emotional phone call to Jess and her tough conversation with Tom.

She'd been shocked when he'd put his head round the door of the summerhouse and asked if she fancied a cup of coffee. She'd never seen him look so wretched and broken. She'd followed him inside the house and listened to him spill out how unhappy he was. Instinctively, she'd pulled him into a hug then said fiercely, 'You have to fix it, Tank, you don't have any choice. You know even better than I do that the two of you belong together – you're a team. Plus you have the twins to think about. You can't throw all of that away because of one rocky patch.' Her words had seemed to have little effect, however, and she'd banged down her coffee cup in frustration. 'Tom, I will not sit

321

here and see twenty years of happiness go down the drain! You love Jess, right?'

'Of course I do! But I'm just not sure that's enough,' he'd added miserably.

'Then make it enough. Make her see how much you love her. Make her see how much you love her for being an amazing wife, a brilliant mum, a successful business-woman, a ridiculously good friend. And for being as flawed a human being as you are. Neither of you are perfect, but as long as you are both determined to try to make things better, then maybe love is enough.' Hannah had looked up at Tom's face and saw that the tears pricking her own eyes were mirrored in those falling down his cheeks. She'd squeezed his hand and brushed the sleeve of her jumper across her face. There had been a beat of silence while they both pulled themselves together, then suddenly an idea had struck Hannah and she'd sniffed then grinned at Tom. 'What if you planned a party to celebrate ten years of being married? You could renew your vows and everything! Jess and I were just talking about this a few weeks ago before my wedding.'

'Would she really like that, do you think?' Tom had asked. 'I don't want to get this wrong and make her more angry and frustrated.'

'She'd love it!' Hannah had grinned. 'I'm not saying it's going to solve all your problems, but it's about showing you care. Although, instinctively, she'd want to organise every single detail herself − but you can't let her. She's such a control freak but we all know sometimes she goes too far – she just can't help herself. What do you think?'

'I think it's a great idea,' Tom had replied, the first smile Hannah had seen in a long time hitting his face. 'But I'm worried she'll end up wishing she *had* organised it all herself.'

'Then you'll just have to make it the best party ever.'

Hannah stepped off the bus outside G-ma's sheltered housing block and made her way to her grandma's flat. When she'd called G-ma the previous evening and asked if she fancied an early lunch, she'd been subjected to some robust questioning about why she wouldn't be at work and what had happened that necessitated a daytime visit, but she'd managed to brush her off at least enough for G-ma to say, 'Okay, well, if you're sure, Hannah darling, you know I'll never turn down a free lunch, and we can talk about what's actually behind all this when I see you!' Hannah had had to smile as she said goodbye and hung up the call; G-ma might be in her late eighties and physically not as strong as she once was, but she was still a wily customer, just as she'd always been.

'It's me, G-ma,' Hannah said now into the intercom, and immediately the door clicked and she was granted entry. Her grandma was already dressed in her smart coat, complete with bejewelled brooch, and clutching the LK Bennett handbag Hannah had saved up to get her from duty-free for her eighty-fifth birthday a few years before, as she knew the old lady had coveted a posh bag her whole life. Her hair was freshly set by the lady who did the rounds of the sheltered-accommodation block twice a week, and she was sitting in the wheelchair she used when she needed to go further than the rooms in her flat or a car parked outside. She immediately fixed Hannah with a beady eye.

'You're looking lovely this morning, G-ma,' Hannah said, as she bent to give her a kiss on her cheek, the familiar scents of Nivea cream and powder tickling her nose.

'And you're looking rather shifty, my darling. I knew something was going on. Out with it!'

'Detective G-ma strikes again!' Hannah laughed. 'Let's at least position ourselves in the restaurant with a glass of wine in our hands before you interrogate me any further. Are you ready to go?'

Hannah pushed her grandma out of her flat and a few hundred metres down the road to the large garden centre with its pretty café that was a big hit with residents of the sheltered housing block and their relatives alike, as it not only served excellent scones with clotted cream, but also had a licence to sell alcohol.

'I've been dreaming about a nice big glass of Chardonnay all morning!' G-ma sighed as she sipped the large white wine Hannah had immediately ordered for them both. 'Now, young lady, are you going to tell me what's going on? Is it that handsome husband of yours?'

'How did you guess?'

'The way your smile hasn't reached your eyes today, the set of your chin because you don't agree with something he's said or done, the way you keep checking your phone to see if he's sent you a message.'

'I'm waiting to hear from Jess, actually!'

'Is she still thinking of selling the dating application? In fact, let's come back to that and focus on you and Toby. What's happened?'

Hannah took a deep breath and let it out as slowly as possible before she began speaking. 'It feels like he's unable to talk to me about anything important. Any weirdness or awkwardness between us, he'll just gloss over and pretend didn't happen so we never actually talk about real things. Of course there's going to be weird and awkward conversations – we've only known each other a few weeks and are still trying to work out who the other person is, but it's like he has to pretend that everything's perfect between us, especially when we're with other people. And then when I do question him about something or disagree with what he's done, he just totally shuts down and won't speak to me.'

G-ma looked at her keenly. 'And what was it you disagreed with?'

'His parents suggested we go to theirs for the whole of Christmas and he immediately said yes, without even asking me. I was planning to go to Australia to see Dee. He just didn't get why I was so annoyed.'

'I see. And what did you say when he didn't understand why you were so put out?'

Hannah took a long swig of her wine. 'I may have said

I was beginning to think the whole marriage thing hadn't been the best idea.'

'And what did he say to that?'

'That's the problem; he didn't say anything. And I've heard nothing from him since. Again, he just won't engage when it comes to anything important.'

G-ma fixed her with a thoughtful gaze. 'Did you ever ask Toby if he wanted to come to Australia with you?'

'Well, no. He seemed very clear we were spending Christmas with his parents.'

'So you didn't actually suggest that both of you went to see Dee?'

'No. It didn't really cross my mind to.'

G-ma gave her another long look and paused before she replied gently, 'And do you not think it should have crossed your mind to invite your husband on your travels?'

Hannah shifted uncomfortably in her seat as G-ma's words hit home, and she was glad that the waiter chose that moment to come over with their lunch.

Once they were left alone again, G-ma said conversation-ally, 'Have I ever told you about the first argument me and your Gramps had?'

'No. You two never really argued, did you? You've always said that Gramps would take himself off and smoke his pipe in the shed when he needed to let off a little steam – liter-ally, ha! – and when he came back you'd both be ready to compromise.'

'And that's true, to a point, darling. But of course we

argued! We were like any other couple – neither of us were saints. And, yes, we learned the art of compromise over the years, but my goodness we had a few humdingers to start with!'

'You've never told me that,' Hannah said, putting down her knife and fork.

Her grandma sighed a little. 'Hannah, darling, I fear I may have presented a somewhat idealised view of my marriage to you as you were growing up. And don't look like that, Robbie and I were just as much in love as I've always said we were – I still am in love with him and always will be. But I never wanted you to think that we had some kind of miracle relationship where we never disagreed or I never thought he was being foolish or selfish. Of course there were times that I thought those things of him – and he thought them of me. But we got through those times. And the more we did that, the more we realised we didn't need to have the argument in the first place – if we'd told each other how we were feeling from the beginning, more often than not we could have saved ourselves the row further down the line.'

Hannah stared at her grandma, her brain a whirl of half-questions and mixed-up thoughts. She took another sip of wine. 'How did you know?' she asked simply.

'You mean how did I know that Robbie was The One?' G-ma replied astutely. 'I had a feeling deep in my chest. Ever since meeting him at the village fete on the Saturday and him coming round for tea with my mother after church on Sunday. It was like my heart was telling me not to let this man leave.' She blinked watery eyes at her granddaughter and reached for her hand. 'But, Hannah, just because you didn't have that feeling doesn't mean Toby isn't The One. Everyone is different, even the time we live in now is different. The important thing is that you're happy. You have to find your own path to that happiness, and that might be a different path from the one I travelled with your Gramps. Maybe Toby isn't The One for you, but also maybe he is. Only the two of you can work that one out. But I'll tell you this: I may have known Robbie was The One that very first day I met him and that never changed, but what did change was my love for him; it grew every single day we were together. And that's because we both put everything we had into it.' She squeezed Hannah's hand. 'Can you hand on heart say you've put everything you've got into your relationship with Toby?'

Hannah looked down at her plate and was silent for a few moments, before replying, 'No. But neither has Toby. I can change how I go about things, but if he refuses to talk to me, what more can I do?'

'How hard have you tried to talk to him in the last few days?' G-ma asked quietly.

'Well, I ... *Fine*, I haven't tried to talk to him either,' she sighed.

'Hannah, darling, you are sometimes more like your mother than you imagine. The only person I've met who is more stubborn than her is you! Are you really going to give up and run away from something so important? Either you or Toby has to be the one to make the first move, and why shouldn't it be you?'

Silence stretched between them as Hannah wrestled with her thoughts. 'Fine, okay, I'll be the one to make the first move! But what if he still refuses to talk about the important things?'

'Tell him how you feel,' G-ma said simply. 'And don't use any of that iMessage or Skype rubbish. You need to speak to him face to face. Allow yourself to be vulnerable. You can't let your worry about him rejecting you stand in the way of your happiness.'

'I'm . . . I'm scared,' she whispered. 'I don't know if I can do that, G-ma.'

'You can and you must,' G-ma said firmly. 'Promise me, Hannah darling. Promise me you'll at least try.'

Hannah sighed and knew when she was beaten. 'I promise,' she said quietly. She felt her grandma's hand relax in hers and suddenly G-ma looked every one of her eighty-eight years, which made Hannah feel terrible. She shook herself. 'Let's have coffee back at the flat,' she added. 'I'll get the bill and then we can go. I might even watch that terrible quiz show with you, if you don't mind me beating you, that is!'

'You'll be lucky!' G-ma replied, but without the vigour she usually would have shown.

As Hannah washed up their mugs an hour later, leaving G-ma snoozing in front of the TV, she felt both guilty at wearing her grandmother out, but also weirdly like a weight had been lifted from her shoulders. She gave her a gentle kiss and made sure her tablets were on the kitchen table for when her carer popped round later, then quietly shut the front door behind her.

Hannah rested her head against the window as the musty bus creaked its way down the road. She'd never broken a promise to G-ma in her whole life, so she reluctantly pulled her phone from her pocket and began composing a text. Twenty minutes later, as the bus pulled up at her stop, she jabbed the 'Send' button, and quickly shoved her phone back into her pocket, determined not to check it for at least the five minutes it would take her to get home, open her door, kick off her shoes and fall into her sofa.

When she finally dared to look at the screen, she immediately saw a notification: Toby had replied.

Chapter 24

Jess

Twenty-four hours earlier than she'd planned, Jess battled to find room for her case on the train and eventually sank gratefully into her seat. At the B&B, she'd finally fallen asleep in the early hours of the morning, and not even a long stint under the power shower and a cooked breakfast had done much to make her look or feel rested and revitalised. But Jess knew that, as well as attending her business meeting, her break in the Lake District had been necessary. It had given her the time and space to realise what was really important to her, from her family to her job to her own mental health. But as the train trundled towards Manchester, she knew too that the next hours and days weren't going to be easy for either her or Tom, as they faced up to the realities of what needed to change.

Jess hadn't been in touch with Tom since the twins' FaceTime call the previous afternoon, so he didn't know she was coming home early. She considered treating herself to a taxi from Piccadilly Station, but the thought of arriving on her own doorstep so soon made her heart thump in her chest uncomfortably. So she lingered in the station, gazing pointlessly at bags and shoes she was never going to buy in shops she would never normally have given a second look. Finally, after doing a lap of the concourse, she got on the local train that would take her towards home. She only allowed her mind to turn to the conversation she knew she needed to have with Tom once she was walking over the railway bridge and making her way down the road. Acid rose in her throat as she slowly and deliberately found her keys and unlocked the door.

'H-hello?' she called in a voice that sounded strangely unlike her own. She heard a door opening and his unmistakable footsteps coming closer. 'Tom?'

'Jess! You're home!' Tom didn't question why she was standing frozen in the hall, coat still on, suitcase beside her, on a completely different day and at a completely different time than she'd told him a few days before. He wrapped his arms around her and held his lips against her hair. After a beat, Jess felt her whole body instinctively soften at his touch and she lost herself in him. For a long moment, she breathed in his woody smell, his comforting warmth and the slight stubble on his soft skin. She was home. But then she made herself pull away from his embrace. Seeing the surprise on his face, she touched his arm gently.

'Tom, we need to talk.'

*

Strangely desperate to have the conversation she had been putting off, Jess would have gladly spilled the contents of her heart right there and then in the draughty hallway, but perhaps sensing the seriousness of her impending speech, Tom had insisted they go into the kitchen and have a cup of coffee, and that she take off her coat and boots.

'Otherwise it looks as if you're not staying!' he'd joked, before he'd realised how inappropriate his words were, given the last few days.

An awkward silence reached out between them.

Now, looking around the kitchen, Jess was surprised how tidy it was. Sure, there were a few mugs on the side that she would have cleared away, and a pile of post on the table she would have already sorted through, but she'd been expecting a bombsite on her return.

'Here's your tea,' Tom said, his smile not reaching his eyes. Jess took the No.1 MUM mug from him and wondered whether he'd picked that specific one intentionally.

'Thanks.' She took a sip of the scalding liquid then set it down on the table. 'I did a lot of thinking while I was away, Tom.'

He looked at her with frightened eyes, but nodded encouragingly. 'That's good. Did it help you, do you think? The time to think, I mean.' They both smiled as he fumbled over his words, their expressions acknowledging they both knew how hard it was – and would be – to say the words they needed to say.

She nodded. 'It did. Being away made me realise that

things can't go on the way they are.' She saw the fear increase on Tom's face and she reached for his hand. 'Neither of us have been very happy over the past few months, have we? I love you, Tom, but if I'm being honest, lately I'm not sure how much we've *liked* each other. I know we would both lay down our lives for the twins, no questions asked, but I don't think either of us are being the best parent to them while we're constantly arguing.'

'Jess, I don't think—'

'No, Tom, please let me finish,' she said urgently. 'We can make this work, I know we can, but we both need to be prepared to change. We're not the same people we were when we were fifteen, or even when the twins were little. I'm a mum, a wife, a friend, but also a business owner who wants to make a success of all the hours of toil and sacrifice I've put into it – but not at the expense of my family. And it's the same for you – you're a brilliant dad, a great husband, but you also have a fledgling business that needs your care and attention if it's going to succeed. But I think we're both struggling with all of these roles. I feel like I'm failing at being a mum, a wife, a friend and even though Save The Date is doing okay now, I feel like I'm failing at that too because I'm not giving it my full attention. And it's making me unhappy. I don't want to spend another week, month, year or whatever feeling like this; like I'm letting everyone down.'

'You're not letting anyone down, Jess!' Tom burst out. 'I'm the one letting us all down by not bringing in enough

money or spending enough time with the kids. Or appreciating everything you do for us enough.'

Jess swallowed the lump at the back of her throat as she
saw the tears at the corner of Tom's eyes, and squeezed his
hand even harder. 'I think we both agree neither of us are in
line for an award any time soon, but all the more reason to
change things, don't you think?'

Tom swiped his hand across his eyes. 'Yes, definitely.' Jess
saw him take a shuddering breath in and he squeezed her
hand back. 'I feel like I haven't been honest with you for the
last few months, Jess.'

Now it was her turn to widen her eyes in fear of what was
coming next.

'No, nothing like that,' he reassured her. 'Christ, I don't
have the energy to so much as glance at anyone else – not
that I ever would,' he added hurriedly. 'What I meant is that
I haven't been honest with you about how I'm feeling either.
Seeing Save The Date develop over the last few months has
been amazing because I know how much work you've put
into it, but as the business has grown, so has your need to
have everything perfect around the house. It's felt like you've
not allowed yourself to switch off at any point, and in truth,
I've been really worried about you. I didn't know how to
help because you didn't let me in. You tried to cope with
everything on your own and shut me out. And that made
me feel like utter shit.'

Although he spoke softly and without any menace what-
soever, Jess felt each of his words hit home like little arrows.

She stared in shock at her husband. 'I . . . I had no idea that's how you were feeling. Or rather how I was making you feel,' she stuttered.

'I know. And that's my fault for not being honest. Or forcing you to let me help, rather than taking a step back and letting you become more and more stressed. I'm sorry, Jess.'

In truth, Jess didn't really know what to say. She'd always been one for making sure things were 'just so' and she knew that lately she'd felt like she was having to be the one to make sure both the household and the business were running smoothly, but she'd thought that was because Tom had stopped doing even small things round the house and obviously Save The Date had taken off with the wedding and all the publicity around it. To hear from her husband that she had largely been the architect of her own stress by not letting anyone help had shaken her more than she could articulate.

Seeing her floundering, Tom reached for her other hand, too. 'Look at me, Jess. I love you and I will always love you. But I've stood by and watched for too long as you've become a shadow of your former self. You shouldn't have had to resort to taking a week away from the family for me to realise what more I should be doing. But I was scared – for me and you. All I really care about is your happiness. It doesn't matter if we don't have piles of money, it doesn't matter if the kids don't get top marks for some poxy geography project all the other parents have spent the night making, and it certainly doesn't matter if the washing-up from the night before is left on the side. I know we don't want to live in a pigsty, but we have two amazing, boisterous children who make a mess just eating an orange from the fruit bowl, so we're never going to live in a pristine home. And, to me, that's okay; it's enough that we're doing our best as busy, working parents. I'm just worried that you think it – or rather you – are never enough.'

Tom stopped speaking and swallowed hard, this time not filling the silence left between them. Jess knew it was her turn to be honest.

'You're right: I do feel like I'm not enough. I dropped out of uni unlike you and Hannah and everyone else we seem to know. You have a degree that proves you're qualified to make a living from what you love – I don't. When I started Save The Date, I had no idea what I was doing, but I spent so long pretending I did, I'd almost convinced *myself* it was true. And then my small but steady little business began to get into trouble and the bank started making threats, and at the same time our relationship became more strained and I found it harder to keep all the plates spinning. I started to question how I could expect to successfully help people to find their happy-ever-afters when my own marriage was in trouble, but instead of facing the problem head-on and talking to you like an adult, I threw all my energies into making a success of Hannah's blind-date wedding to prove I wasn't a failure. But even then I couldn't enjoy what was happening because I knew Hannah's happiness was so tied up with Save The Date's success, and Save The Date's success was so tied up with Hannah's happiness that if one plate stopped spinning, it would all come tumbling down, and not only would I be failing as a wife and mother, I'd also be failing as a friend, employer and breadwinner. I feel like I haven't been fulfilling any of my roles properly.' She pulled her hand away from Tom's to reach for another tissue before continuing. 'Being away this week has made me realise I don't know who I am anymore. If I'm a rubbish mother, crap wife and self-serving friend, then what kind of person does that make me?'

Tom barely let her finish her sentence before he said angrily, 'You're not rubbish or crap or self-serving. You can be stubborn and too determined to do things on your own and afraid to ask for help. Jess, you need to put yourself first sometimes. Your happiness matters. I'm just as guilty of burying my head in the sand; I could see what was happening and failed to do anything about it. Please believe that it's not because I didn't want to, it's because I was scared of doing the wrong thing and making you even more unhappy. I was scared of . . . of losing you.'

They were both crying now and reached for a tissue at the same time, before sob-laughing at how ridiculous the situation was.

'Look, Jess, I am as much to blame for all of this as you. We seem to have fallen into roles that don't reflect who we are and we've taken each other for granted. Your control-freak tendencies might have gone into overdrive, but I hold my hands up that I've not been pulling my weight. I've felt worn down and exhausted, although I know you must have been feeling that even more so. All week I've been replaying what I said to you on the way home from ParkRun, and every time

I think about it, it gets worse. You are the best mum to our children and we are all so lucky to have you. And I am so happy they are growing up with you as a role model, both as a mother and a businesswoman.'

Jess blew loudly into her tissue and they both laughed. 'And as a nose honker!' she said. 'I wish we'd had this conversation six months ago,' she added, as Tom nodded. 'But maybe it took something to tip me over the edge before I could face up to it all.'

'And that's what we need to change,' agreed Tom. 'I can't bear the thought of you being unhappy and not talking to me about it, whether it's to do with the kids, or us, or the business. We're in this together, Jess, I promise.'

'I know,' she said sadly. 'Or at least I realise that now anyway. I love you, Tom, and I love Sam and Lily with every fibre of my being, but I'm not just a wife and mother. If I'm honest, I think I still need to prove to myself that I'm capable of excelling in my career too. Hopefully selling Save The Date will not only give us some much-needed money, but will buy me a little time. Time to spend with my family, as well as time to spend working out exactly what it is I want to do. Being in the Lakes made me realise that time is the most important commodity in all of this. I rushed into starting the company after I was made redundant and I knew I had to make it work no matter what. Hopefully, if I can now sell it I'll be able to take the time I need to find something I'm truly passionate about.'

'And I will support you with everything I've got. But

maybe being all of those things – a mum, a wife, a success-ful woman at work – doesn't have to mean being "perfect", Jess,' Tom said gently. 'Everyone's idea of perfect is different. Surely being happy is the most important thing? And know-ing that you're not the only person responsible for everyone's happiness. We're a team, the twins are also on our team, as is Hannah and so are our parents. You don't have to be super-woman on your own, even if you are a super woman to me.'

Jess walked towards the school, hand in hand with Tom. She'd trowelled on a ton of foundation and concealer to hide the worst of the 'I've spent twenty-four hours crying' evidence, and had accessorised with her brightest scarf and the fluoro yellow trainers she'd bought on a whim because they were in the sale at John Lewis and Lily had told her she would be embarrassed to be seen with her wearing them. As they reached the growing huddles of parents at the gates, Jess wondered why she and Tom didn't both come to pick the kids up more often. They'd chosen to walk rather than drive and she already knew there'd be grumbling when the twins realised they'd have to wait longer to get their hands on the all-important snacks at home, but it was grumbling she couldn't wait to hear.

She and Tom kept their hands entwined until they saw two excited children rushing towards them and they stretched out their arms.

'Mum! You're back! Did you bring us a present?'

Chapter 25

Hannah

A grey and windy Saturday afternoon in late October wasn't the best time for an emotionally charged walk around a city centre marina, Hannah belatedly thought as she pulled her scarf higher up her neck and battled her way through the Northern Quarter. Especially as she was already ten minutes late and she couldn't remember if there was anywhere to shelter from the Manchester elements. But at least it wasn't raining. She hurried towards the water and almost walked smack–bang into a man with his coat zipped up as far as it would go and his head down against a particularly fierce gust of wind.

'Sorry!' she gasped. And then, 'Toby?'

They stood, just inches apart, winded by the sight of each other.

'Hannah!'

Her mouth opened and closed as she grappled with what

to say. Toby seemed equally dumbstruck, until a sharp gust whipped round them, and he grabbed her arm to steady her.

'There's a nice bakery down the road, shall we go there?'

Hannah nodded, still unable to speak as rain suddenly began spilling from the sky as if a hose had been turned on and sprayed directly in their faces. She followed Toby at a sprint and they both arrived at the café dripping. Hannah peeled off her coat and faffed around placing it on the back of her chair as she tried to force her breathing to return to normal. Thankfully, Toby went to the counter to order them coffee and by the time he came back bearing a muffin and a huge pastry covered with strawberries, Hannah was mostly recovered.

'I couldn't decide which you'd prefer,' he confessed.

'Thanks, they both look yummy,' Hannah said, smiling at him shyly. They picked at the cakes as they waited for their coffees to be brewed and frothed, but finally they had flat whites in front of them and had exhausted all conversation about their pastries.

'Sorry I was a bit late,' Hannah began. 'I hope you didn't think I wasn't going to come.'

'No, you said you were coming, so I knew you'd come,' he said. 'Though I got there a bit early and wished I'd thought to suggest we meet somewhere a little warmer,' he added ruefully.

'Bloody Manc weather.' Hannah grimaced. There was a silence and they both reached for their drinks. 'Thanks for agreeing to meet me,' she started again. 'Look, Toby, I owe you an apology. No, hear me out,' she added, holding up her hand as he tried to show he disagreed. 'However frustrated and upset I was, I should never have said what I did. I can't imagine what you went through when Emma died – it must have been truly awful, and I know it's something you'll carry with you for the rest of your life.' She swallowed hard before continuing. 'And I definitely don't regret getting married. But honestly, I don't think I'd properly considered what would happen after the wedding, or after the honeymoon, when we both returned to our normal lives that suddenly another person was a significant part of. I wasn't prepared to feel so awkward, so unsure of my own feelings, let alone yours, so unequipped to be a wife. But now I can see that it's hardly surprising I felt like that – and still do feel like that, if I'm being honest. I mean, it's not every day you marry a man you've never even seen, is it! But maybe that's okay. Maybe it's okay that we both feel a bit weird about everything and don't know how to react to certain situations; maybe it's okay that we get things wrong sometimes simply because we've not been in this position before; and maybe it's okay if one of us has a freak-out every so often. But we have to talk to each other. You're the only other person on the planet who can truly understand how I'm feeling – because you're going through this too. So maybe if we tell each other what we're thinking and are honest with each other, we can see where this crazy, mad situation takes us?'

Hannah stopped speaking and looked at Toby, aware that now she had laid her cards on the table, he could still send everything crashing to the floor. She gripped the handle of her coffee cup.

'You're right,' he said instead. 'This is a crazy, mad situation and we were kidding ourselves if we thought we were prepared for it. And I'm as guilty of getting swept up in the wedding and immediate aftermath as you are. It's always easier to focus on those fun, exciting details than it is to face the scary big picture.' Hannah nodded in agreement, but gripped her mug even tighter, aware there was more to be said.

'But we do need to look at the bigger picture and be more honest with each other, as you said. So we need to talk about Emma. Or rather, I need to talk about Emma.' Toby took a gulp of his drink, but then carried on speaking. 'Two and a half years ago I thought I had everything, but then Emma lost control of her car and skidded into a tree on the way home after a night out. She hadn't been drinking, but it was late and foggy and she was killed pretty much instantly. As much I had loved her, I was angry with her for a long time after she died because that night she took away not only her future, but mine.' He picked up his cup but didn't raise it to his mouth. Hannah didn't speak as she wanted to give him space, and just as she was starting to feel uncomfortable about the silence between them, Toby placed his cup back down and looked up at her.

'It took me a long time to come to terms with the fact it was an accident and to forgive both her and myself. Maybe if I'd been in the car with her I'd have been able to stop the crash from happening. I'll never know. But what I do know is my life changed completely in that moment. For eighteen months I thought it had changed only for the worse. But gradually, I began to find my way back to living again and tried to redis-cover the fun, loving, interesting man I used to be. Then when Melissa strong-armed me into applying to be part of Save The Date's project and I got deeper into the process, I realised that maybe there was light at the end of the tunnel. Meeting you changed everything again. Suddenly I saw that I could have another long-term relationship, another future. But I realise that I've been trying to race towards that future in my head in the hope that, that way, nothing bad will happen to take it all away from me again. I'm not exactly the same person I was before Emma died, but that doesn't have to be a bad thing. And just because I find another woman attractive and funny and smart and funny – oh, I've already said that!'

Hannah laughed and blushed, but allowed him to continue.

'It doesn't mean I'm disrespecting Emma. I think I've finally realised that. Does that make sense?'

'Yes,' Hannah said gently. 'It makes perfect sense. And while we're being honest about everything, I think I've built up this feeling in my head that I'll never live up to this amazing woman you were engaged to and thought you were going to spend the rest of your life with. And instead you ended up with me. That night at your house I felt this huge pressure to live up to the woman you wanted me to be. I'd started to believe that I'd always be second best to Emma; that I wasn't worth all that waiting you've done.'

She raised her gaze nervously to meet his and was relieved to see he was smiling, but there was also sadness in his expression.

'I'm so sorry that I put that extra pressure on you; I should have thought before I spoke, especially at that moment when we were ...' He tailed off, and they shared an embarrassed smile. 'You and Emma are two very different people, Han,' he said quietly. 'But I never want you to feel like you're in competition with her, and I know she would want me to be happy. In fact, I think you'd have really got on with each other, if that's not too weird to say. She'd have loved how funny you are and how you care so deeply about your friends and family. She's still a part of my life and always will be, but this is about you. And from everything I already know about you, I am so glad you are here.'

They smiled at each other again. 'I'm glad I'm here, too,' Hannah said. She glanced over to the table next to them and was met with eavesdropping gawps from the two women sitting there, though when they saw her looking, they immediately busied themselves pouring another cup of tea from their pot. 'It looks like the rain has stopped.'

Toby nodded. 'And the wind doesn't seem quite so intense.'

'Maybe we should brave a bit of fresh air?' Hannah suggested.

'Good plan,' Toby replied, smiling at her.

Hannah dug her hands into her pockets as they wandered round the edge of the marina, her mind retracing the steps of the conversation she and Toby had just had. It seemed to have gone well and they were both obviously making an effort, but there were still things they hadn't talked about that she knew needed to be addressed.

'I've been thinking a lot about why travelling has been such a big part of my life,' she said as they walked past a couple of swans serenely paddling in and out of the colourful boats moored up along the brick walls. 'And I think maybe it started out as an escape from real life and the need to get away and spread my wings, but now it's become part of who I am, part of my DNA. And it's not because I want to run away from my job or my family or my friends – although I admit it definitely was at one point when I was younger – it's because I want to *add* to all of those things; to enhance them with my experiences of visiting new places and trying new things. I guess what I'm saying is that there's no need to feel threatened by it all, and if we do it together, it can be something that helps bind us as a couple. But I also get that trekking around Chile for three months and living out of a backpack might not be your thing. Hell, I'm not even sure it's my thing anymore, if I'm honest – I've done enough camping to last me a lifetime! But we need to talk about our dreams, our bucket lists, our future, otherwise every time one of us makes a decision or expresses a preference, it could come as a huge shock to the other person and rock everything we've been trying to build between us, don't you think?'

'I know. Or rather I do now,' Toby said a little sheepishly. 'Melissa had a "chat" with me a couple of days ago and told me off because she said if I didn't actually tell you how I was feeling then I couldn't expect you to read my mind. So, yes, I have been feeling, well, threatened I suppose is a good word. About the travelling stuff, I mean. And I obviously shouldn't have agreed to Mum and Dad's offer to stay with them over Christmas without talking to you first. So I apologise. Melissa also made me realise that I'd probably want to murder them both after four days, never mind two whole weeks, so it was never going to work anyway.'

'I owe you a bigger apology,' Hannah said quietly. 'It was horribly selfish of me to agree to go and see Dee without even asking or really even thinking about you. I feel terrible about it now. I suppose I'm so used to only having to think about myself, and speaking to Dee made me realise how much I missed her, as well as Oz, so I didn't stop to think how you would feel. I'm sorry.'

'That's okay, I'm starting to understand where you were coming from, so it makes sense to me now,' Toby replied. 'I guess it's similar to how I reacted to my parents' suggestion we stay with them. I didn't think about what you might want, just what the easiest thing for me was. I've spent the last two years trying to convince my parents I'm okay – even when I wasn't – so I've been saying yes to whatever they ask. Sometimes I'm not even sure what are my own decisions and what I'm doing just because my family think I ought to.'

'They clearly care about you very much,' Hannah ventured.

'They do, and I sort of felt that when Emma died and I

fell apart, I let them all down. So since then I've been trying to do everything I can to make it up to them.'

'You've nothing to make up to them, Toby. Grief is a long and painful process, especially when you lose someone so suddenly. You need to not be so hard on yourself.'

He smiled. 'You sound like Melissa.'

'Then it must be true if we're both saying it!'

'I'm not sure that quite follows, but thank you.'

There was a short silence during which a huge gust of wind wound its way through Hannah's limbs and into the furthest recesses of her coat, making her shiver beneath the darkening sky. 'Well, at least one good thing came out of you doing exactly what your family told you.'

'And what's that then?' asked Toby, a smile creeping across his face.

'You agreed to marry a woman you'd never even seen before, enjoyed a week of absolute luxury in sunny St Lucia, and then got to spend a Saturday afternoon freezing to death in the middle of rainy old Manchester with said woman, that's what!'

Toby grinned, turning towards her so their faces were almost touching. 'You're right.'

'Toby, can I ask you something?' Hannah asked softly.

'You mean you don't think we've done enough soul-searching for one day?' He smiled. 'Of course, ask me anything.'

Her heart hammering and more aware than ever of just how close they were, she whispered, 'Would you like to come to Australia with me sometime?'

He gently touched his lips on hers and then answered so softly she wondered if she'd imagined it. 'Yes, I would love to.'

Hannah stroked his face before pulling him towards her. Suddenly, immediately above them there was a crack of thunder, followed by a huge flash of lightning. Within seconds they were being pelted with jagged balls of hail. They reluctantly moved apart.

'To the pub?' Toby suggested.

'I thought you'd never ask!'

Epilogue

Two months later

Hannah looked around at the throngs of people all along the harbour. The walkway was full of families, friends and couples, their faces lit up with smiles and awe as the last of the early fireworks filled the sky. She glanced over to the bar where Dee and her partner Ade were ordering the drinks before the next wave of celebrations began in Sydney Harbour, with all the boats lighting up in a perfectly choreographed dance, followed by the iconic midnight fireworks display with the bridge at the centre.

And she squeezed Toby's hand.

'What a year!' she said, looking up at him and smiling.

'I don't know what you mean? It's been such an *uneventful* twelve months . . .' Toby teased.

'Sure, just a *few* things going on.' She grinned. 'My new job is exciting, that's true. As much as I loved Save The Date, when I knew the sale was definitely going through I actually felt relieved to be starting a new chapter of my life. Although the downside of working for a teenage outreach charity is having to pretend I'm cool and down with the kids all the time.'

'Don't worry, they'll see through you immediately,' Toby quipped.

'Oh thanks! What else has happened over the last twelve months? Well, there's the fact that in a matter of weeks I'm going to be bridesmaid for my best friend *again* – though this time I definitely won't be getting off with any hot barmen. Well, at least that's what I've told Jess.'

'I'm *very* pleased Jess and Tom are renewing their vows, but I've already made them promise to employ only ugly bartenders, so I don't think your luck is going to be in, I'm afraid. Anyway, hasn't something else interesting happened in the last year maybe?' he smiled, leaning towards her playfully.

'Has it? No, there's nothing I can remember ...' She squealed as he started to lightly tickle her. 'Stop it! You know I can't deal with being tickled under my ribs – *Tobes*! Fine, yes, something else quite exciting happened this year, you're right.'

'*Quite* exciting?'

'Sorry, *very* exciting. I have a new sister-in-law! Oh, and a new mother-in-law and father-in-law, both of whom made me feel very welcome for the few days I stayed with them over Christmas. And, yes, I suppose it is pretty exciting that I have a new husband. Happy now?'

'Very happy, thanks.' Toby beamed before adding more seriously, 'I am really happy I met you, Han. I know it's not been easy for either of us over the past few months and there's no magic wand to make everything perfect immediately, but I'm having fun being on this journey with you and seeing where it takes us.'

'Me too,' Hannah replied, wrapping her arms around his neck and leaning towards him. 'And I'm excited that this journey will very soon take us up to Queensland and the Barrier Reef with Dee and Ade. I can't wait to take you swimming with the fish.'

'Nemo's got nothing on us! And I can't imagine a better way to start the New Year.' He leaned into Hannah for a kiss.

They were interrupted moments later when Dee and Ade returned with their drinks. Hannah laughed as her friends teased them, then poked out her tongue. 'Shut up, I'm just starting the next twelve months as I mean to go on! Right, Husband?'

Toby grinned and leaned in to kiss her again, 'Right, Wife.'

Acknowledgements

Well, what an eighteen months it's been (and, no, for once I'm not referring to a certain pesky virus). Since the ebook of my debut novel came out in July 2019 and I first got to see my paperback on a shelf in an actual bookshop two months later, it's been quite a ride. And I feel so lucky to have a whole team of friends and family – both in the book world and in 'normal' life – who have come along with me on this ride.

Thank you to my agent Tanera Simons, who has so often been on the receiving end of an essay-length email containing the line: 'I know I might be overthinking this and apologies in advance for the stream of consciousness, but . . .' – and has not even once sent me a sarcastic message in reply. Writing this book has been a much richer experience for having you in my corner, and your encouragement and suggestions gave me the self-belief to find my way through Hannah and Toby's story. I'm so proud to be part of #TeamTanera. Thank you, too, to the whole team at Darley Anderson who work so hard.

An absolutely massive whoop-whoop to my Simon & Schuster crew. My biggest thanks go to my talented editor Bec Farrell, who knows how to raise people from the dead (yep, she's that powerful), how to tell me things aren't quite working in the most constructive (and kindest) way, and how to curb my overuse of the word 'ooh' (as well as 'ahh'). This book is at least a million times better than it would have been without you. I'm hugely grateful for Alice Rodgers's input and hard work (I will definitely never confuse half-sister and stepsister again thanks to your brilliant intervention!), and I am forever indebted to the all-round superstar that is Sara-Jade Virtue – I could not be happier that I now get to work so closely with you. The second I clapped eyes on Pip Watkins's cover design for *Married At First Swipe* I instantly adored it – in fact, you could say it was love at first sight! – so thank you, Pip, for being such a cover whizz. While we're on the subject of whizzes, a massive shout-out to the S&S publicity and marketing teams, especially brilliant Becky McCarthy and amazing Amy Fulwood who have worked so hard to create standout campaigns for my books.

It has been an absolute privilege to meet and connect with so many fellow authors over the last few years, and I want to say a particularly big thank you to every writer who has supported me by reading and blurbing my books, sharing my posts on social media and offering me congrats and advice when I need them most. Understanding that you all feel the same highs and lows on your own writing journeys has stopped me from going (too) mad.

It's hard to put into words (and I know that's what I'm supposed to be good at!) how much it means to me that so many bloggers have taken the time to read and review my novels, be part of blog tours and post beautiful pics of proofs and finished copies of my books on their channels for the sheer joy of it. I am so very grateful. Thank you to all the super-hardworking journalists and reviewers on magazines and newspapers who are drowning in jiffy bags and TBR piles (I hear ya!) but have still found the space to feature my books. Your support is invaluable and I will never get tired of opening the pages of my favourite mags to see my beautiful cover staring back at me.

I wouldn't be the person I am today without all my friends and family (you're to blame for all the bad bits, obv!) and each and every one of them has played a part in my author journey, from my best friend Beth buying up every copy of my books in West Yorkshire and the whole *Fabulous* team turning out to support me, to my mum and sisters proudly cheering me on (and spreading news of my books far and wide on social media and pulling them to the front on bookshop shelves) and my mother-in-law Pat reading a chapter every night even though she isn't really sure what Instagram or dating apps actually are.

Thank you, Steve, for the last twenty-two (twenty-two? God, how did that happen?!) years together – yes, I know you keep saying you'd get less for a life sentence, but hopefully you agree that doing time with each other has been fun. Here's to another twenty-two (maybe you'll get round to reading one of my books by then!).

Finally, thank you to YOU. Readers are everything to an author, and to know you opened this book and got to the end (and hopefully enjoyed reading the pages in between) means the absolute world to me. On those days where I stare blankly at my laptop screen and despair of ever writing a coherent word again, just one Instagram message from a reader telling me how much they loved meeting my characters is enough to send flamenco ladies dancing across my computer and love hearts glinting in my eyes. So if you read this book and enjoyed it, please do let me know – and I will send you all the emojis in reply.

Claire x

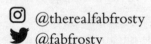 @therealfabfrosty
@fabfrosty

If you loved *Married at First Swipe*, don't miss out on Claire Frost's debut novel

living
my best
li^fe

This life-affirming and hilarious novel is the perfect balm for the Insta-weary mind – get ready to shatter the illusion that is #LivingMyBestLife

Recently dumped by her boyfriend of ten years, **Bell** is struggling to move on. Haunted by #blessed on social media, she can't help but compare her life to those she follows online, wondering where she is going wrong . . .

In the world of social media, **Millie** is the successful online influencer @mi_bestlife. But in real life she's just a regular single mum trying to make ends meet. Her Instagram feed is far more #Best*Lie* than #Best*Life*.

It isn't until Bell and Millie's paths cross that they begin to realise what they're both missing. Can Millie prove to Bell that life online isn't always what it appears to be? And in return, can Millie learn that she needs to start living for the moment and not for the likes?

'A fun, fresh debut that manages to be both quirky and deep' MILLY JOHNSON

AVAILABLE NOW IN PAPERBACK, EBOOK AND EAUDIO

SIMON &
SCHUSTER

booksandthecity.co.uk
the home of female fiction

NEWS & EVENTS | BOOKS | FEATURES | COMPETITIONS

Follow us online to be the first to hear from
your favourite authors

bc
booksandthecity.co.uk

@TeamBATC

Join our mailing list for the latest news, events and
exclusive competitions

Sign up at
booksandthecity.co.uk